D0612414

First published in print in 2021 by Solaris
an imprint of Rebellion Publishing Ltd,
Riverside House, Osney Mead,
Oxford, OX2 0ES, UK

www.solarisbooks.com

ISBN: 978 1 78108 834 0

10 9 8 7 6 5 4 3 2 1

A CIP catalogue record for this book is available
from the British Library.

Cover design by Head Design.
Interior illustrations by Gemma Sheldrake.

Designed & typeset by Rebellion Publishing

Printed in Denmark

SHADOW IN THE EMPIRE OF LIGHT

Jane Routley

SOLARIS

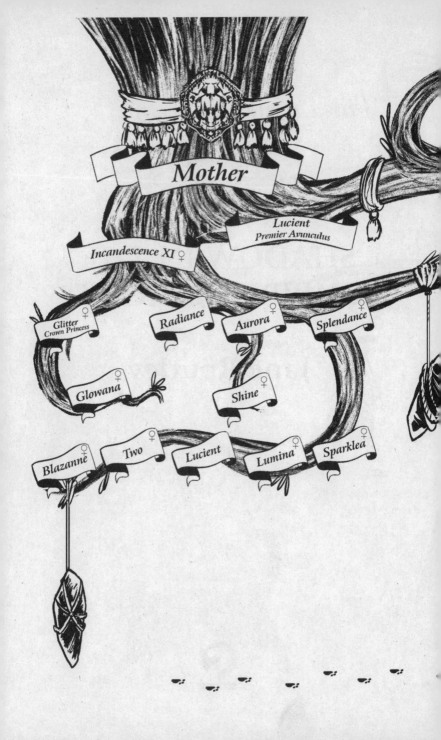

The Lucheyart Family

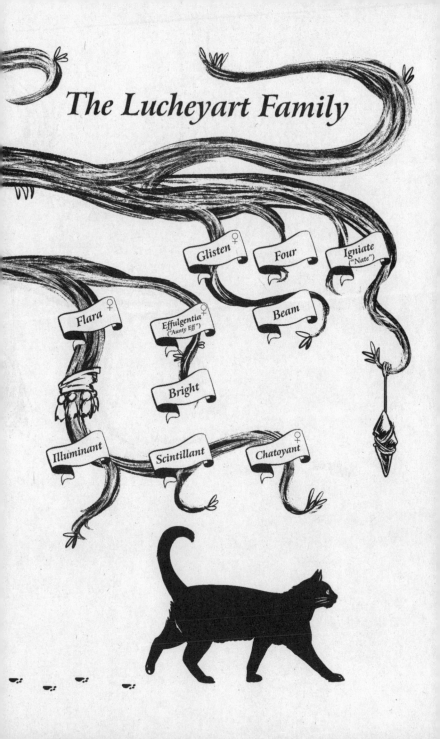

To my partner, Terry Cooper

CHAPTER ONE

IT'S NOT WORKING, I thought at Katti as I broke up the clods of earth with the hoe. The heavy swallowed anger still burned in my chest, no matter how hard I thought of the family as I smashed.

I'm hardly surprised, she thought back at me. *It's mud, not relatives.* Her thoughts held a certain paw-shaking disgust at the word 'mud.' Katti considered herself a mighty hunting cat, far above such distasteful mundanities as breaking up clods in the fields with the peasants. She had only come out with me because of the chance of catching tasty little animals in the hedgerows. Her thoughts were full of mystification as to why I would choose to do fieldwork on this of all mornings.

But I had to do something. I was so teeth-grindingly

angry at my family that I wasn't sure I could face them without creating some terrible scene that would make us all homeless. It's a bad idea to punch someone in the face when they have complete financial power over you and the people you love, no matter how much they deserve it.

If I could only calm down a bit, I thought at Katti.

My dear young human, I can't imagine fieldwork… Her focus suddenly switched away from me. I looked up. Her elegant grey head was turned towards the estates' entrance.

"They're here!" shouted one of the peasants.

Oh, no. Already?

It was only midday, far too early for the Blessing party to arrive. Yet a gleam of light had appeared in between the pair of tall trees that marked the entrance, showing that someone was travelling under magical power.

Katti leapt up and streaked away towards the carriage. Praying it wasn't the family but wondering who else it could be, I ran over to my horse, scrambled onto it and took off after her, leaping over the ditch at the edge of the field and up onto the track. The peasants working round me had dropped their hoes and were also running towards the road. A solitary phaeton without horses, a light carriage that carried only a couple of people, came sweeping up the drive way between the bare early spring trees. Ladypraised. Not the family. Who then?

It's him. It's him! came Katti's gleeful thoughts back to me.

But who?

10

The blue body and black hood of the light two-seater vehicle were unfamiliar to me, but I recognized the mage sitting in the driver's seat, and my heart leapt with joy.

Waving and shouting, I urged the horse forward faster. On the roadway before us the phaeton pulled to a stop and settled on the ground. The crystal embedded in the mage's forehead went dark.

"Shine!" Bright's round face split into a grin. "How's my favourite ghostie-girl?"

Normally I hated being called 'ghostie-girl,' but to hear Bright's teasing voice again was so wonderful it didn't matter today. He leapt out of the phaeton and held out his arms. His crystal lit up again and I felt his power snatching me off the back of my horse. Reaching out, I threw myself through the air to be caught in his arms. He squeezed me and swung me around.

"How are you?" I cried, hugging him tight and kissing both his cheeks. "What are you doing here? How long are you staying?" The true situation stabbed at me. Bright was the reason for all my anger at the family, and he was in danger. "Oh, no! You've got to go. It's Blessing time. Impi and the others will be arriving in a couple of hours."

"Thanks a lot," laughed Bright. "I just arrive and you're telling me to go away."

He was damp with sweat, as any mage would be after a long drive, but it was the dear familiar stink of my beloved cousin, so it didn't much matter. He looked pale and tired, but his eyes were much livelier than when I had last seen him, and all the bruises were gone. The dusty tan of his military robe suited him and his arms felt muscular as he replaced me on the ground.

"Bright, it's Blessing time..."

"I know, I know. I'm going to come and go. I've got something to give you. Wait a minute and I'll show you."

He turned away to shake hands and exchange greetings with the peasants who had run over the fields behind me. Since he'd grown up here at the Willow-in-the-Mist Estate, my noble cousin knew everyone by name and was still well liked despite the scandal. He had a lot of questions to ask and answer.

While he was distracted, I turned to the other seat where Stefan Graceson, Bright's valet, was sitting.

"You both look great," I said. I'd known Graceson all my life, but after not seeing him for so long I was struck again by how gorgeous he was, with his high cheekbones, huge dark eyes and lovely curly hair. As children, the Graceson brothers and Bright and I had played together and, later, Graceson and Bright were inseparable. I'd always known that Bright loved Stefan more than anyone else. I'd accepted it as part of my cousin. If only the family had, curse them. What was it to them anyway? Bright was honest, loyal and kind—a wonderful person and surely a credit to his family.

"Military life agrees with us," murmured Graceson. "He's so much happier now he's got something to do. He's been saying the disinheritance may have been the best thing that ever happened to him."

"Shine, get someone to take your horse back to the

house," interrupted Bright. "I need to discuss something private with you."

"I'm all ears," I said, giving the order to one of the peasants.

Katti was sniffing at the trunk of the phaeton. *Something smells very strange in here*, her thoughts told me.

Graceson shooed Katti away as he climbed onto the back and sat on top of the trunk. I took his place beside Bright, calling Katti to sit between us. She almost reached our shoulders.

"Lady!" exclaimed Bright, reaching across to rub her cheeks. "Look at you, you gorgeous cat. You're enormous."

She had the size of her wildcat sire and very likely her dark tufted ears came from him too. But she had the long tail of her mother and the soft smoke grey fur of a domesticated cat. Katti allowed Bright to rub her neck and cheeks. She liked him; she said he gave good neck rubs. But oddly enough she almost never spoke in his head, so he turned to me for information.

"Is she full-sized now?"

"She's had her first litter of kittens, so I guess she must be."

"That's a relief. Wouldn't want her to get much bigger. She must terrify visitors."

Quite true, thought Katti smugly.

Bright settled himself into place and crossed his arms, and his face took on the glaring, jaw-clenched look of a mage at work. The crystal embedded in his forehead that marked him as a mage lit up as he called his power out. The phaeton rose into the air and turned towards the forest that covered the sides of our valley. We flew high enough over the fields not to disturb the neat furrows in the earth below. Once the phaeton was flying straight, Bright was able to drive and talk at the same time.

"So when are they due?"

"The family? Not till nightfall."

"No need to rush off, then. Are they still as appalling as ever?"

"Worse," I said. "Apparently our Holy Matriarch was so smoked at Plainsofgold, she almost fell over during her first Blessing. Lumina's as horrible as ever and I hear Klea has run off to join the theatre. And Impi still rules the roost."

"*Cursed be the family where the consort holds sway,*" quoted Bright. "I'm glad I'm out of the whole ghastly thing."

"You really prefer military service? Isn't it limiting?"

"It's less limiting than life at Elayison. Hanging about smoking dreamsmoke and ranting on about nothing, and everyone spying on you. If you do your job on the frontier, they don't ask any questions."

"Promise?" I asked softly. "You're not just...?"

"I'm not just saying it. I'm loving it there. Best thing I ever did." He squeezed my wrist. "You can stop worrying about me. Honestly. Impi and the rest have done me a favour."

He smiled at me and it was a smile I could believe. He seemed like his old cheerful self. Some of the weight seemed to leave my chest and I found my eyes tearing up. I blinked.

"We going to the tree house?" I asked, to cover the moment.

"Such a perspicacious little coz!" He laughed.

Little coz indeed. I smacked his arm. I was two years his senior. Twenty-three and still on the farm. And likely to remain so now.

The phaeton slid over the river that fenced our lands off from the forest, and in under the canopy of the trees. The lush undergrowth swayed as we manoeuvred between the tree trunks. So close to the edge of the forest there were no puffballs or mine shafts to look out for. I felt Katti's mind fill with the possibility of small tasty animals and squeezed the back of her neck to remind her to stay put.

I love travelling by magic phaeton. I'd have had to take the much longer route via the bridge and the path if I'd been alone. Now in a few moments we reached the single spreading fig tree where, as children, Bright and I had had a secret hideaway. You could curl up on the deep beds of leaves that collected between its huge roots, and make little houses. The fig tree's spirit felt sleepy and sort of motherly. Bright laughed at me the time I told him that, but I was certain it was true.

It looked like children still played here. I myself rarely visited now, because it always made me melancholy. When we were little, I'd always assumed that I'd grow up to be a mage, inheriting my mother's estate and title, and that Bright would act as uncle when I set up my nursery. Now here I was ten years later, no magic powers, no nobility, no inheritance and no children. And Bright kicked out of the family for being a man-lover. *Dust, dust, all dreams are but dust.*

Bright turned the phaeton as we landed, so that the fig's lower branches hid the back of it. He relaxed and the crystal blinked out.

"Graceson, release the luggage!" he cried, mock dramatically, as Katti and I jumped out.

Katti gave a chirrup. *Something is alive here.* She darted around the back of the phaeton after Graceson.

"Oh, drat, call that cat to heel," cried Bright. "Graceson, look out!"

"Katti!" I darted in under the branches and saw Katti jumping up on Graceson's back as a hooded figure rose out of the large trunk and gave a yelp of alarm.

"Down, Katti, down," I cried, seizing her collar. "Bright, what's this? Did you arrest a rogue on the way here?"

"Better than that," said Bright. He looked round to check that no one could see us and waved his hand so that the figure's hood fell back. Despite the canopy of branches, it was quite light in here, so I saw the figure's horrible pale face and hair clearly. Its weird blue-coloured eyes were wide with surprise.

I'm ashamed to admit I squeaked.

Very well, it was an actual scream, but only a small one.

Katti hissed and pulled back. I squeezed her neck consolingly, trying to send calm to her—which wasn't easy because I didn't feel very calm myself. I'd never been this close to one of these pale foreigners, unless you count the one who sired me, who'd gone by the time I was a year old.

"Lady! Is that a ghost? Is it real?"

"Of course. Get down, outlander. I won't let the cat hurt you."

The outlander jumped out of the trunk and landed with a reassuringly corporeal thud. His joints even creaked, as he stretched his back and legs. These pale outlanders from over the Bone Mountains in the west had come to the Empire of Light about thirty years ago, full of clever inventions and pretty trinkets to trade for crystal. Every outlander in the country was registered and limited to a strict trading path; only a few of them came at a time and the Imperial Government kept stern watch on them—as well they might. Most of the peasants feared these pale folk as escapees from the land of the dead, and at first there had been panic and attacks.

"You can touch him, if you like," said Bright. "He's human."

"I..." What if he put an enchantment on me, the way an outlander had enchanted my mother? You've spent too much time among superstitious mundanes, my girl, I told myself. I put my hand on his cheek and was intensely relieved that it felt like any proper-coloured cheek. He even needed a shave.

"No wonder people call them ghosts. What a horrible colour! Like a fungus."

The outlander glared at me.

"I can speak your language," he said with a perfect accent.

I jumped back with another embarrassing squeak.

Graceson poked the ghost with a finger. "You have no manners," he hissed. "The lady is of noble lineage. Address her as 'marm.'"

"I beg pardon," said the ghost, and swept a surprisingly good, if rather stiff, bow. "I am at your service, marm."

"Let's have a seat, coz," said Bright, stripping off his riding gloves. "Come on, Graceson, I'm starving and thirsty."

The valet nodded and turned to rummage in the luggage compartment.

Bright spread his cloak between two of the largest roots at the base of the tree and threw himself down on it. I settled down beside him and wriggled my back into my old accustomed place. The outlander didn't sit but stood over us, rubbing his back and groaning softly.

"Sit, friend Shadow," said Bright.

From a noble, such words are an order, not a request, but the ghost said quite simply, "No, thank you. I have been cramped up in that trunk and my back is killing me." He stretched out and bent back.

"Don't worry," murmured Bright to me. "He doesn't mean to be rude. He's very blunt."

"But where'd you get him from? And what's he doing in your luggage trunk? And out here? Are outlanders allowed outside the capital now?"

"He's unregistered," said Bright. "Apparently he and his friends came from their own land without letting our government know about it. He says they were intending to come and go through the Endless Desert without really entering our borders. They've been investigating crystal smuggling. They were asking questions at a mine in the borderlands and got caught up in some kind of attack. The other ghosts were killed, but one of the miners rescued this one and dumped him at our outpost. Ran away before I could question him—the miner, I mean. I went up to see the mine site before we came here. Shadow's telling some version of the truth. The place was a mess, and the attackers had at least one mage with them. Shadow said he thought they took most of the miners prisoner. Thanks, Graceson."

Graceson offered us a little travelling tray holding stuffed marrow-blossoms and metal beakers of red wine. Since we were alone among friends, once we had been served, he sat down and took a beaker for himself. I notice he didn't serve the outlander, though he had poured a beaker of wine for him. Clearly Graceson didn't regard the ghost as noble. That presumably meant the ghost had no magical powers: he certainly had no crystal in his forehead.

"Anyway," Bright continued, "I kindly offered to take him back to Elayison in secret so that his embassy could get him home without a diplomatic incident."

The ghost snorted. "For a consideration."

"Yes, that's the best thing. He's going to find your mother for us."

"What? But she's dead." I didn't know that for sure, but she'd gone off with my outlander sire to visit his homeland when I was barely twelve months old, telling Auntie Eff she'd be home in a couple of months. Apparently she'd been fascinated by the ghosts. Eff had always said she'd adored me and would never have stayed away so long if she'd been able to come back. I'd long assumed that she'd died on the journey through the Bone Mountains, which was supposed to be very long and extremely hazardous. Everyone in the family called her 'poor dear lost Aurora'—except Granny, who refused to believe she wasn't coming back.

"If Shadow can find proof of what happened to her in Ghostland, Granny will have to sort out her estate and you'll finally get your allowance. And you'll be able to get out of here. See, I told you I'd make it up to you for being disinherited."

This whole idea was so surprising I didn't know what to say. I struggled to close my mouth and say something useful.

"You can't take him to Elayison," was the best I could come up with. "You're in exile."

"You did not say—" began the ghost.

"Shut up, both of you!" Bright glared at me and then at the ghost. "I can't take you. But Shine here can. She's not in exile."

Trust a mage not to consider the obstacles.

"Bright, I can't go anywhere. It's Blessing time."

"So? You stash this fellow somewhere until the festival is over. And then you set out. Simple."

The house was going to be packed to the rafters with the family and their ravenous servants, sticking their noses into everything, snooping all over the estate and hunting all through the forest. And the peasants would be too frightened of the ghost for me to stash him at one of their houses. Yet Bright said it was simple. Cursed mages! Life just isn't real for them.

"And before you say 'but' again," said Bright, "I've got the money for the tickets." He held out a fat little purse.

"Ladybless, did you rob someone?" I took the purse. It contained about ten lumins. I whistled. "Did you actually *win* at cards for once?"

In the background, Graceson rolled his eyes.

"No," snapped Bright. "The commander gave me an advance on my pay. I'm her little bright-eyed boy. She loves me."

"What, you mean you managed to make love to the commander?" The family's problem with Bright was not only that he liked to sleep with men, but that he'd refused to be unfaithful to Graceson even with women. Since he was only a man and not important to the lineage, it was a mystery why the family had made such a fuss about it. Plenty of noble men didn't do their duty.

Graceson had been thrown into prison on a trumped-up charge, but Bright had managed to bail him out. Despite this being perfectly legal, there had been a scandal over their relationship and the prison sentence. Bright had been given an ultimatum and when he refused to give up Graceson, he was disinherited. The family had hushed up some truly dreadful scandals in the past, so why they had to make an example of Bright was still a mystery to us. Eff said she saw Auntie Flara's fell hand in the deed.

"What my lord is saying is that he's the best mage in the regiment," interjected Graceson smoothly.

"Not that that's hard," Bright's round face split into a cheerful grin. "A more pathetic collection of smoke rats, drunks and arrogant shitheads too stupid to follow a mundane commander's orders, you could never hope to find. Almost makes me believe the stuff Mother says about mages being too decadent to govern properly."

I stared at the purse. Elayison! Even for a short time, it would be fabulous. And I might be able to save some of this money. Because, like it or not, I'd have to come back. I wasn't going to leave Auntie Eff here on her own. Not now she'd lost all hope.

"You've really thought this through," I said, touched by Bright's planning. On the whole mages don't do planning, even for their favourite cousins.

"Don't sound so surprised. I'm doing my best to sort out Mother too, but that's a bit of an uphill battle now. How is she, by the way?"

The light tone didn't fool me. The way he was rubbing his hands together gave away his anxiety.

"She's fine, though missing you," I lied. No point in telling him how shattered Auntie Eff had been by his disgrace. As anyone would be if her only son had been exiled from the capital, disgraced, beaten up, and forced to join the army in a frontier regiment to make a living. Eff had been counting on her noble son to sort out her own exile, not to join her in it. "She'll be over the sun to see you, Bright."

Bright jumped up. "Good. Let's get on up to the house. Back in the trunk, Shadow."

"So his name's Shadow, is it?" I asked. Mages often nicknamed people to suit themselves.

"No. It's something awful... Say your name for us, would you, Shadow?"

The ghost opened his mouth and let out a long stream of sing-song sounds that sounded like swear words.

"Wha...!" I gawped at him open mouthed. "Lady! Say it again slower."

Bright grinned. "You'll never learn it. Their language is awful. I've decided to call him Shadow 'cause he's a ghost."

"You might as well do the same," said the ghost. He smiled ruefully. "Cultural correctness seems to be an unknown concept here."

"What did you say?" I asked for a second time.

"Don't worry about him," said Bright. "He's some kind of scholar in his own country and I beginning to suspect he's as big a radical as Mother. He says weird stuff all the time, but he's pretty well behaved on the whole." With another grin, he whacked the ghost on the back. "He's even housetrained. Can you believe that?"

The ghost rolled his strange light eyes as he turned to climb back into the trunk. Clearly he understood Bright's teasing; I hoped we'd understand each other.

CHAPTER TWO

"FINDING MY MOTHER is a bit of a long shot, isn't it? Why are we really helping this ghost?" I asked Bright as we drove back to the house.

"An unregistered ghost sneaking over the border and wandering about the country would make things very hard for Great-Uncle in the Great Council. The conservatives would have a field day." Even out here in Willow, I knew how much the ghosts were distrusted by our leaders. They brought interesting inventions and trinkets, but most of the mages felt we didn't need them. Apart from that, there wasn't much else they had to trade for the crystal they seemed so interested in. Many mages thought we should forbid them to enter our Empire and instead trade with them in the desert outside our borders. As it was, they were limited to living in Elayison and every one of them had to be registered.

"So it's about politics?" I was surprised. Bright had always denied any interest in such things.

"Guess I'm my mother's son after all. We need to open up to the ghosts. Trade with them. Maybe follow your mother and travel to their land. They're a clever folk and they have lots of good inventions we could use."

"Radical! You *are* your mother's son. Still, can't see why you would help Great Uncle out. He didn't help you."

"He did help me. There just wasn't much he could do by the time he found out."

"Really? You didn't tell me this."

"Hey—you drained those fields by the river. When did you do that?" asked Bright. Apparently, the subject of Great Uncle Lucient was closed.

I told him how I'd paid the peasants a small money wage to help me with the ditch digging. "Eff's right about that. They worked so much harder for a money wage. I wish I could persuade Impi to switch from indenture farming to money. The estate would run so much better."

"You shouldn't be spending your money on that. You'll need it when you leave,"

"I'm not going anywhere. I can't leave your mother alone. She'd have no one to talk to, and you know she'd never cope with the estate."

Immediately I'd said it, I was sorry, because Bright flushed with guilt.

"She's got Thomas," he retorted. "He's trustworthy and great with numbers. If you stay here because of me I'll never forgive myself. Or you."

"No, Bright. Really. I'm not staying because of you. I... haven't decided *what* to do."

This was an arrant lie. I knew exactly what I wanted to do. Just before Bright had been disinherited, I'd accepted an apprenticeship with a merchant friend of Eff's and was already packing to go on my first trading journey along the Spice Road. My noble family would never have stood for one of their own going into trade, but Eff and I hoped that I'd be away across the sea before they knew anything about it. I'd even bought a journal, intending to write a really exciting travel book like the ones I was addicted to. The apprenticeship was still a possibility and I longed to go, but I knew I wouldn't.

After Bright had been disgraced and left us for the frontier, Eff had gone to bed for days. Her correspondence had gone unread, her students at the peasant school had gone untaught, she'd even stopped eating. She was better now, though still inclined to wander sleeplessly about the house at night. No way was I abandoning her when Bright was so far away.

The trees opened out to reveal the final stretch of driveway up to the manor house.

"Willow-in-the-Mist!" Bright sighed. "I love this place."

I shot him a startled look. As children, we had talked incessantly about getting away from here and going somewhere exciting.

"You've no idea what a lovely place this is till you've left it," he said.

Willow-in-the-Mist *was* pretty. The original towering six-storey stone eyrie, the traditional sort of dwelling for mages, was almost seven centuries old, built in the time of Civilising when mages first settled in this country. About two centuries ago, some surprisingly capable member of the family had added a long double storey wing so that the mundane members of the family didn't have to climb endless flights of stairs to get to their bedchambers. She'd built a deep summer veranda along the front using similar coloured stone so that the whole place had weathered to a warm tan colour. It was one of the most graceful and comfortable manor houses in the district, enhanced by the delicate tendrils of wistful vine that covered it and the backdrop of orchards, forest and the jutting peaks of the Secret Mountains.

In the olden days, members of the family had retired here annually to escape the summer heat of Elayison, but during my lifetime they'd always preferred to go to the coast. Ladybless! At least we only had to put up with them for short, infrequent visits.

"I shouldn't say that sort of stuff," said Bright. "I'm still hoping you'll come up to the frontier and join my regiment. I could get you a good position in the quartermaster's office. We could really use someone organized. I could be Uncle when you started your family. The way we always planned."

That old dream.

"Thanks for the offer, cousin dear, but to be honest,

burying myself in some dusty little military outpost isn't my idea of seeing the world," I said.

"You're sure that's what it is?" he asked. His face was pinched and the phaeton jerked to a stop and thudded to the ground as he turned to me. "Your sons would be perfectly safe. I'm not what they say."

"Bright, how could you even think such a thing?" I was shocked and hurt. Then understanding dawned. During the scandal and the disinheritance, family members had said outrageously horrible things about him. Clearly they'd said them to his face as well.

"I'd never... Of course I trust you," I put my arms around him and gave him a good hard squeeze and a kiss on the cheek. "Look, I could ask for no better Uncle for my children, but I want... I'm not ready to settle down. And don't say you'll wait for me. If you find someone else who wants you to act as Uncle, go ahead."

My words seemed to reassure him. The phaeton rose into the air and continued its onward course.

"I can't see that happening," he said, smiling wryly. "Not to me. Now look, promise me you're not staying here. They're never going to pay you, you know. As long as you run this place for free, Impi will let you. You ought to stop. Let the place go to pieces. Go on strike the way Mother's friends are always saying people should. They'd have to hire someone and they'd stop taking you for granted."

"Oh, Bright, you know I can't do that. The peasants rely on the place. I couldn't bear to see them go hungry."

"Well, promise me..."

"I promise, I promise. Give me time to work something out."

"If you start your family here, you'll get stuck and you'll always be at their mercy," muttered Bright darkly, as we reached the house.

Servants had been hanging out of all the windows watching us come up the driveway. As we reached the stairs, a couple of footmen ran down to meet us. They looked remarkably fine in the tight trousers and low cut jackets of their Blessing uniforms.

"Hmm, nice," murmured Bright, appreciatively. "Graceson, see to the luggage, will you?" A couple of flustered-looking stablehands rushed round the side of the house dragging a chariot cart. Clearly they'd been caught on the hop without enough time to harness horses to it.

"Take it away," called Bright. "I'm not staying long. Merely a flying Blessing visit." He climbed out of the phaeton. As he landed on the ground, he staggered and slumped back against the blue side panel with a huff of exhaustion. His face gleamed with sweat.

"Bright, how long have you been driving?"

"All night."

I was impressed. For a lone male mage to carry himself and a phaeton for so long was quite a feat. No wonder Bright was exhausted. Mages, especially males, usually marshalled their power by sharing a long journey with another mage and taking regular rest breaks.

"All night! Why didn't you bring someone else?"

"Whew, what a journey! I'm done for," he cried,

ignoring my question. He struck a pose and waved imperiously at the footmen on the step. "*Bring my mother to me and let her feed me cherry cake and wine,*" he cried, quoting from an old poem of war and heroism.

"I think I can hear her now," I said, listening to the hubbub that had arisen in the house. Eff's exuberant voice carried a long way. "She sounds almost pleased. What *can* she see in you, I wonder?"

"My genius, of course," laughed Bright. "Carry the trunk up to Marm Shine's room," he told the hovering footmen. "Graceson, see to it. Now Shine darling," he added loudly, "I'm trusting you to dole out only two of the books in that trunk to Mother every week. Otherwise she's going to get through them too fast."

He winked at me and I managed to nod and smile without looking too mystified. "Quite the intriguer, aren't I?" he whispered, so that I finally realised that we were supposed to be pretending that the trunk was full of books. Well, that would stop the servants snooping, I supposed; Eff's favourite books were powerfully dull tomes about politics and peasant rights.

Bright turned and shambled away up the stairs as Auntie Eff came bursting out of the front door and rushed down the steps, laughing and extending her arms.

As usual, her white hair was coming loose from its bun and sticking out in a wispy halo around her face. She had both sets of spectacles on again. Today her work tunic and pants were covered in flour. I loved Auntie Eff, but no one could ever call her elegant.

31

"Darling mother, you've lost weight," cried Bright, hugging her. Thank the Lady—he didn't know the half of it.

"Pish! I could say the same for you, horrible boy," cried Eff, laughing, kissing him all over his face and surreptitiously wiping her eyes. With a painful flutter in my chest, I realised that it was the first time I'd seen her laugh since Bright's disgrace. "And stop quoting poetry. You know there are no cherries at this time of the year. Come on. Tell me everything you've been doing. Oh, you're filthy. Come, you must have a bath while you tell me what you've been up to."

Cherry cake may have been absent, but there was wine and Bright was soon being plied with all sorts of other dainties that had been prepared for the Blessing party. I left them alone and ran upstairs to my room. I met Graceson coming down.

"Want to come back and hide in my room?" I asked, knowing that he would be trying to avoid Auntie Eff, who blamed him for Bright's inversion.

"I'll wait for him in the stable," he said.

"Stefan," I asked, as he turned to go. "Do you ever hear from your brother?"

"Still in the army, I think," said Graceson. "I don't know where. If I see him, I'll give him your best wishes, shall I?"

I went up the rest of the stairs, filled with curiosity and trepidation at the thought of dealing with the ghost on my own. Also excitement. I loved to hear about new places, and nowhere was as unknown as Ghostland.

The trunk was sitting open and empty at the foot of my bed.

"Outlander," I called softly as I closed the door behind me. "It's me, Marm Shine."

"Here," called a voice and the ghost slid out from under the bed, clutching a little orange and blue backpack that was definitely of foreign make. He slid right into Katti, who had been peering under the bed at him.

"*Sha, Sha, Sha,*" he said in his funny language. "She's huge."

He smells very fearful, thought Katti. *I fear I am too magnificent for him.*

Smug old Katti. I refrained from reminding her of her terror when the ghost had first appeared. Cats have very sensitive pride.

"Don't worry," I told the ghost. "She's big for a hunting cat, but she's very friendly to people. She won't hurt you unless you hurt her first. Or me. I'm her cub as far as she's concerned. I'm afraid you may be spending a lot of time together."

I helped him up off the floor. He was my height, bigger than the few outlanders I'd glimpsed before. The strangest thing was his hair, which was the colour of straw.

He must have known cats, because he politely offered Katti his hand to sniff, before tentatively reaching out to stroke her head. He wore rough cotton miner's clothes. I brushed the fluff and dust off his back. He had lovely muscles, but the pale skin... Argh!

"You have not got anywhere better I can hide? In case someone comes in?"

"Looks like you'd be safe under the bed. Clearly no one ever goes under there. And Hilly promised me they'd swept everywhere. But come…"

I pulled aside a screen to reveal a wardrobe built in to the wall and pushed aside the clothes. "There's this." I opened the narrow secret cupboard in the wall behind the rack.

"This is nice," he said, looking at the little seat.

"It's a lover's hide."

"A what?"

"Lots of these old houses have little secret cupboards for lovers in the wardrobes," I said. "I don't know how ghosts are, but Empire men get can be very tiresome about each other, so sometimes it's simpler that they not meet. Saves all that pointless chesting and fighting."

The ghost stared at me wide-eyed. Then he shook himself and said, "So anyone looking for me would guess this cupboard was here?"

"Possibly. Probably," I conceded.

"Do you have anywhere else?"

"Why would anyone come looking for you?"

"Your cousin didn't mention that we were attacked on our way here? Someone wanted me dead so badly that they set on your cousin's phaeton. Bright's co-driver held them off while we escaped."

That explained why Bright pushed himself so far and so fast, without another mage to take turns at propelling the phaeton. But would the attack have been personal? The roads were full of bandits and rogues.

"Well, they're not going to come and get you here," I reassured him. "Especially not during Blessing time. The place will be lousy with mages."

"Please! You must believe me," he said. Curiously, even though he was a complete foreigner whose feelings should have been a mystery to me, I could sense how real his fear was.

"Well, there is this," I said. Beneath the window was a sliding panel triggered by pressure. In the wall cavity behind there was room for an adult to curl up, chin on her knees. I pulled out the little calico bag lying on the floor where once I'd hid my travel savings. It was empty now—the money spent on draining those new fields and a doctor for Eff. The empty feel of it in my hands made me sad and a sigh escaped me before I could stop it.

The ghost didn't notice.

"So who knows this is here?" he asked.

"Me, Bright, Auntie Eff. Maybe Thomas and Hilly the housekeeper. This used to be my uncle Batty's room, before he died. He had a weakness for Holy Wine, but sometimes he had terrible visions. He'd crawl in here when the hallucinations got too bad. Apparently the pressure of the walls helped. You press at the bottom like this to open it and it closes itself."

"This seems better," said the ghost, squeezing into the little space.

"I brought you some food," I said, handing him the food I'd purloined from Bright's meal. It seemed best not to tell Eff about the Ghost. That way she would have deniability if he was found. "I'm not going to be around much this evening. Neither is anyone else."

"I have arrived in the middle of some kind of event, have I not?" He crawled out of the wall cavity and took the food. After sniffing it, he started eating, gingerly at first and then with increasing gusto.

"Only the most important time of the year. The head of the family travels to all the family estates and walks around the fields blessing the seeds so that they'll be fertile in the coming year."

"So is he the only one coming? The head of the family, I mean."

"She!" I frowned at him, because really, what a stupid grammatical error to make when he spoke the language so well. Though of course he hadn't been in our country very long.

"Of course. Sorry. So is she the only one coming?"

"Oh, no. She brings all kinds of other mages and family and their servants. Fifty-odd people all told. Lucky it's not more, otherwise I'd have to give up my room and you'd have to stay in the trunk."

There was a knock on the door. The ghost dived back under the bed.

"Marm, Lord Bright is leaving and wishes to bid you farewell," called the servant through the door.

"HE'S GOING TO be fine, isn't he?" said Eff as we watched Bright drive away. Her eyes were glistening with tears.

I put my arms around her. I too was relieved that he seemed happy. Perhaps I could manage the coming Blessing days without shouting at anyone after all.

"I've been so worried, and there was nothing to be worried about," she murmured. "He doesn't need our stupid family after all." She gave me a little reassuring pat on the shoulder and pushed me gently away. "Now all I need to do is get *you* sorted out."

"I'm fine." I said. "Nothing to sort out here." I wondered what would happen if the family found out that I had an illegal outlander in my room. Could we be in any more disgrace? Was that even possible?

One of the servants at the upstairs window let out a shout. "Marm! There's a rider coming up from the village. The noble ones must have come over the pass."

"Oh, pish! The family. Just when I was feeling better," groaned Eff. "At least now I won't mind so much when they make snide remarks about my son."

"They'll be gone in four days," I said putting my hand through her arm as we went up the stairs. "Who knows? We might even have some fun. It *is* Blessing time, after all."

CHAPTER THREE

BACK IN MY room, Shadow seemed to have made friends with Katti, who was sitting on a chair by the window. He scratched her absently behind the ears as he bent and peered out of Uncle Batty's old telescope

He has a wonderful touch, Katti thought contentedly. I wondered if he was good at touching in other ways, and moved right away from that thought. That was one curiosity that was never going to be satisfied.

"They are your visitors up there, are they not?" he asked, pointing towards the gap in the hills that was Red Cat Pass. He spoke our language well, but in a very stilted way.

I took a look through the telescope. Sure enough, five huge carriages were flying in stately splendour along the road, so stuffed with people and finery that they looked like window boxes full of bobbing flowers. The magic crystals in the foreheads of the driving mages were bright even in the daylight.

"Ladybless! Look at those hats. They're even bigger than last year. Each of those sods must be wearing three times our annual earnings."

"And the one on the flying golden throne in front is...?"

"Our Matriarch," I said. I noticed that she was causing her crystal to glow with a golden light—a reference to the Lady of Light whose priestess she was. "That's Auntie Splendance. Say one thing for her, she knows how to put on a show. Even in a daylight entrance like this, there'll be something to thrill the peasants. Not that they take much thrilling; nothing much else happens round here."

I took another look through the telescope and snorted. "Rose pink. Does she think she's the Blessed Lady herself? Well I suppose she is, in a sense. I bet there'll be yellow streamers and yellow petals when she comes up the front drive. Wonder where she'll get the petals from, this early in the season? Well, time to be serious. Help me off with these boots, will you? Pull. They're too big so I wear extra socks and they get... whoops! That's it—are you hurt?"

Shadow had sprawled on the floor pulling off my second boot, but seemed undamaged. I started getting changed.

"So the Matriarch is—?"

"The head of our family. The font of our blessings and our fecundity. The representative of the Holy Lady of Light on earth. My legal guardian too, for all that means."

He was staring at me in a funny way and his skin had flushed a bright red colour.

"What?" I asked, pouring cold water into the basin so that I could sponge the dirt and sweat off my chest and neck.

"Nothing," he said, turning his back and returning to looking out of the telescope. "So who else is there?" he asked, as I pulled my white linen under-tunic on.

"Let me see." I took a turn at looking out of the telescope. "In the carriage behind Splen's throne are other family members. The big one's Great-Uncle Igniate. He's the Avunculus."

"That is...?"

"He's the uncle, or in our case the great-uncle, responsible for protecting the children and household. He's the one who should have organised a university education for me. Next to him is Blazeann, Splen's eldest daughter who will probably be Matriarch after her—she's already added three magely daughters to our family line and the Elders favour her. Next to her is her sister Lumina. Curse Lumina; why does she always have to come?"

"You do not like your—what is she, your cousin?"

"That's right, she's my cousin. The meanest of the whole rotten bunch. Every time we're in a room together, I start tripping over furniture and dropping cups."

"What? You mean she makes this happen with her magic? A bit petty."

"It's against the law, too, such as it is. I'd be a sad little skeleton still locked in a cupboard at the Family House if it were up to Lumina. Fortunately, cousin Lucient went and got help."

I took another turn at the telescope. "Good, Lucient's here. I knew there was a reason I didn't run off to the hills. He's Lumina and Blazeann's brother. Auntie Splen's son. He's in the second carriage with that pig rat."

"That who?"

"Lord Impavidus. The one with the flashy gold and blue feathers on his hat. Typical. He's Auntie Splendance's consort. The unspeakable rooster shouldn't be anyone important in her household, but he certainly knows how to make his presence felt. No I'm not going spoil my mood with thinking about him. The two other men are... One of them is Cousin Scintillant, Splendance's nephew."

I felt a flutter in my belly and my heart gave a little twitter of happiness. Stupid cursed heart. I changed the subject quickly.

"The other I can't tell, he's got his face turned away. Ah, it's Lord Illuminus. He's Scintillant's brother. Voice like warm velvet, but what a grouch. Curse it, didn't know Illuminus was coming. I wonder if Thomas counted him. I'd better get down there."

I pulled on my leather body shaper. "Could you lace me up?"

The ghost proved quite adept at lacing. It was nice

to have someone to help me and even nicer to have someone new to talk to.

"So this Lucient let you out of the cupboard?"

"Oh... He was just a toddler then, so he was too short. But he went and got Klea to help. She's another cousin. She's not bad, though I hardly see her anymore—she's fallen out with the family and who can blame her, but Lucient... Lucient's a sweetie. He always brings me lovely books and he gave me that map." I pointed to the large map of the Empire on the wall. "Could you pull a bit tighter? I'm trying to get a bit more cleavage going." I looked in the mirror. "If only I wasn't so small and skinny and pale. Why'd my mother have to mate with a ghost? Sorry, nothing personal."

I opened the wardrobe and pulled out my silken day over-robe. Mine was bone-coloured silk, to make my skin look darker. It was cut down from a much older robe, but the seamstress had done a good job of matching the red-and-gold embroidered flower pattern, and normally I was pleased with it. As I pulled it on, I wondered how long it would take one of the cousins, Lumina probably, to remind me that I'd worn the same robe last year.

Shoes, shoes—there they were.

"So, how about the other four carriages?" asked the ghost.

"Retainer mages and mundane servants. Are you any good at doing hair?"

"I can try. Give me the comb. There are lot of these retainers. Does everyone travel with so many?"

"This is the Lucheyart family."

"Sorry. Forgive my ignorance. You are related to the Imperial family?"

I grinned at him. "My grandmother's the Empress."

"What! You're ONE *of* the Imperial family?" His hands fell to his sides as he stared at me. "*Ka, ka, ka!* I'm really *sha sha sha!*"

"What's the matter?"

"I was trying to keep away from the centres of power. Avoid a diplomatic incident. And now here I am with a royal." He shook his head. "*Ka, ka, ka.*"

"No, you're not," I said. "You have to have magical powers to be noble or royal. Look, Auntie Splen is miles from the throne. Four people at least. Ours is a junior branch. And Eff and I are both mundanes, which means we have no power at all. You couldn't be further from the centre of power, more's the pity. So don't worry. All you've got to do is hide for the next few days and no one important will know. Come on. Can you do a braid?"

"How can you speak our language so well and not know how these things work?" I asked as he braided my hair. I loved having my hair done and he was quick and neat.

He sighed. "It's very complicated. We were here to investigate crystal smuggling through the desert. We weren't meant to come within your borders in any meaningful way. So I didn't bother ..."

"Marm Effulgentia says you should come down now," called a servant through the locked door.

44

"Hell! Reckoning time, I suppose. So what do you think? How are my breasts?" I adjusted my cleavage to show off what there was to its best advantage. I had my pride. And a pointless longing for Scintillant to fall madly in love with me and want no one else.

Shadow started to laugh.

"What? Do they look stupid?" I peered anxiously in the mirror.

"No, no, they look lovely. I mean, how should they look?" he asked. He'd gone bright red again.

"Dark. At least they should match my face. I've been rubbing walnut juice on them all week. No, look properly. Why are you being such an idiot?"

He started to laugh again. "I apologise. It is not you. Things are so different here. You look wonderful. I thought it was your natural skin tone. Really."

I MADE IT back to the top of the Eyrie stairs and Auntie Eff's side just as the stately cavalcade of carriages flew around the curve of the driveway.

In the old days, the family had arrived after dark in a burst of torchlight and fireworks, but after Splendance (and Impi) took over, thrift dictated a more sedate daytime arrival. However, Auntie Splendance still managed to arrive in a cloud of yellow petals. They were silk—specially made, I'd warrant.

(Later that evening I saw one of the junior retainer mages levitating them up into a shining cloud of dancing yellow and blowing them into a trunk, no doubt to be kept for the next religious festival. Ladybless, that pig rat was a pinch-purse.)

The mundane peasants, who had assembled on the gravel before the house in their best cotton smocks, loved the petals and cheered at the top of their lungs.

"Blessings. Blessings, my children!" cried Auntie Splendance, waving languidly. Her voice, magically amplified, carried out over the crowd.

The Blessing party's silken robes shone brilliantly in the late afternoon sun. Tumbles of colourful feathers and bows adorned their huge hats. Because they were mages, there was not a single speck of road dust on their lace-edged shirts, fine leather body shapers, gorgeous silken robes and cloth-of-gold imperial flowers. The retainer mages and servants who filled the carriages behind them were almost as brilliantly dressed, although with slightly smaller hats.

Several special chariot carts had been driven out from their place in the coach house, and each retainer mage responsible for driving a magical carriage carefully landed it on one. That way the magical carriages could be taken round to the coach house without any nobles having to soil themselves by visiting such a humble part of the estate.

The family's servants scampered down the steps at the back of each cart so that they could be ready to rearrange mages' robes and trains and brush off non-existent bits of dust, while the family floated delicately out of their seats.

Eff let out a huff of breath. "Right. Four days and they'll be gone."

I couldn't tell if she was muttering to me or to herself. I squeezed her arm and she patted my hand. I noticed that my teeth were clenched and that I was glaring at Lord Impi, so I directed my eyes downward and breathed out.

Our servants had formed an avenue of welcome at the bottom of the Eyrie steps. Willow-in-the-Mist normally only had two servants, but we got in a lot of extras from the village during Blessing time—mostly young peasants from the estate who helped out in return for the chance to catch the eye of a mage and make their fortunes.

My gaze strayed into the phaeton where Scintillant was seated. He winked and blew me a kiss and—oh, curse it!—I could feel myself blushing and my treacherous mouth turning up at the corners. So much for giving him the cold shoulder. But I was not going to offer him a flower. Finish. End of story. No more.

Once the servants were in place, Auntie Eff and I managed to process down the Eyrie stairs quite elegantly, despite having no servants to rearrange us. By the time the procession of mages approached us, we were down at ground level, kneeling on one knee, heads bowed, leading the obeisance that the assembled peasants made every year to welcome the noble mages.

Our Matriarch had never been one for formality, and she didn't seem to be holding Bright's disgrace against us. Probably couldn't remember it, even. As she did every year, she raised Eff from her obeisance, hugged her and kissed her on both cheeks. They were, after all, sisters, and had grown up together until the accident of magical inheritance had raised Splendance to the nobility and left Eff behind as mere gentry.

Auntie Splen looked the same as last year: thin, ever so slightly unsteady on her feet, eyes vague, long hands fluttering.

"Darling Eff," she cooed. "How lovely to see you. You're looking so well and the place looks divine. All these sweet villagers. So charming. And Shine. Sweetheart, a little kiss for your Matriarch. Are you eating properly? You always look so pale. Impi, darling, we should get this girl to a doctor, don't you think?"

"My dear, have you forgotten she's a half-breed ghost?" murmured Lord Impavidus. He dwelt on the last three words. "No point in wasting money on doctors. She'll always look like that." (Every year, every single year, the same conversation, almost word for word. I tried to see the funny side, but never could.) I kept my eyes lowered in case my hatred for the man who had had Bright beaten and exiled leapt out of my eyes and kicked him.

Auntie Splendance blinked, tried to focus her eyes, gave up and went back to being benignly floaty.

"Oh, well, that's all right then, isn't it? But she is very pale." She patted my belly. I kept my eyes downcast, trying not to pull a face. (Lady of Light, this too. Was I to be spared nothing?) "No babies yet, darling? How sad. More meat, darling. More loving. But more meat, definitely. Might help your colour, too." She patted my cheek and drifted away up the stairs.

"Yes, do something useful with yourself," muttered Lord Impavidus at me as he stalked past.

Him and his snide slights. One of these day I'd...

"Yes, my lord. Thank you, my lord," I said as blandly as I could, looking at the ground. My tone sounded impertinent to me and it must have to Impi too, because he stopped. I tensed myself for a confrontation, knowing I had to keep my tongue between my teeth, but he merely hesitated a moment before bounding up the stairs behind Splen, catching her elbow as he went so that her dithering pace sped up.

"Careful," said Eff in my ear. "Remember he's the power in the household. I don't want to see both of you disowned."

I shut my mouth on the seething cauldron of anger inside. I could have sulked and smoked like lots of the gentry did after they failed the crystal test. Instead, I'd pulled myself together, learned how to use a mundane weapon—the crossbow—and went back to running my mother's estate. Thanks to my hard work, the place was paying its own way for the first time in years. What was that if not useful? In three days' time, I'd have to face Impi across a desk while he went through our accounts, carping all the way. How was I going to do that without shouting at him over the way he had treated Bright?

Lord Igniate (known to those of us who have the dubious privilege of being related to him as Great Uncle Nate) wafted past us on his floating chair, rumoured to contain a chamber pot so that My Lord didn't have to leave his chair while gaming. Lady Splendance's daughters, Ladies Blazeann (who always wore red) and Lumina (who always wore purple), sailed past us in a swish of silk with their noses in the air and a murmured a perfunctory "Blessings" each. Lord Illuminus passed by with a grunt. But my dear Lucient came at me with open arms and a cry of "Blessings, darling Shine."

I was about to throw myself into those arms, when I was seized from behind and wrapped in a huge bear hug.

"Shine, my dear little cousin," cried Scintillant, pulling me off balance (how apt) and giving me a big kiss. "You get more gorgeous every year. Blessings, Blessings, my pretty one."

How had such a dour pointy woman as Auntie Flara produced such a cheerfully raunchy son as Scintillant? Judging from his body shaper, tight black breeches and bulging codpiece, Scintillant was still a ride rat. Why, oh, why did he have to be so pretty? And so lovely in bed? Why, oh, why did my heart always flutter so when he was around? I had to face up to the fact that I was no one special to him and that was it. Finished. Over. Never again.

But if I was too unfriendly, it would have encouraged him. He loved a challenge, did Scintillant. So I hugged him back. He was extremely athletic, broad shoulders, slim hips, all the trimmings, and his arms felt lovely and strong. He always smelt delicious too.

"Oh, you luscious thing!" he cried. "How are you?"

"Scintillant!" called a stern voice from above. "Could you please come up here?"

Cousin Lumina was standing at the top of the stairs, frowning.

"And Lucient," she continued, "Mother wants a pipe packed."

"Oops," muttered Scintillant, frowning comically. "Noble cousin calls, darling." He patted my cheek and leapt away up the stairs. "Yes, yes, cousin dear!" He smiled into Lumina's glare and gave her a firm kiss on the cheek. "I remember perfectly what you said, but I don't care what people say. She *is* luscious."

He gave me a quick wink as he slid his arm through hers and pulled her behind him into the house. Lumina shot me a scowl over her shoulder as she went. I turned away quickly to hide the stupid grin on my face. Ladybless, I was pathetic. Lucient was gone and I hadn't even hugged him.

A man standing at the bottom of the stairs smiled at me warmly, the light of admiration in his eyes. The smile, coming on top of my meeting with Scintillant, confused me, and I looked away. When I glanced back, the man was walking away towards the servant's door. He was a mundane dressed in the dark, sleek clothes of a secretary, which showed off his lean figure. I wondered if I might have a chance for some fun there, and remembered the ghost in my room.

Auntie Eff was hard at work greeting the retainer mages, nobles of new or impoverished lineages who made up Auntie Splendance's retinue. It was my tedious duty to help her. The new ones gazed at me curiously while they mouthed the ritual politenesses.

"That's the one they call Ghostie. You know, Aurora's mistake," I heard one tell another as she nodded at me. "Otherwise, just another mundane."

Heard that before too.

After that came a handful of gentry, mundane members of the Imperial Family like us. They lead happy lives, drifting round the Family House in Elayison, helping out in the archives or the wardrobes, or as secretary companions or nursery stewards—a life I was as entitled to as they were, but had never been lucky enough to have. And never would, probably. Instead I would be spending my life out here being a country bumpkin.

"That's the third of Lord Impi's kin I've seen today," muttered Eff in my ear as the last one filed past. "Sod is filling our house with his sister's children."

I was only half listening. Melancholy was tugging at my edges. *Aurora's Mistake.* Why wasn't I a mage? Why was I motherless? If only I could leave Willow-in-the-Mist. If only I didn't have to see the family twice a year.

The sleek shape of Katti appeared at the top of the stairs. She sat down and curled her tail elegantly around her hind legs.

Too many stupid people making annoying noise, she thought at me.

You could say that again. She must have felt my mood, for as I passed, she stood up and pushed her head into my hand. Comfort flowed out of her.

You are mine, her thoughts said. *Do you need to be anything more?*

What would I do without her?

CHAPTER FOUR

USUALLY, THE BOTTOM of the Eyrie was a cheerless stone hall, with the echoing vault of the tower rising above it like a giant chimney. But when the family visited and it was put to its proper use, we unpacked all the furnishings and it was filled with low couches, rich carpets, cushions and tables. The tapestries were hung back on the walls and the space became warm and comfortable... but very loud. The wooden stairs and balconies leading to the rooms on every level of the tower echoed with the thumps and shouts of servants carrying luggage up to the rooms above, and of retainers using magic to levitate the bigger articles up to the appropriate floors. The hum of people in the hall below was already rising to a roar as everyone tried to hear each other above the din.

The family, at the eye of the storm, had flopped onto the brocade-covered couches in the centre of the hall. Our servants were already moving among them handing out wine and teacups and little meatballs on sticks. I checked with Thomas that all was well with the accommodation, and that Tane the Blessing cook hadn't gone home in a huff. As far as I was concerned the family could starve, but it was Eff they'd take it out on and she'd borne enough.

"Sweetie," said a voice in my ear as Thomas turned away. And there was Auntie Four and Cousin Two with Great Uncle Five, all the mundane members of our family who usually came along at Blessing time. In a large traditional family like the Lucheyarts, the same first names got used again and again. To prevent confusion, the mundanes were simply known by the place they came in birth order.

Cousin Two was Auntie Splen's daughter—Lumina and Blazeann's sister—and acted as a kind of secretary to her mother. She was skinny and beaky but a keen follower of fashion, and had dyed her hair white, which looked odd against her dark skin but very striking. She told me it was ghost fashion—all the rage in Elayison. Auntie Four, who was Eff's favourite sister and her main source of family gossip, enveloped me in a warm lavender and wintergreen hug, and gave me a bag of sweets. As usual Great Uncle Five offered to take me newt hunting. He had retired from active service, but he came for the natural history opportunities. Their fussing and exclaiming soothed my wounded soul. The most powerful members of the family were pig rats, but there were some nice ones, too, and it was a pleasure to see them. I let myself drift along with their chatter.

Unfortunately, that meant that when they fluttered away to check on their sleeping arrangements, I found myself standing, completely exposed to criticism, in among the family's couches.

Auntie Splendance was sitting back taking deep appreciative draws from a long thin smoke pipe, while Lucient packed another one. Blazeann was scanning the manservants, pleating a cloth of gold flower in her hand. She already had three daughters, but the Imperial family could never have enough. To win the gamble of breeding girl-children with magical powers, you had to have a lot of entries in the pool.

Lord Impavidus, who was standing surveying the scene with an offensively proprietary air, raised his hands and clapped. A silken canopy spread out from the landing above us, floating over to the opposite landing to be tied to the banisters by waiting servants. That was new— and what a good idea! Suddenly it was much quieter in the hall.

"This place is a dump!" Lumina's voice rang out loudly in the sudden quietness. I felt my jaw clenching.

Eff, scooting past, gave me a grin and a wink and turned to Lumina—who already had a huge plate of dainties on her lap—and solicitously inquired if she had enough to eat and drink.

"Oh, yes, Lady Lumina," added Impi, "watch your weight. You know how inclined you are to porkiness."

All quite needlessly, since Lumina was obsessively careful of her weight. The maids told me she often threw up her meals.

Lumina flushed and threw the plate of dainties onto an occasional table. His second snide remark for the Blessing period; we were off and racing. I headed for the door before Impi could start picking on me.

A hand caught mine. Lucient smiled up at me from his couch and pulled me down beside him.

"Sweetheart, I've brought you some lovely travel stories. Come and hear about them." He had a tendency to tell me the whole contents of whatever book he was reading in mind-numbing detail, but he did read some interesting books.

Lucient's valet leaned over and held a lighted taper over my cousin's long elegant smoke pipe. Lucient took a long appreciative pull. In the last couple of years he seemed to have become as big a smoke rat as his mother.

"Ah, just the thing! Now I've brought you one about the pagan tribes of Omorod and a lovely one about the archaeology of Parratee. The city was first settled over two thousand years ago, would you believe? Will you take a draw?"

I took a draw from the offered pipe. A hot unfamiliar taste filled my mouth and I coughed.

Lucient thumped me on the back. I seized the glass of water which the ever-capable valet presented.

"Sweetheart, so sorry. I should have thought. It's the new dreamsmoke the ghosts have introduced. The most marvellous dreams, but it's so strong and burns so hot.

You need to take little pulls. Or a lot of people use a water pipe. What's that? Are we to have no peace?"

With a creak, the huge iron doors of the Eyrie had swung open again.

"Shine! Shine!" cried Auntie Eff, rushing towards them. "Someone else is arriving. Oh, Lady, first one extra mage and now another. Thomas, quickly! Make up another couple of rooms. No, I don't know where we're going to put another mage! It looks like one of Flara's lineage. Ah, yes! Lady Chatoyant. And she has Lady Glisten with her. Oh, no, that's two!"

I was taking such great pleasure in whispering to Thomas that he should move Impi's noble nephews into the stable with the mundane menservants to make room that way, that I took a while to notice how Lucient was tugging my arm.

"Shine, stay with me. Please!" he hissed.

"I have to go and greet her."

Lucient pulled me back.

"Shine's staying with me, Auntie Eff."

I shrugged at Eff, who had more important things to worry about and flustered away.

"Let her go," purred Lumina. "I'll protect you from Toy."

"Even I'm not smoked up enough to believe that, darling sis," scowled Lucient.

Lumina flicked his cheek, a playful gesture on the surface but hard enough to make him wince. As she flounced away, I hissed, "What's going on? Are you getting me into trouble?"

"No, no, Toy never notices gentry. Me, on the other hand, she claims to be absolutely smitten with. I can't shake her off."

He didn't seem her sort. Chatoyant was active and busy. Lucient was... not. He caught my raised eyebrow and didn't take it as an insult.

"I don't think she really wants me, but she knows I'm in line to be the next Avunculus. Bloody Flara's get; they're all so ambitious."

"But if you take Toy's keys, she'll do all the work of being Blazeann's Avunculus. Could be an easy life for you, Lucient," I said.

"Easy life! The woman's a fiend. She wants me to give up dreamsmoke. And the theatre. And she wants sex *all the time*. She believes in only mating with mages." He shuddered. "Can we pretend to be having an affair, please? Where's your flower? Quick, pin it on me."

"I haven't got one," I giggled; the smoke must be going to my head. "No one's going to look at me."

"Oh, poor little Shiney," cooed Lucient, grabbing my cheeks and wobbling them just as Scintillant and Illuminus's sister, Lady Chatoyant, sailed into the room in a swirl of green silks. She was tall and thin and looked like a hawk. An attractive hawk, of course. All mages were as attractive as money could make them. She shot me the sort of look that would melt glass. Oh, Lady, what had I let myself in for? She was followed by a tall magnificent mage with masses of grey hair.

"Hmmm, Great Aunt Glisten. I wonder what she wants," murmured Lucient, enfolding me in a warm smoky embrace and rubbing his head against mine. Suddenly he stopped and hissed in my ear, "That prick. Blazeann has told on Mother. That's why Glisten's here."

"What?"

"There was an unfortunate incident at Plains-of-gold. Cursed Blazeann, she's so frothing to be Matriarch, she must have sent to the Council and complained that Mother's unfit. Prick, prick, prick."

Another teacup tornado among the mages. The distinctly cold undercurrent in the greeting Splendance and Impavidus gave the new arrivals seemed to support Lucient's story. The moment she dropped Lady Glisten's hand, Lady Splendance rose and announced that it was time to dress for dinner. The crystal in her forehead lit up and she floated upwards, passing through the gap between the silken canopy and the staircase full of scampering servants towards her room at the top of the tower. This was the signal for the rest of the visitors to follow, which gave our household the chance to clear all the divans to the side of the room and bring out the long trestle tables for the meal.

"Come on up to my room and have some fun, sweetheart," said Lucient, as loudly as possible. He put his arm round my waist and his forehead crystal shone as we rose into the air together.

I adore flying.

The new dreamsmoke must have been strong. It took me several attempts to remember that I wanted to ask Lucient the details of what happened at Plainsofgold.

"Oh, nothing very terrible," he whispered in my ear. "Mother hasn't quite got the hang of this new dreamsmoke's strength. Had some in the night, was still completely smoked in the morning. Could have happened to anyone. And anyway, Blazeann covered up, and the mundanes never noticed."

"Auntie Splendance smoked dreamsmoke the night before a Blessing?" I hissed. I didn't share Lucient's relaxed attitude to the Blessing ceremony.

"Oh, don't be such a prude. There's no rule against smoking before the Blessing. And Mother's not used to sobriety. She gets horribly depressed. Sweetheart, a little frolic?" he added loudly, as we floated past Toy. "Give us an appetite."

He peppered my cheek and neck with kisses.

From the look Toy gave us, I suspected she wasn't fooled.

"Lucient, no offence but I hope you don't seriously want to do anything," I whispered as we floated over the fifth floor balcony rail and in through the doorway.

"Oh, no! Heavens, sweet thing, I mean, pardon me, I love you madly of course, but as a friend only. Anything more—"

"It'd feel like incest, wouldn't it?" I whispered.

"Indeed," he said. "I wish everyone was as sensible as you."

LUCIENT'S ROOM HAD already been decorated with his own linen, carpets and wall hangings, and a little maid called Sharlee had his dreamsmoke bowl all mixed and ready for him. That ghost dreamsmoke was strong. I didn't have any more, but Lucient did, and the smoke in the room seemed to scramble my brain completely.

I lay on Lucient's bed and giggled. Lucient's maid bounced up and down beside me, making the springs creak suggestively while Lucient read bits from his favourite books to me. Time passed without my noticing it. Lucient's valet, Busy, found a pretty little cloth rose for me to pin to Lucient and dressed me in a set of Lucient's dinner robes, which added to the fiction that we'd been 'treading the Blessing path' together. The sleeves of the robe were quickly folded and sewn back so that I could eat without trailing them into my food. Such lovely fussing.

Somehow, I found myself seated back at the dinner table with no clear memory of how I had got there. Busy had told Thomas to ensure I sat next to Lucient, and on my other side was Great-Uncle Igniate. At least he was an easy dinner companion, belching and rumbling happily away about his main obsessions—food and gambling. Since Blessing food was all meaty baby-making food, the fare could be lean for those avoiding fertility. But dear Hilly seemed to have made all my favourite vegetarian nibbles this year and brought them to my side herself. I started having the sort of good time a person is supposed to have during the Blessing festival.

There was no sign of Scintillant, so I couldn't torment myself by counting the flowers pinned to his robe. Best of all, Impi was picking on Cousin Illuminus, who apparently had joined the party yesterday without any warning, "expecting poor Marm Effulgentia to accommodate your whims with typical thoughtlessness. And after all the disappointments she's had to suffer."

Impi's further inevitable snide remarks about Bright cleared my head. The meal also helped. By the time we rose from the table and drifted into the drawing room for smoke and liqueurs, I'd remembered how much I hated the people who controlled my life.

Toy was no real danger to Lucient tonight—the women mages of the family spent the Blessing nights in chastity and prayer in order to preserve their powers— so I was able to slip away without his protesting. But as I was scurrying back to my room to check on the ghost, Thomas caught my arm.

"Bright's in trouble," he hissed.

CHAPTER FIVE

NOTHING COULD HAVE got my attention quicker.

"Bright's still in the village. He was too exhausted to go far tonight. The innkeeper waived the Blessing rule and said he might stay at the inn. News has got about and Grumpy's come to complain to Lady Splendance."

Thomas dragged me down the passageway towards the entrance hall of the house as he spoke.

"Oh, Lady! Where are they? Does Impi know?"

"Look out," hissed Thomas, pulling me into a nearby room as the door of the drawing room opened back along the passage. Katti was snoozing by the banked-up fire. She lifted her head and gave a brief mew of enquiry before deciding our human business wasn't interesting.

Through the half-open door, I saw Impi floating past along the passageway and into the great hall of the Eyrie. Most mages walked when they were on the level, but Impi had to make a show for the peasants. Silly rooster.

We crept down behind him to see what was going on.

"Good evening, good fellows. Blessings upon you." Impi was at his most urbane. He landed and strutted forward, shoulders back, hips square, all in blue and red and gold like some cheap village cock. He shouldn't even have been there; this sort of thing was the duty of the Matriarch, or failing her, the Avunculus, Great Uncle Igniate.

Not that the villagers cared. A mage was a mage to them. As Thomas and I crept out and huddled in the shadows where the passageway opened into the Eyrie, I heard the rustle and thud of mundanes dropping to their knees. Impi stretched out his bejewelled hand, and each of the villagers shuffled forward on their knees to kiss his ring.

Sure enough there was Grumpy the blacksmith, a hulking fellow with a huge belly and a perpetually scowling slit of a mouth—and backing him up were four of his drinking buddies. Always sitting round in the inn complaining the world was doing them wrong when they should've been home helping their sisters.

It made sense that Grumpy would rat on Bright. Bright's valet, Graceson, was Grumpy's nephew and their scandalous relationship did Grumpy no favours in the village. I wondered if he realised that his nephew would come out far worse in any brush with my uncle than Bright would. Perhaps he didn't care. *Men are strange cattle,* as the saying goes.

Impi waved his hand languidly at the villagers.

"Please rise. How may I be of service to you, my fine peasants?"

Amazing how he could make the most innocent words sound belittling.

"With all due respect to your lordship, we come to tell you we don't hold with mages staying overnight in the village, 'specially not during Blessing time. We'd be very beholden to you if you could make our representation to the mages concerned," said Grumpy.

"Mages?" asked Impi. "What mages?"

"Lord Bright," muttered Grumpy. "We don't hold with it, whatever Jar Ellasdaughter says. It breaks our sacred agreement. No mages overnight in the village, that's how it's always been."

"Lord Bright is lodged in the village?" said Impi calmly. He flicked an imaginary piece of dust off his sleeve. "How very interesting."

"Thomas, quickly, get my horse saddled," I hissed. "I'll be there in a moment."

Thomas ran away down the darkened hall.

I darted back into the breakfast room. Katti had sensed my urgency and was up already, stretching her back into an arch. By the light of the banked-up fire, I scribbled a note of warning and tied it securely round Katti's collar, all the time telling her to go to Bright in the village inn. If she went straight there, she would get there very quickly, but cats are easily distracted and I knew I had to follow her to be sure.

I shoved open the glass door to the breakfast room and she shot past my legs and lopped away towards the village while I ran round to the stables.

I KEPT THE horse at a canter most of the way despite the track being dark and rough underfoot. All the time I was peering back over my shoulder, certain that the mages would set out immediately. When Bright's relationship with Graceson had finally become a scandal, Impi had had his retainers thrash him in the street. They'd hurt him so badly that Bright'd been too concussed to use magic and had had to come back to Willow by canal boat. I still remembered the swollen eye, the broken nose and the dark bruises. Graceson said he'd pissed blood at first and it was two days before he could heal himself enough to walk properly. Impi had promised a repeat performance if he ever set eyes on Bright again.

My one consolation was that Impi would want to gather help and he would need to be selective in who he chose for such a sensitive family mission. The women would be praying tonight and unavailable, and he would not want to involve mere retainer mages. This gave me some hope of beating them there.

As I cantered down the dirt track that was the village's main street, I was cheered to see no sign of crystal light behind me. The tap room of the big whitewashed inn at the village centre was noisy with drinkers, but everything else seemed quiet. I leapt off my horse and ran into the inn.

"Where's the mage?" I cried to the little serving boy, who was passing through the front hall way with a tray full of dirty plates.

"Parlour or—"

I didn't hear the rest of what he said. I dashed up the stairs and barged in through the private parlour door crying, "Look out. Impi's coming."

"Why, my dear!" said a languid voice. "Unpleasant news, no doubt, but surely not cause for alarm."

I found myself facing not Bright, but another of my noble cousins, Lady Sparklea, the one who'd let me out of the closet all those years ago. The only decent one of the lot. She was standing by the fire in riding boots, plain travelling clothes and a merely medium-sized hat: yet she still looked stylish. Klea always did.

"Oh, no! Sorry, I—"

There was a crash from upstairs and an explosion of magic. Without pausing to think I blurted out, "Bright's hiding upstairs. Impi and the others have come to beat him up. I have to help him. He's almost exhausted."

"You can't go up there," shouted Klea, as I dashed back towards the door.

I felt myself seized by her power and pulled back as she raced past me and up the stairs. I went after her, only to run into her back on the top step.

"What are you going to do?" I asked, uncertain of her loyalties. As children, she and Bright and I had all been great friends, but it was a long time since I'd last seen her.

"Rescue Bright, of course," cried Klea, pushing me back against a door at the end of the corridor. "I told you to stay."

She had her hat pulled down over her head and was tying a kerchief over her nose, covering everything but her eyes.

Further down the hall, a door hung shattered on its hinges and sounds of shouting and breaking wood came from the room. Even as Klea flew towards the broken door, a burst of power shot out, blurring the air and blasting a hole in the wall of the corridor. Klea threw herself in at the door, power already forming between her hands, and almost tripped over a large animal shape that came streaking out through her legs.

"Katti! Here! Good girl!" I shrieked, as the blast of magic rocked the whole inn.

As I tried to reach out and catch her, someone touched my arm. I jumped so much, I missed Katti and she fled away down the stairs.

"Shine, stay in here," cried Graceson. He'd come out of the other room. He had a loaded crossbow in his hand and he was making for Bright's room.

I seized his arm. "No! You stay. A mage has gone to help Bright." Even as I spoke, the whole inn rocked to another blast of power. Graceson and I clutched each other.

"For Mother's sake, put that thing down," I cried over the sounds of shouting and smashing.

Graceson pulled the bolt out of the crossbow. "I smell smoke," he said.

The fire or candles in Bright's room must have got away—inevitable in a magical fight with so much air swirling around. Even as we smelt the smoke, it began to fill the corridor. Graceson and I tumbled down the stairs as quick as we could, both screaming "Fire! Fire!"

Not that we needed to. The last of the villagers were already rushing out into the street. People were screaming and shouting. The round figure of Jar Ellasdaughter could be seen organising a bucket line from the well. Someone was running towards the inn carrying a ladder.

As Graceson and I ran towards the well to help, a hole burst in the thatched roof of the inn and two figures shot out and streaked away across the sky, arm in arm. Burning straw flew everywhere as three more figures burst through another part of the roof and shot off in the same direction. From the speed of the first couple, I was certain that that was Klea in the front, which meant that Bright was most likely safe. I eased out a sigh of relief.

Jar the Innkeeper was screaming, "Shitty mages!" and shaking her fists at the sky. "What about my sodding roof, you scabby roosters?"

Her voice was drowned out by a roar of flame as the fire streamed up through the thatch.

She looked angry enough to forget my rank, so I abandoned the idea of helping out and took up the idea of running away instead. Graceson must have had the same thought. As I was looking fruitlessly for my horse—which clearly had long since bolted for home—he seized my arm and dragged me down an alleyway. Liking his plan so far, I broke into a run and followed him as he sprinted along a couple of dark muddy lanes.

We quickly found ourselves at the edge of the village. By the flickering light of the burning inn, we could see the village temple nestled under its huge Holy Tree.

We both leaned against the tree and coughed smoke out of our lungs.

"That was my lord in the front, wasn't it? Do you think he'll get away?" asked Graceson. He was completely devoted to Bright.

"That was a female helping him," I said. "No way they'll catch them."

"Ladybless," breathed Graceson. He pushed open the temple door and drew me in after him.

The village priest, a very old man, was sitting on a pallet on the floor beside a brazier. Our village was too insignificant to have a female priest. He lit a taper and looked up at us.

"My boy. How wonderful to see you," he cooed in a voice like dried husks.

"Most Holy Zostre," sighed Graceson. "Thank the Lady, it's still you. You must be the only person in this village happy to see me."

CHAPTER SIX

WE VISITED WITH the priest for the rest of the evening. Graceson recounted the tale of his meeting with his mother, Grace, and of her reproaches. Though he told the story in a humorous way, I could sense the pain beneath it and squeezed his arm. He and the priest began exchanging news about places and people I knew little of, so I left them and wandered into the temple proper. In the flickering light of the votive lanterns, I could see spring leaves and a few early flowers heaped around the feet of the statue of the Bright Lady of Light. But most villagers still believed in the old spirits of place and of nature they had worshipped in the days before Magekind had arrived from out of the rising sun and brought the civilising influence of the Lady of Light, and the temple reflected that. Clustered around the feet of the Lady and huddled in niches in the walls were dozens of little statuettes dedicated to tree spirits and well spirits, to Mooncat and Grain Boy.

Zostre, a village man himself, understood this. If truth be told he was more an old-style shaman than a priest of Light. Grain Boy helped make the crops grow, so I could see the point of him, but Mooncat was a forest spirit who never seemed much use to me. Yet it was a popular spirit in our district, with little shrines all over the forest. It always seemed to me that the villagers had more belief in Mooncat than even Our Bright Lady.

I lit some incense and made a prayerful obeisance to the Bright Lady and to all the other spirits as well. I was officially a Light worshipper, but I had never seen the Bright Lady of the Sky except in her guise as the sun. I had, however, seen things in the forest—shapes rising from lakes and glowing lights moving among the night trees. Sometimes I sensed a personality in trees and other supposedly inanimate things. I could not help believing in spirits. I'd never told anyone except Bright. Auntie Eff, like most educated people, dismissed spirit worship as arrant superstition.

"The gentlewoman is welcome to take my mattress for the night," offered the priest. "Please, I press you to stay. The spirits of Mooncat are restless at night." Regretfully I declined. I was worried about the ghost alone in my room and also about what would happen if Impi found out I'd come to warn Bright. Eff's allowance was the only money we had and Impi kept threatening to have it cut back. Once the village had quietened down, I took a torch from those by the temple door and set out to walk home by torchlight.

Willow was two miles walk from the village. The same cart tracks I'd ridden down so quickly seemed a long way back on foot in the dark, with only torchlight for company. I'd shed my robes before I'd gone out, so I was freezing in my underrobe and body shaper. My dress shoes, which were cheap and flashy, were extremely unsuitable for walking on mud. Curse Bright; he owed me a pair of good shoes.

Worried about where Katti might be, I called out for her a few times, but stopped as the farmland ended and the home forest came into view. The forest surrounding the manor house descended unbroken from the mountains and, despite the river, which acted as a kind of moat, wild cats and grunters would occasionally turn up near the house. No point in attracting their attention.

Or other things. The forest of the Secret Mountains was an uncanny place even this close to habitation. Big pallidly glowing orchids known as corpse lilies hung in the branches of trees like sickly lanterns. The earth around here was impregnated with crystal dust, and magic got into every living thing. Inanimate things moved and creeping animals flew. You heard things talking in strange inhuman voices sometimes.

Tonight, as the trees closed in along one side of the road, I felt certain something was watching me. I wished Katti were there with me to scent danger. *Don't be a coward*, I told myself and kept walking steadily, if a little faster.

Then a twig cracked so loudly that I spun round before I could stop myself.

Padding along the track behind me was the biggest glowing white wild cat I had ever seen. I swear it was as bigger than I was.

I screamed and almost dropped my torch.

It stopped, one shimmering velvet paw in mid-air.

"No!" I cried, trying to sound commanding. I held the torch out towards it. It seemed a pitiful matchstick against such a creature and the hand that held it shook.

It stood there, a few small bounds away. Shimmering. Huge. Real. I would never outrun it and it didn't seem worried by the torch.

It took a step towards me. This wasn't some tame hunting cat, it was a wild cat three times the size of Katti.

"No!" I shouted again; it sounded pleading. "Don't."

I waved the torch around. It took another step towards me.

Suddenly it turned and loped away, with a crashing of grass.

A bright light came skimming around the bend from the house and I ran towards it.

"Help, help!" I cried. The light slowed and hovered above me and I saw it was a messenger mage in one of those enclosed chairs they travelled in. Must have been an important message to have gone to such expense.

"What do you want?" said the messenger, sticking her head out of the window.

"My horse bolted and I saw a wildcat," I cried. "Please help me!"

"A wildcat? Really?" she cried excitedly. Oh, to be a mage, for whom the thought of a large deadly beast delightful rather than terrifying.

"Please can you take me...?"

But she had set out in the direction of my finger, shining a light over the fields beneath her. Just my luck to have met up with a keen hunter.

"Can you take me back to the house?" I shouted.

"'Gainst regulations," she called back. "You go on. I'll stay and keep an eye out for the beast. Go on. You haven't got far to go."

Curse her! Still, it was better than nothing. I set off at a run.

BACK AT THE house, I panted round to the bathhouse, hoping to wash off the mud and smoke and get warm. Alas, it was occupied. The village wheelwright was on his back on the warm boards near the stove being fiercely ridden by a woman retainer mage. Another lad crouched behind her, stroking her breasts and kissing her neck. The wheelwright was a very virile lover— I'd enjoyed him myself—but from the clenched look around his mouth, he was doing his best to last as long as possible and not enjoying it too much. I closed the door as softly as I could and went round to the kitchen.

Thomas was sitting at the kitchen table with Hilly and Jenna. All of them were wearing the long hooded robes of mundanes who did not want to take part in Blessing congress. I was still shaken by my brush with the Mooncat and considered telling them about it. Then I thought better of it. A confession would cause a fuss. Hilly would cover me in sacred amulets and everyone would get anxious about what it meant. And maybe it'd been nothing. Maybe I'd been affected by puffball spores drifting out of the forest and had simply had a vision.

"The women of the family retired to rest some time ago," Thomas told me. "Lord Impavidus and the boys are back. Lord Bright and a mysterious woman escaped—so they say."

"Has he gone over to the right path, Marm?" asked Hilly. Hilly, who had been our nurse, always hoped that Bright would 'come good.' As if he wasn't good enough as he was.

"I don't think that's what it means. Did Impi ask after me?"

"I don't think he noticed," said Thomas. "Though he berated your aunt about letting Bright visit her. In front of everyone. But Lady Glisten defended her, so I don't think she'll lose her allowance."

"If only I could get her away from here," I sighed. No chance of that. Eff had been exiled to Willow for her political activities before I had been born. She wasn't even supposed to leave the estate.

Thomas shrugged. "Give me your shoes, Shine. I'll clean them. Then there'll be nothing to find if they do look."

Dear Thomas. When he'd been young, a cart accident

had crippled his leg and, seeing that he had no future in farm work, Eff had taken him on as a houseman. One of Eff's flashes of brilliance. He would have been wasted hoeing weeds anyway, for he was very clever, managed to learn letters and figures with only a little help from Eff, and had been a better uncle to me and Bright than anyone in the family. And unlike Eff, he always remembered to see there was enough food in the place. He drew me two pails of hot water from the water tank and I carried them up the stairs. Not much chance of getting any help. The servants from the village would all be in with the mages. That was the real reason they were here. Our pay was lousy.

Through the half-open door of the great hall came laughter and the sound of the village band playing sultry music. I saw the shadows of people dancing on the table in the dim light. The night before a Blessing ceremony was one of stern chastity for the women of the family as they conserved their energy to bless the crops, but the rule didn't apply to the men or to any of the retainers. Soon a trail of half-drunk couples would be wending their way up into the Eyrie bedrooms to try for the next crop of Blessing babies.

The last thing I wanted was to witness the village girls working their charms on Scintillant. I went on upstairs. As I was heading down the upper hallway towards my room, the door of Eff's bedroom opened and the nice-looking fellow who'd caught my eye on the steps came out. His eyes widened when he saw me, but that was the only sign of guilt he gave.

"What are you doing?" I asked sternly, knowing that Eff was up at prayers with the rest of the Lucheyart women. Surely this fellow wasn't a thief? A spy for the Elders, perhaps. My aunt read, and secretly wrote, a lot of radical mundane-rights articles.

"Forgive me, lady. I was lost."

The 'lady' confirmed my suspicions. People only call a mundane 'lady' when they want to get around her.

"It's Marm, as well you know," I snapped. "Who are you and who is your lord?"

"I am Hagen Stellason and I have the honour to attend the Avunculus as a secretary, Marm."

A secretary? Rubbish. What would Great Uncle Nate be doing with a secretary?

Hagen bowed again and gave me a smile full of meaning as he rose from the bow. "Might I have the great pleasure of asking for a flower from you, Marm?

Cheek of the fellow. Did he think lust was going to blind me to his lies? Yet I love an audacious man, and he was handsome.

"Not tonight," I said, suppressing a smile. I turned and pointed up the hall to the staircase that led to the servants' quarters. "You're on the wrong floor. That is the way to your room. Or"—I pointed to the closed door of the great hall—"back to the great hall if you wish to win a flower tonight."

"Yes, Marm. Thank you, Marm," I sensed irony in his tone, the rooster. I watched him climb all the way up the stairs to the attic before I went into my own room.

"Shadow," I called softly as I put the buckets down on the floor. "Where are you, ghost?" There came a knocking on the wall under the window and when I pushed open the panel, the ghost tumbled out at my feet.

"You did not tell me how to open it," he panted. "I couldn't get out."

I made soothing noises and showed him where to press the inside of the panel.

"I don't suppose you saw who came in, did you?" I asked, wondering if Hagen had searched my room and why. I often wondered if they thought I was a radical too. Sometimes I even wondered that myself—though I preferred to think that I was simply practical. Let's face facts; serfdom makes for rubbish farm work.

"No," snapped Shadow. "There was more than one. The first one was tapping on the walls and I think he found that Lover's Hide thing. The second scared him off. He was much quieter. I suppose it was lucky I was trapped, because I couldn't be sure when he left."

So handsome Hagen had probably been in my room as well. How very thorough of him.

I wondered who the other one was. My heart twitched at the (unlikely, and I knew it was unlikely) thought that Scintillant might have been one of my visitors.

"More action in my bedchamber than I would have expected," I said, lighting a candle. "Pity I was away. Well I'm going to wash and go to bed. Undo me, will you?"

"No party?" he asked, pulling out the lacing at the back of my body shaper. "I can hear music downstairs."

"No party," I said. "Blessing time is really about mundanes seducing mages. Gentry like me are kind of irrelevant. To everything, really."

"So tell me about this Blessing festival. From your cousin, I got the impression that people have a lot of... um... sexual intercourse during Blessing time."

"Sexual intercourse," I echoed, unable to help laughing at the prissy way he'd put it. "You mean they pleasure themselves stupid." Then I felt mean for laughing, because, after all, he was speaking a language foreign to him, which must be why he often seemed over-formal. So I added, "The Blessing is a fertility festival. People believe it's easier to conceive a child at this time of year. Certainly this is when the peasants eat the most meat and when they've got the best chance of mating with a mage and breeding another mage." I pulled the shirt over my head. "Do you want any of this water? Where have you gone?"

"Yes, thanks. Later," said Shadow. He had turned his back and gone to the window.

I was beginning to suspect that he had some kind of problem with nudity. Different customs, I thought with a shrug. I'd heard there were some tribes in the cold South who pleasured with all their clothes on. Maybe the ghost's land was another such cold place. I sat in my bath and started sponging myself down with lovely warm water. It made up for the chill in the fireless room.

"So are you going to try to get pregnant? Am I in your way here?" asked the ghost.

"Oh, no! I'm not even eating meat."

"Meat? What has meat got to do with it?"

"You can't get pregnant if you're not eating meat. It's simply not possible. Everyone knows... Is it different in your land?"

"We're fertile no matter what. So why are you not allowed to get pregnant?

"Allowed? It's not that. I've been stuck here at Willow all my life, and I want to see the world first. And I don't want to go off like my mother and leave my child to be brought up by other people. Especially not this family."

"This family?"

But I'd had enough of personal talk. I felt uneasy enough voicing the shocking fact that I didn't want to have children. Talking about wanting to see the world first reminded me that I had no plans to leave Willow for as long as Eff needed me. Depressing.

"This second pail of water's for you," I said, pulling my night shirt on. "You can use the basin and this washcloth. Help me pour the dirty water back into the pail. There's a clean wash cloth and towel in that chest."

He took the washing things behind the screen. The sound of him splashing around made me curious, but when I peered over the screen to see what his naked body was like, he squeaked and held the towel over his prick.

"Do you mind?" he said.

"What?"

He sighed. "Ghosts do not like to show their naked bodies," he said patiently.

"Oh, fair enough. I was just curious. You look like a normal man."

He signed again. "Yes, I have no tentacles anywhere. No, not even out of my behind," he added, adjusting the towel so I couldn't see his buttocks.

I left him to it. If I stood in the right place, I could still see him in the mirror without his knowing. He was nicely shaped, but it was difficult to get over the sickly paleness of his skin. The sweet way he was enjoying his wash made me feel unfair for spying on him. He was as dependant on me as a child would be and deserved the same respect.

I threw myself down onto the bed. My legs ached. Never walk two miles in evening shoes.

"Are you any good at massaging feet, Shadow?" I called, as I heard him pouring out the water.

"I have had some experience," he said.

"Would you rub mine, now you've finished washing?"

"Certainly."

"I hope you won't be offended if we don't make love afterwards," I said, as he approached the bed. "I only want a massage."

He looked startled, but since that seemed to be his second most common expression, I didn't inquire.

"I do not mind at all," he said, as he settled himself on the bed at my feet. "I think it would complicate matters if we were to become sexually involved."

"Sex-u-ally involved," I laughed as I sounded out the entire huge phrase. "You're so adorable. I begin to see what my mother saw in ghosts. You've gone all red again."

"This is a taboo subject among my people. Sexual intercourse, I mean."

"Really? How do you get baby ghosts?"

"We do it plenty," he snapped, though his mouth was turned up at the corners. "But without talking about it all the time. Are there no taboo subjects for you people?"

"It's not really polite to bandy about the name of the man who sired you. Although everyone talks about my sire. Not wanting to have children is definitely wrong."

"Do not worry. Your secret is safe with me." He was a good massage-boy, with nice strong thumbs. "I suppose sex between men is taboo too. This is why Lord Bright has been exiled, is it not?"

"Bless, yes! How did you know? About Bright, I mean. He's very discreet."

"I could see they were a couple. It is quite common among our people. No one worries about it. Love is love."

"That's very reasonable of you." I felt oddly comfortable talking about this dirty subject with him. "So do you pleasure men? What do you do exactly?"

"No, no! It is not mandatory. Just accepted. But I understand why it's disliked here. Your whole culture seems to be about getting women pregnant. I get the impression it's difficult for you to conceive."

"Of course. Isn't it the same for your people?"

"No, it is quite easy."

"Really? Now that makes sense."

He laughed. "I am glad you think so."

"Eff told me that my mother had no intention of getting pregnant, that she wasn't even eating meat and yet your countryman's seed made her flower. You must be very fertile. Well, I don't want to compound her mistake by getting pregnant to another ghost. So no loving. Lady knows what they'd say about another half-breed."

"*Wqhucla ir hariti*," said the ghost. "Look, no sexual relations is totally fine with me. I am not some kind of animal, you know."

I felt the sting of rejection. Most men adore making love and get sulky when you don't want to. Was I so ugly? I told myself to toughen up. You can't be attractive to everybody. And who knew what ghosts liked?

"I guess I do look rather strange to you. Like you look to me."

"Exactly," said the ghost as if relieved. "Nothing to be hurt by. Let us just be friends. Hey, now tell me about this Blessing ritual. Can your mages really make seeds more fertile?"

"The peasants certainly think so. If the seed doesn't get blessed, they won't even sow it. Auntie Eff says it's all rubbish, but—"

A loud knocking sounded at the window. Shadow gasped, dived off the bed and rolled underneath it.

I pulled open the curtains and was astonished (and delighted, curse it) to see Scintillant hovering outside.

"Happy Blessing time," he shouted, waving a bottle of sparklewine at me. "Let us tread the Blessing path together."

I shook my head. "Tired," I mouthed at him and made to pull the curtains closed.

Of course it didn't do any good. Mages can do exactly as they like and Scintillant simply lifted the latch of the window with magic and pushed it open.

I pushed him back as he tried to come in.

"No, you don't," I said.

"Oh, Sweetie. You're looking so lovely tonight."

"Go away. I'm sure there's plenty of others slavering for it." I shouldn't have added that last bit. It sounded petulant.

"Jealous, darling?"

"No. Just tired," I snapped.

"Oh, Sweetie, I'll pep you up." He stroked my cheek with his finger tip. "You know I can."

No point in arguing with him there.

"Look, I don't feel like it," I said.

"You're mad at me, aren't you?" He stroked my cheek. I pulled away from him. "Oh, sweet thing, what did naughty Scinty do to you?"

Annoyed by this baby talk, I pushed and managed to dislodge him from the window.

He floated in the air outside, laughing.

"Get out of here," I shouted. "I'm not giving you a flower this Blessing. Do you get it? You'll have to have one less notch on your belt."

This made him laugh even more. "Who told you about the belt?"

The moment I spoke, I was annoyed with myself for telling him. "Lumi showed me. Get out of here and leave me alone."

"The rat." He sounded even more amused. "She gets so jealous." He put his hand on the window sill. "Did you get jealous too, sweetie? I like the sound of that."

A red spike of anger went right to my brain.

"Piss off, weasel dick," I shouted. I tried to slam the window shut, caught his fingers which made him yelp, opened the window to push him back and slammed it again, this time unimpeded.

"You rotten little—" roared my cousin. A gust of magic flung the window open. The curtains flew back into my face and I lost my balance and staggered backwards.

"Curse you," I shouted, straightening up only to discover that his light had gone.

Really gone. After I stuck my head out the window to check, I felt like crying. Did he have to give up so easily?

"Are you all right?" whispered the ghost from under the bed.

"Of course," I said, through the annoying lump in my throat. Stupid ride rat. I hoped his feelings weren't too hurt over the weasel dick remark. For Lady's sake, why did I even think that? Scintillant didn't have real feelings. Only ride rat urges. And I was better off if he was offended.

I must have let out a groan as I closed the curtains. Shadow reached out and touched my foot.

"Are you sure you are all right?"

"Yes," I said. "I'm just a stupid woman with a weakness for someone completely unworthy."

"So, like everyone else in heaven and earth," said Shadow.

I couldn't help smiling at that. "So this happens to ghosts too?"

Another knock on the window sent Shadow shooting back under the bed before he could answer.

My heart leapt for joy at this sign of Scintillant's attachment to me, but when I opened the curtains I found Lord Illuminus, Scintillant's older brother, floating there by crystal light, looking concerned. Concerned for me? I doubted it.

"What's happened?" he asked as I opened the window. His voice was distinctive, rough as gravel, but warm at the same time. It was the only thing I liked about Illuminus. "Are you hurt? Was Scintillant trying to force himself on you? You shouldn't have to push him out. You're a woman of the lineage, not some peasant girl."

Ah ha. Illuminus was obviously trying to get one over Scintillant. The usual family politics.

"Oh, Lord Illuminus, I was never in any danger from Lord Scintillant and you know it. It was a Blessing tiff. Don't go telling Lord Impavidus."

Because the odd thing was that despite all his snobbery, Impi was very strict about the Great Pact and made Auntie Splendance deal very severely with any forcing of mundanes by mages.

"Impavidus doesn't need me to go running to him with tales. He knows what Scintillant is. He's really not good enough for you, Shine."

I stared at him. This from Illuminus, who had never said a polite word to me before.

"You look a bit upset, Shiney." He put his hand through the window and took my hand before I knew what he was doing.

"I'm fine," I said firmly but politely. "Thank you, Lord Illuminus."

"You don't want me to stay with you," he said. "I'd be very honoured."

Blah, what was this? I wasn't even fertile and yet the men were all over me. And Illuminus, of all people! I mean, he was well enough looking, but eww, what a snob.

I turned my face away. "That's very kind of you, Lord Illuminus."

"Call me Illuminus, please," he said softly. He had caught my hand again and was covering it with sloppy kisses. "I don't know what it is. Tonight my eyes are open to how very attractive you are."

He'd have to be a bit more consistent if he wanted to get into my bed this Blessing Time.

"Thank you, Lord Illuminus," I said firmly, pulling away again. "But I'm exhausted and really want to sleep alone tonight. I'm sorry to disappoint you after you've been so kind."

"My loss, sweet lady," he said benignly. "Sleep well." He used magic to close the window. I pulled the curtains shut and lay down in bed.

The gleam of Illuminus' crystal shone through the curtains for a few moments before he flew away.

I sat up.

"He's gone," I said softly.

"Are you sure?" hissed the ghost, not moving beneath the bed. "Who was that? Is he a friend of yours?"

"My cousin Illuminus," I said. "Lord Illuminus Lucheyart. Slime rat."

"That man tried to kill me," moaned the ghost. "*Hwitl ka ka*. I am a duck who sits."

CHAPTER SEVEN

"WE WERE AT the mine because we'd hoped to find clues to crystal smuggling there. Earlier they'd told us to stay out in the desert, but then instructions changed. We slipped in over the border hoping come and go quickly without anyone knowing."

Strange how he talked about the border as if there were some kind of definite moment when you were out of the Endless Desert and into the Empire of Light. There was no physical boundary and almost no people in those trackless wastes. Bright's fort at the edge of the desert was the border post. It had only been set up fifty years ago to keep an eye on the comings and goings of the ghosts, but given that it was a pinpoint of settlement in a vast area of sand, all kinds of comings and goings could be taking place out there. Though the lack of water would be a serious limitation.

"We did it that way to avoid offending your government," whispered Shadow.

We were laying side by side on the floor under my bed. He wouldn't come out, nor talk above a whisper, after the incident with Illuminus, so since I was curious about his story I had crawled in there to join him. There was no need to keep a lookout in case Illuminus came back. You can always tell where mages are by the shining of their crystals. And if Illuminus tried to come in without using magic, I would hear his tread on the creaky old boards.

The ghost was holding something in his hands, a small shiny metal tube. When I asked him if it was a talisman, he said it was. I hoped it was comforting to him.

"There were three of us. Our leader asked to speak to the head of the mine. When she came out, she asked if any of us was a healer. A man had been hurt in a rock fall. Bad wounds with gangrene already set in. Since I was the trained healer, I went off to see to him."

"Really?" I asked.

"Yes," said the ghost in an offended voice. "I may seem ignorant to you, but I am good at healing."

"No, it's not that. People are scared of ghosts. The sick man would have thought you were the spirit of death come to collect him."

"True. But your folk also believe that we know a lot about healing, and we do. I trained long and hard to learn it. How could they not have a healer at that mine? We would have had one. That poor fellow had awful injuries, but easy to treat if you knew what you were doing. Anyway, just as I started to patch him up, the mine was attacked. Masked mages and a whole lot of men with crossbows."

"Rogues. You get gangs of them in frontier lands."

"One of the masked men was your cousin. And before you ask, I saw his face, as well as hearing his voice. One of the miners hid me under the floor of the room where I was operating. Your cousin took his mask off to wipe his brow and I saw his face through a gap in the floorboards. Just now I thought I knew his voice, so I took a look at him from under the bed."

Illuminus did have a very distinctive voice. Some injury to his throat as a child made it low and husky. But why would Illuminus be helping rogues? He was a Lucheyart, for Lady's sake! We owned most of the crystal mines in the country. It was the source of the family's power. Why would he help destroy one of our own mines? Could the manager have offended him somehow? Or a bet? That seemed irresponsible, even for one of the mages.

"And before you ask how, I could see his reflection clearly in that mirror on the wall over there." He shook his head. "*Wilkhkje, wilkhkje, wilkhkje*! He must suspect I am here."

I could feel the tension in him. "Don't worry, the place is full of mages who can protect you from him."

"Yes. All his relatives."

I laughed ruefully. "Just 'cause we're family doesn't mean we get along. Plenty of people here would happily see Illuminus disgraced. His own brother Scintillant, for a start. They fight all the time—proper punch-ups. Then Blazeann and he have some kind of feud going on, and Lucient would happily help us because he's a sweetie. If you're really certain it was him, we could take you out of here and show you to everyone and get you a real protector."

I felt him relaxing.

"I know! Great Aunt Glisten is here. She's one of the Council of Elders. No one goes against her. She'd be perfect."

His arm tightened again.

"No, she would not. *Djthlyer*. She would be the worst."

"Why...? Ah! The whole diplomatic incident thing."

"We were not doing any harm. We wanted to find out how the crystal is getting out. Black market crystal is causing our government all kinds of problems..."

"But how do you know it comes from here?"

"There is not anywhere else."

"Really?"

He sighed. "Is there any point in my telling this story if you don't believe a word I say?"

"No, I believe you. I'm amazed. I didn't realise."

"That is how the Empire of Light has so much dominance in the world. They control all the crystal and most of the enhanced mages. If they wanted to run the whole planet they could. But I guess there is no point in conquering places when you've got such a hold over people. So tell me, can you do anything to stop him coming in and getting me?"

"No. All he'd get would be a lecture from Impi. Although killing would be more serious. He'd have to stand trial for that. Hey, why—?"

"I suppose that means he is not certain that I am here. Actually he might have been one of the people who searched this room this evening. In which case he might be almost sure I am not here. I suppose it would be safe enough to stay."

"I still find it hard to believe that Illuminus would be smuggling crystal," I said—gently, so as not to upset the ghost again. I was thinking aloud more than talking to him. "It's treason and he's undermining his birthright. Crystal is the basis of Lucheyart power. Shola's pact centres around it."

"Tell me how this Shola's pact works, exactly."

"Oh, you know. Well, I suppose you don't, do you? Once upon a time there was war between mage and mundane. Rogue mages enslaved the mundanes, and peasants had to run away and hide in forests and hills. There was famine and uprising and also the hunting down and assassination of mages by bowmen. Shola was the first Empress, the one who brokered peace with the mundane leaders and killed off the rogue mages for them. Shola's pact gives protection to mundanes, and any mage who doesn't sign and uphold it has their crystal removed, loses their powers and is driven out as a rogue."

"And this would happen to your cousin if caught smuggling crystal? Would he be punished?"

"He would certainly be stripped of nobility—that's what happens when you lose your crystal."

"Is that for good?"

"Not really. Most people get it back after a while if they behave themselves. But for treason—crystal smuggling—I don't know. But the risks are huge, Shadow, and what for?"

"Money."

"But..."

I shook myself. I was starting to believe him, although the suggestion was outrageous. All our lives we'd had it drummed into us how wrong it was to help rogue mages get crystal. Rogues did terrible damage: they ransacked farms, they killed people, some of them were just plain mad.

"It doesn't make sense."

"You are not going to run off and ask him, are you?"

"Oh, no. If his prick was under my foot, I'd stamp down hard."

The ghost winced.

"Let the rat look after himself. I don't care what happens to this family after Bright. They can burn for all I care."

"So even if you doubt me, you will not tell anyone else? The fewer people involved in this, the better. All I want is to get back to my embassy in one piece."

"Fair enough," I said. "Though if Illuminus is searching for you, you'd be much safer with Lady Glisten guarding you."

"Not Glisten Lucheyart. The political outfall would be terrible. No, Illuminus seems to be being discreet at the moment. He clearly does not want you to know about his activities. There is protection in that. And he cannot know that I know who he is. *Ka ka,* I am freezing." He had been shivering for a while, even with me pressed against his side. Some of it must be fear.

"It's a cold one, true enough. Are you going to come out and hop into bed? We can keep each other warm."

I realised how that must sound only when he made one of his embarrassed noises. Curse it, I'd forgotten what an odd creature he was. I felt foolish at being so insensitive after our earlier conversation.

To cover it up, I said, "Mind, if you get a stiff prick in the morning, don't expect me to help you sort it out."

He laughed. After a moment he said, "No need to worry. I have taken it off for the night."

"What? You mean... It's detachable?"

He laughed softly. The sod was teasing me.

"You lying rat!" I hissed, smacking him and trying not to laugh. Soon we were both giggling helplessly.

"You people are so blunt," he explained, when we'd got our breath back.

"You're lucky I don't insist on seeing it," I said. "Come on. I promise not to interfere with you. I'm too tired."

"I would rather stay here," he said. "It's not you. I feel safer down here."

"Suit yourself. Pretend to be a chamber pot, then," I said.

I crawled out from under the bed, and passed him my quilt. I put my winter cloak on the bed and crawled under the remaining covers. All the other spare blankets were spread out among the guests. As I tried to get my feet covered, I wished Katti were here to keep me warm and hoped she was safe. I remembered I hadn't heard all of the ghost's story.

"So how did you wind up with Bright?" I asked in a low voice.

"Once the rogues were gone, I crawled out and looked around. Our chariot was destroyed and the others... They were dead."

His voice went husky. I put my hand down over the side of the bed, and after a moment he squeezed it.

"I... I... finished binding up the miner I had been working on. I did not know what else to do, and he had a chance of survival. Anyway, by the time I was done, other miners had crept out of hiding to see what had happened to their mates. One of them took me down to your cousin's regiment and left me there."

I remembered something else I wanted to ask.

"So is Ghostland like the Empire of Light?"

"Not at all. It's like one big city. Your land is much prettier. We don't have many mages, and magic doesn't give you any advantages. The rulers are mundanes like you and me, and everyone is supposed to be equal under the law, which they sort of are. We all get to vote for our rulers, who are replaced every three years. Anyone can stand for leadership if..."

It sounded like the perfect world Auntie Eff was always going on about. So as usual, I fell asleep.

CHAPTER EIGHT

KATTI WAS PURRING and nudging my head just as she did every morning and like every morning I moaned and batted her away. Instead of ignoring my objections as she usually did, she jumped off the bed, her mind full of curiosity.

Why is he there?

Then a woman cried, "What are you doing under there? Bright Mother! What on earth?"

My eyes sprang open. I sat up to find Lady Klea crouching on the floor beside me. Magic shone out and Shadow was pulled out from under the bed. He flopped around on the rug like a badly landed fish, spitting out his spiky-sounding language. I reached down and helped him upright.

"What in hell's name is that?" asked Klea.

"It's a ghost. He's unregistered. A secret. For Lady's sake, Klea, don't tell anyone, will you?"

"Of course not. Where..."

Why do you speak with her when I am here? thought Katti, purring imperiously and nudging the back of my head again. *I require food.*

Her fur was cold but she seemed perfectly well, unharmed and unperturbed by the night's terrors.

"Oh, you lovely girl!" I cried, rubbing Katti's cheeks. "Thank you, Klea. Where'd you find her?"

"She's been up in Marellason's hut all night, with me and Bright," said Klea. "Well, well. A real live outlander. What are you doing with a ghost? And why under the bed?"

Katti was purring so loudly in my head I could barely think.

"Very well," I cried. I got up and let her out of my door. "No, you'll have to get Hilly to feed you," I told her. "I'm busy."

She flicked her tail at me in a distinctly unimpressed way as she padded away down the hall.

"I'm busy," I repeated to her receding hind quarters.

"Does she talk to you?" murmured Klea in my ear, stopping me from closing the door. "You lucky thing. Is it nice?"

"Mostly, yes, but when she's hungry it's a pain."

"Anyone else out there?"

"Not a soul," I said, after a quick look up and down the hall. "Too early."

Even to my ears I sounded reproachful.

Klea grinned, pushed the door closed and swaggered back to the bed. Swaggered because she was wearing the most amazing boots, tight up to the knee and wide and loose at the top. Even if they weren't the height of fashion—though they probably were, knowing Klea—they *looked* stylish. So did the pale silk shirt and matching black waistcoat and coat she was wearing. I started to feel a bit shy of Klea. She'd become so elegant and beautiful. For a most of my winters at the Family House we'd been great friends, allies against the older cousins and dour Auntie Flara, who was Matriarch in those days. When I was twelve, Bright and I had stopped going up to the Family House for some reason never explained. I'd hardly seen her since, but she'd always acted like a friend to me whenever we did meet. I'd always felt that she had a good heart and her rescuing Bright yesterday confirmed this.

"I've been up for hours. Tried to get your cousin's carriage back but it's still at the inn and Impi's nephew is watching it. So Bright decided to fly home on a log of wood."

I felt a rush of relief knowing Bright was safe.

"You found Graceson?"

"Oh, the lover, yes. Isn't he gorgeous? They're happily reunited." She was the first person I'd met who referred to Bright's inversion without a grimace of disapproval.

"Thanks for last night," I said. "Was Bright hurt at all?"

"He was fine. Just used up. So tell me about this outlander," she said, flopping down in my chair, putting her feet on my dressing table and eyeing him.

"His name's Shadow," I said. "And he can speak our language, so don't be rude about his looks. So what are you doing here? Or are you not here?"

She took off her hat (no feathers at all on this one, and it looked much better for it) and smoothed out her hair. Which was a shock, because it was clipped short below her ears.

"Klea!"

She grinned. "Daring, isn't it? It's ghost fashion. Apparently the women all wear their hair short." She nodded at the ghost. "You're extremely fashionable, Sirrah Shadow. And so would a half-ghost like you be, Shine, if you came down to Crystalline. Why don't you come when Blessing's over? We could have some fun. I'm in the theatre now."

"Lord Impavidus wouldn't allow it."

"What's that to do with him? You're not under his guardianship."

"Yes, I am."

"Didn't your mother leave you...?"

"My mother's not officially dead, so I can't inherit an allowance and she's not here to send me to university or make any other provision for me. Your mother is my guardian."

"You poor thing. No one like Impi for using the pocket to pull the strings, is there? Well, maybe I can help you. I've got a favour to ask you. If you do one for me, I'll do one for you."

"How big a favour?"

"I want you to find something for me."

"No, how big a favour will you do for me? Shadow and I want to go up to Elayison after Blessing Time. In secret."

"Of course. I can take you there."

She agreed so easily that I regretted not asking for something more. Though mages being mages, who knew if I'd end up getting any favour at all?

"So what's this thing you want me to find?"

"A messenger, a woman, came here with a letter yesterday, yes?"

"A lot of people came here yesterday. Chatoyant and Aunt Glisten even came up from Elayison."

"She was a messenger mage. Up from Crystalline."

"Oh, yes. I saw her."

"I don't know who she came to see, but she will have given them a letter of mine and I want it back. I would have taken it off her, but as you know I got sidetracked helping your cousin. I can't come here myself and search it out. That'll set whoever it is on guard and I'll never get it back. So I need you to find it and bring it to me."

"What's in the letter?" I asked, naturally curious.

"I'd rather not say." Klea looked at her hands. "A private matter. A *delicate* private matter. You'll recognise the letter because it's got a crouching unicorn seal on it. So you'll find it for me?"

I'd seen this a hundred times before. Klea would have written something rude about the wrong person or something like that and now she would be worried that someone would use it against her. The feuds mages got themselves into... Probably when I got the letter and, of course, had a sticky nose into it, it wouldn't even seem important to me. Anyway, it was an easy enough task, and I already owed her a favour.

"No problem. I'll take a look around."

"You're a darling," she said, smiling brilliantly at me. It didn't seem fair that someone could have magic and such looks. And she was a wonderful singer, too; apparently in Crystalline, people paid money to see her sing. "I'd better go back to my little hideout. Got any food?"

"There is some cake and some fruit left," said Shadow. He pointed out the remains of the food I'd given him last night

Klea's eyes widened. "He really does speak our language. Is he normal 'down there'?"

"Do you mind?" he snapped.

"I beg your pardon?" said Klea, opening her eyes.

"Shadow, at least address her as 'my lady,'" I told him. "He's got no manners but he doesn't mean any harm. Ghosts are very shy about their pricks, apparently."

"Modest, you mean," snapped Shadow. "And if you will forgive me, my lady, people will be up soon. Perhaps if you are worried about discovery..."

"It's Blessing time," I told Shadow. "Everybody'll be asleep until well into the morning."

Klea grinned. "No, our pale friend's right. Best be careful." She shoved the food in her pockets and pulled her kerchief over her face. "Now if you find the letter, how can you let me know? I know, pull one curtain closed in your window. I'll be checking. And please don't let anyone know I'm here, will you? This family's a snake pit."

I nodded my agreement and she jumped out the window. I expected to see her flying out over the lawn, but she actually flew discreetly along the side of the house away from the Eyrie until she reached the cover of the trees clustered at the other end.

The pale morning sun glistened on the dewy grass. Tendrils of morning mist hung over the trees. A lovely day for the Blessing ceremony, and the heavy dew would mean the ground was perfect for planting. A deer was digging at my strawberry plants, but as I picked up my crossbow to shoot, it scampered away. Great Uncle Five came pottering across the lawn, having been up newt hunting since before dawn. I didn't worry that he might have seen Klea leave my room; since she wasn't any kind of amphibious animal, he was unlikely to pay any attention to her.

"This is a beautiful place," said Shadow from his vantage point well back from the window. "Is the rest of the Empire like this?"

"Most of the Empire is warmer and greener than here. Don't you like Klea?"

His eyes widened. "I... I felt... she treated me like some kind of toy."

"That's just mages. Power makes them frivolous. But I think she's pretty reasonable. No chance she'll be on Illuminus' side, anyway. She loathes all of Flara's children. Let's see if we can scare up some breakfast."

I dressed, put my towel and underwear in a basket and ran down to the bathhouse. Once I'd chased out a half-naked peasant lad who'd obviously spent the night curled up in a towel against the boiler, and emptied and cleaned the baths from the night before, I had a quick bath myself before people started using up the hot water. Then I checked that the boiler was stoked and that there was still plenty of soap, and ran up to the kitchen to make sure everything was going smoothly.

Of course it wasn't. Tane the Blessing cook and our normal cook Hilly were having one of their quarrels.

"How can I cook for such misers? The shame! The shame!" Tane was wailing at the ceiling, while the empty griddle smoked. The servants holding the empty serving dishes stood around waiting with varying degrees of impatience.

"This bacon has to last four days," shouted Hilly, arms spread over the front of the larder door. "They can fill up on eggs."

I looked over the bacon on the table and thought it was plenty, but told Hilly to open the larder and get out another dozen rashers anyway. Tane had to have a win, otherwise he would sulk. That sometimes led to his getting drunk. We couldn't afford to eat much meat at Willow, so nobody was very good at cooking it. Since Tane was the cook at the village inn and the person in the village who had most experience of cooking meat, we always had him cook for us during family visits. He was good at it too. But he had this weird conviction that people would go hungry if he didn't cook everything in sight immediately. In the old days, this meant that we always ran out of meat before the final day and had to buy it in from the neighbouring estates—at huge cost. A few years ago I'd hit upon a system of locking up the larder and having thrifty Hilly dole it all out day by day. It saved a lot of money and kept Tane much more sober, but Ladybless, the kitchen dramas.

Oh, bacon! I loved it and I only ever saw it during a family visit. Once Tane had finally cooked some, I bundled a rasher into a roll and gobbled it down before thinking of the ghost. Under the pretence of being very hungry I shoved a couple of extra rolls and some cheese into my basket and ran back up the stairs. I met Thomas on the way and managed to find out that it had been Lady Chatoyant who had received the messenger mage from Crystalline. Thomas was so busy sorting out breakfast that he didn't pry into why I wanted to know.

Katti, who had returned to the room, was unimpressed that I hadn't saved any bacon roll for her, and curled up on the bed and ignored me, but Shadow was happy to have the bread and cheese. He asked me all about the map I had on the wall. It was so lovely having someone listen to me going on about my dreams of going on the Spice Road that time melted away. Then I realised I'd be late and, pulling on my green Blessing robes, I hurried down to the Dining Room which had been set up for family breakfasts.

I could hear the argument in progress all the way down the stairs. (Ah, Family. Such joy!) When I recognised Auntie Eff's raised voice, I broke into a run.

"What's happening?" I asked Thomas, who was standing impassively by the door.

"Innkeeper's been here demanding recompense for her inn. Lord Impavidus thinks we should pay," muttered Thomas, out of the side of his mouth.

"My dear Marm, I merely follow orders." Impi was at his suavest. No sign of Splendance or Great Uncle Igniate, who would be the proper source of such orders.

"*You* burned the inn down. Lady Splendance should pay the woman," shouted Eff.

Most of the rest of the mages were in the room, eating the Blessing breakfast of eggs, beefsteak and bacon and watching this performance with the interested air of an audience at a play—except for Great Aunt Glisten, who looked disapproving, and Chatoyant, who was whispering something clearly startling to a wide-eyed Blazeann.

"Come, come, my dear Effulgentia," sneered Impi. "We all know you are skimming the top off the estate to keep you and Shine in luxury."

"In *luxury?*" screamed Eff. "Luxury? We don't even have wax candles, you..." Her fingers gripped her breakfast plate and I thought she was going to throw it at him. Both Thomas and I stepped forward. The movement must have brought her back to reality, because she stopped, took a deep breath and said in a softer tone—but through gritted teeth, "Forgive my tone, my lord. The foolish innkeeper has upset me. But I do think the bill is down to you. Any court of law would find that the inn is your responsibility."

"Well, I do not. We were protecting the youth of the village from your son's vice. You should have brought him up—"

"I shall pay!" cried Blazeann. "Yes!" she continued, standing up and confronting the astonished eyes of everyone in the room. Her voice broke a little under Impi's outraged glare, but she kept on bravely. "I... I do not agree with your... with my mother's decision in this, Lord Impavidus. It is neither Aurora's nor Eff's responsibility."

She pulled one of her rings off her finger and held it out to Eff, her hand trembling.

"Yes," added Chatoyant quickly. Her voice was perfectly calm. "Lady Blazeann rightly feels that if Lady Splendance is determined to shirk responsibility for her consort's actions, then rather than bring shame on the family, she should pay. Bravo to you, Cousin. At least someone cares about Lucheyart honour."

She started clapping. Great Aunt Glisten joined her and all rest of the family joined them. Nobody much liked Impi. One or two of the retainers clapped as well, but the rest looked anxious, torn no doubt between offending Impi, who was currently the real power in the family, and offending Blazeann, who might one day be the family's leader. (Poor sods. It couldn't be easy.)

Blazeann smiled and nodded at everyone. Eff stood there, mouth open. Thomas nudged me.

"Quick, get the ring," he hissed. I stepped over, prised the ring out of Blazeann's hand and went round the table to give it to Auntie Eff. If it was real, it could pay for at least three new inns. Or an inn and four new workers' cottages. And a new downpipe on the kitchen wall too with any luck. Blazeann probably thought of it as a cheap little ornament.

By then Eff had recovered enough to come back round the table and kiss Blazeann on the hand. I stuck close to her because Lord Impavidus looked ready to explode. So I was able to overhear Chatoyant saying softly to Auntie Eff, "We'll be wanting a receipt for that, Eff, and a return of the money you don't use. One must keep a close eye on the pennies."

She smiled at an approvingly nodding Lady Glisten. Shit-eater.

Impi sucked in a breath. Here came the tirade. Eff and I both took off out of the dining room so fast, we almost knocked over the servants bringing in the hand-washing bowls.

Before Impi could really get into his stride about how much he regretted joining our family and how much of a burden keeping us respectable was, the Blessing ceremony started. A great light burst from the top of the Eyrie, a light so powerful that it spread all the way to the bottom of the tower and down into the passageway to touch even us. The silken canopy had been removed and a glowing figure came floating down the Eyrie's central well, bringing light with it as it came. A mage in full flight is a true marvel.

"Come, mortals all," shouted Lady Splendance in a mighty and enhanced voice. "Witness the blessings of the Lady of Light."

As Auntie Splendance reached the bottom of the tower, trumpets were sounded and the huge door at the front swung open so that she could be framed in the doorway. She was wearing the cloth-of-gold robes of a High Priest. Peering out from behind her, I saw her light and the reflected light from the robes glowing on the faces of the peasants who had been gathering outside the house since dawn.

They let out a loud cheer.

"Blessings on you all," cried Splendance.

Even with all I knew of her and our family, I still got a lump in my throat. I found myself crossing my hands above my heart and murmuring my thanks for the Lady of Light's Blessings.

Then Lumina, brushing past me, trod hard on my foot and gave me the nasty grin that told me she'd done it deliberately.

CHAPTER NINE

ACCORDING TO THE legends, before the Light Mages had come, the people of this land had been wandering hunters living hand to mouth in a trackless forest. The Light Mages had brought agriculture and the easier, more civilized life that came with it, interbreeding with the local people and populating the land with contented farms. At least that's the story. Our priests tend to gloss over the major stumble that was the Crystal War, but lots of folk songs telling of those times get sung around tavern fireplaces.

But the Crystal War had brought Shola's Pact, which required mages to do something useful with their power. Every Blessing festival, the Matriarch, in her role as High Priest, leads the other noblewomen of the family in reciting the words of Blessing over the sacks of grain and seed potatoes. The sacks rose into the air and glowed as they did so, and—aided by the attendant mages—distributed themselves among the baskets of those waiting to sow them in the earth.

The Matriarch blessed the fields themselves before the crops were sown. The sowers were always the older peasants, those wearing the long hooded robes that indicated they did not wish to take part in the Blessing congress.

Did the Blessing make a difference to the harvest? I'd never heard of anywhere where the crops didn't get blessed in spring. The peasants swore that unblessed grain came up slower than blessed grain and that unblessed fields were less fertile. While most of the aristocracy regarded peasants as stupid and ignorant, experience made them extremely wise in the ways of nature; I'd learned to respect their knowledge in such matters. Certainly the orchards always blossomed a couple of days after the ritual had been completed. If the harvest was poor, the peasants could always trace it back to some misstep or wrong word of the previous spring's Blessing ritual.

I always felt hopeful for the future after a Blessing ceremony, and this year I really longed for that feeling. I dreaded yet another year at Willow, even though I knew I mustn't leave Eff alone. I nodded my head at the respectful bows of the peasants (as well they might bow—they had a very good deal with me and Eff running this estate, as they must know if they took a look at our neighbours) and tried to take pleasure in how well the fields looked. I'd worked hard, chivvying the peasants to till the soil and keep the ditches clear, and the result was good. But I couldn't quieten that little voice in the back of my mind that said, *Like last year and the year before. The same old, same old until the end of your life.*

However, I had a task to perform today. As soon as the procession set off for the second field, I ducked through a thin place in the hedge and ran back to the house.

On the way, I passed the place where I had seen the big wild cat the night before. The Mooncat—I had started calling it that. Had it even been real? I stopped and looked around the place where I thought it had happened. Something large and heavy had run across the pasture here. I wasn't a good enough tracker to say what it.

Focus, woman! I told myself. A light night puffball vision was not important today. I had more important things to think about. If I could find this letter for Klea, and she kept her promise to take us up to Elayison, that would be so much easier than keeping Shadow hidden while we travelled on the canal boat. And Klea was always good fun. Maybe she would take me down to Crystalline for a little visit after we'd dropped off Shadow.

Although most of the mages were at the Blessing ceremony—the retainers were always expected to show up—Great Uncle Nate and Cousins Illuminus and Scintillant had not attended, which meant I needed to be careful. I avoided the kitchen, too. Most of the servants were out with the Blessing procession, but I could hear Tane pottering around; if he caught me, he'd want to tell me of all Hilly's heinous crimes against him. So I crept into the house through the small door in the side of the Eyrie.

Three of the local servants were standing round a pile of sheets in the centre of the Great Hall. Luckily they were too absorbed in gossiping to notice me creeping past.

"Lord Scintillant always gives babies," crooned one of them, rubbing her belly.

Curse Scintillant. Of course he'd found someone else to tread the Blessing path with. Probably several someones, knowing him.

"Well he's not going to do so right now, is he? So how's about you help me with this?" replied another.

At least I knew where Great Uncle Nate was. I could hear his snores echoing down the Eyrie. He snored so loudly that he slept during the day so as not to disturb anyone else's sleep. In the gaps between his thundering grunts, all was silence as I crept up the stairs. The doors to Illuminus' and Scintillant's rooms were closed. This meant nothing, of course; Scintillant especially was notorious for never sleeping in his own bed.

The mages brought extra furnishings when they came to inhabit the Eyrie. Though we did our best, Willow's furnishings had become very threadbare in the twenty-five years since they'd been bought. I stopped to admire the tapestries on the stairs and wondered if I might be able to scrounge some of the old ones. The house was draughty in winter.

Despite arriving late and without warning, Chatoyant and Glisten had been given rooms befitting their station at the top of the Eyrie. Eff was good at organising a noble household into correct rankings, which was ironic considering all her years of radical pamphleteering.

Chatoyant's room was hung in elegant green silk, as luminous as cat's eyes and as delicate as their paws. The hangings felt lovely, but I only stroked them for a minute before I set to searching the room. I quickly found her small treasure chest. Unfortunately it was locked with a fiendish little mage-proof lock. Nothing could actually keep a mage out of your things, but if the chest was not opened using the correct combination, a mage-proof lock leaked a sticky coloured powder that stained everything inside, so at least you knew when someone had been prying. No chance of getting at Toy's valuables discreetly, but in the hopes she hadn't put Klea's letter in her treasure chest, I began searching the rest of the room.

I was keeping an ear open for approaching footsteps, but I heard nothing until suddenly Great Uncle Nate's snores became louder. I looked up from where I was crouched on the floor, my hand feeling under Chatoyant's mattress. Hagen Stellason, the supposed secretary, stood in the doorway smiling at me. Then he closed the door between us and left me to it.

In a fright, I rushed out into the hallway.

"What are you—?" I cried, seizing his arm.

He turned and clapped his hand over my mouth.

"Shhh, you'll get yourself caught," he hissed.

I glared at him and pulled away the hand.

"You should show more respect to one of the lineage," I muttered. "What are you doing here?"

He sighed. "The mages asked me to keep watch on their possessions while they were here. There's been pilfering in other places. I heard a noise and came up to check."

I found that *very* hard to believe. The mages would never have been so easy-going about pilfering. They'd have struck back so hard I would have heard of it even here.

"Is that what you were doing last night?" I hissed back at him.

His glance hardened. "Do you want me to tell your cousin you were searching her room?"

"I could tell Lord Impavidus about you in my Aunt's room," I said, feeling even as I said it that it was a weak threat.

To my surprise he grinned. "You're a feisty one," he said. "What if nobody told anybody anything? I promise you, I'm doing nothing that would harm the family and I'm doing it for a good reason."

"Very well," I said, trying to be dignified.

"Have you finished your search?"

"I don't know what you're talking about," I snapped. "I was simply straightening the bed."

"Of course you were, O woman of the lineage. I'm sure you make all our beds." Despite myself, I liked the teasing look in his eyes. "Have you finished your 'tidying'?" he continued. "I could keep watch for you while you finish. We mundanes should try to help each other."

"Thank you, I'm fine."

He took my hand and kissed it. Something about that kiss, or maybe it was the way he looked up at me over my hand, went right to my belly and made me tingle. Impressive.

"Go back and tidy up and I'll keep watch."

I almost went. Then I turned and said, "I don't think I will."

"What? Don't trust me?" He smiled. "Very good. You'll go far."

He stepped around me, opened the door of Chatoyant's room and looked inside.

"A nice neat search. Very good for a beginner."

He pulled the door closed again and leaned against it.

"How are you planning to spend the rest of this Blessing day? Might I be a part of it?" he said softly.

His gall was arousing. I could almost picture us...

I shook myself.

"As if anyone would believe an ambitious man like yourself would even look twice at me," I sneered, more strongly than I intended.

"That's a sad way of thinking," he said. He came up close and his fingertips rested gently on the edge of the door by my cheek. "You're extremely lovely. The man who finds himself in your bed..."

At that moment Katti let out an ear-splitting yowl of anger and fear inside my head.

"Katti!" I cried. I'd never heard her thoughts from such a distance before. I ran headlong down the corridor and leapt down the Eyrie stairs two at a time.

There were no servants in the great hall to see me. I found them all gathered in the corridor around the door of my room.

Katti was crouched on my bed, tail lashing, hissing at anyone who approached. Her ear was bleeding and so was her leg. Her mind was full of a huge evil yellow-fanged monster that had to be slashed, and slashed good.

"Another cat. It went out the window," one of the lads babbled at me. "I don't know how it happened, Marm. All the visiting cats are s'posed to be locked up."

"Get down to the stables and see who's been letting their cats roam about," I told him. "They'll have me to deal with."

"Your Katti really showed 'em off." He grinned, lifting his hand to pat Katti and getting hissed at. She didn't have time for niceties.

How had the cat got in here? Had I left the window open? Only then did I think of Shadow.

"Enough," I snapped. "Haven't you all got work to do?"

I flapped them all out of the room, slammed the door shut behind them and waited as their footsteps thudded away down the hall. I even opened the door a crack to check that the hall was empty before I softly called out Shadow's name.

"I'm here," he called out from under the bed.

"Stay there."

I set about soothing Katti so that I could examine her wounds. The tear in her ear was one thing—it would give her a swashbuckling air—but her front leg was deeply bitten. Her skin had closed already over the wound to prevent loss of blood, which would unfortunately also keep any infection from draining away.

"We'll have to get you down to the stableman. Have that dressed," I said to her.

"What?" hissed Shadow.

"I'm talking to Katti. You can come out now. How did another cat get in here?"

"Your cousin, Illuminus brought it. He came through that window with almost no warning. I just had time to drop under the bed. He would have found me had it not been for your pet."

"She's a good girl," I said, patting Katti.

Shadow, still under the bed, seized my ankle.

"Listen. You need to find me a better hiding place. I swear to you, he will kill me if he finds me."

I stroked Katti and tried to think things over calmly. But I was too upset. The intruder mage might have killed Katti if everyone hadn't noticed so quickly. I squeezed her tightly and she rubbed her cheek against me. *I do not die easily,* she thought. Idiot creature; she was no less fragile than I.

"We have to do something. Haven't you got an attic or a cellar or something?" hissed Shadow.

"Not if he's going to use a hunting cat to sniff you out."

He shook my ankle. "Look, take me to one of your cousins. This is too dangerous."

A cousin—

"Klea! Oh, curse it. I should have sent you off with Klea this morning. She's hiding out at Marellason's. You'd be safe with her. And she'd keep your secret."

The ghost groaned.

"Don't worry. She won't hurt you."

"I know that. But she did seem... flighty."

"They're all like that. Nothing's serious for them. But Klea means well, unlike some of them. Listen, a woman mage can best a man anytime, so Illuminus would never dream of coming at you under her protection. If we can only work out how to get you there."

"If you are planning to wait until nightfall, it will not—"

"Listen, I'm not an idiot. I've run this estate for nine years."

"No, no, sorry," said Shadow. He climbed out from under the bed and crouched at my feet. "My life means a lot to me, you know."

I almost stroked his head while I worked out what to do, but I stopped myself in time.

Like most big old houses, Willow-in-the-Mist had a secret escape passage, built in the old days to enable helpless mundanes to escape into the forest in case of a battle between mages or a rogue attack. These passages were supposed to be only known to mundanes, although

I suspect most of my noble cousins could have found it without too much trouble. I had certainly played in the tunnel with Bright when we were children.

The real problem was to get Shadow through a full house and into the cellar. Luckily it was Blessing time. People would assume that a cloaked and hooded figure moving around the house was someone who didn't want to have congress. Even luckier, most of the household's old clothes were stored in my room—Auntie's Eff's wardrobes were too full of books and letters to hold anything else. It didn't take long to get the ghost all wrapped up in an old hooded robe with my spare riding gloves to cover his hands and a scarf over the bottom of his face in Klea's style. I'd been planning to disguise him in the same way on the canal boat.

"Katti, is anyone in the hall?" I asked.

I opened the door, and she limped to it and snuffed the air outside. She sensed a group of male and female humans down in the Great Hall and, curse it, some small creatures up the other end of the corridor. I'd have to get some baits put down before I left for Elayison or we'd be swimming in mice by summer.

Then as we stepped out of my door, Katti's thoughts went blank red with rage and she shot past my legs with a yowl.

"Katti!" I lunged after her, only to be dragged back.

"Shine! Don't leave me!" Shadow's grip on my arm was surprisingly strong.

"Yes, yes, of course. Come here."

I pulled the ghost over to one of the linen chests that

lined the wall. They were completely empty; all the sheets and towels were in use. I thrust him into it, closed the lid and ran after Katti.

A chill breeze blew in through an open window at the bottom of the winding servants' stairs. Katti was balancing on four feet on the windowsill, looking upwards.

He got away.

I took her collar, coaxed her away and pattered back up to get the ghost. To my surprise, he popped out from behind the tapestry at the top of the stairs and scampered down to meet me mid-stairway.

"Someone is in your room again," he hissed.

So this had been a trick to lure Katti away. I felt that grim chill again.

"Marm," said a voice above us. "Might I have a word?" I recognised Hagen Stellason's voice and managed to shove the ghost round the curve of the staircase just as Uncle Nate's so-called secretary appeared at the top of the stairs and came down toward me.

I ran up and met him, blocking his way forward. His eyes widened.

"You didn't answer my question earlier," he said suavely.

It took me a moment to remember his proposition. I laughed at his persistence.

"I'm sorry. I'm busy at the moment," I said.

"That's disappointing," he said.

We stood there and looked at each other. He showed no sign of going away.

"Would you mind if I went down to the servants' hall?" he said

"You can't go this way."

"Really? May I inquire why, Marm?"

His annoyingness started to outweigh his attractiveness.

"No, you may not," I snapped. "Now, you listen. I may be only a mundane, but I am a woman of the lineage and manager of this house. So don't question me. Take yourself somewhere else."

Something like anger sparked in his eyes, and then that little smile was back again.

"Of course, Marm," he said, bowing. He turned and went back up the stairs. Remarkably slowly, I thought. I stood and watched his back till he was almost at the other end of the corridor.

I raced downstairs.

Katti was sitting upright on the open windowsill, her paws neatly in front of her, looking statuesque, and just a little smug. In response to my *Where is he?* she flickered her ears sideways out the window, where empty wine barrels were stored in the corner of the courtyard underneath the windowsill.

"Which one?" I asked, getting the idea.

She got out of the window and stood on the closest one. Luckily it had an old label on it, so it was quite distinctive. She told me that she could smell nothing but wine from these barrels. Good. Hidden here, the ghost would be safe from Illuminus' cat. And now I had an idea for getting him out of the house that would be even better than using the tunnel.

As Katti came back through the window, she snuffed the air. She smelled a male figure, possibly Hagen Stellason, approaching the top of the stairs again.

"Shadow," I called softly.

"I'm here," murmured a voice from the barrel.

"Stay there. Nothing can smell you, so you should be safe. I'll come back as soon as I can. Maybe after dark. Or maybe I'll get them to move you. Yes, that'd work."

I thought I heard a groan.

I was tempted to go upstairs and give Hagen a blast about ignoring my orders, but I was more worried about Katti's bitten paw.

"Come," I told her, and led her down the hall and out into the stable yard.

CHAPTER TEN

I MIGHT NOT be a mage, but I had one small advantage over Illuminus: I was in my own home and had trustworthy helpers. Thomas grouched when I asked him to have the wine barrels moved from the corner of the servants' courtyard. But when I gave him a meaningful look and told him I didn't want Lord Impavidus to find out, he fell over himself to help me. Am I or am I not a master manipulator?

He oversaw the loading of the barrels himself. I watched surreptitiously from the dining room window, making sure I knew exactly which of the barrels contained Shadow.

After that it was a small matter to cut through the woods behind the house, meet the cart of barrels as it passed along the cart track to the village and get Joe the carter to help me offload the barrel carrying the ghost. The fact that the ghost had a sneezing fit as we put the barrel among the ferns beside the road didn't bother Joe. Clearly he had already guessed that there was someone hidden there, but he was a taciturn man and I trusted him almost as much as Thomas.

I waited till the cart had clip-clopped away through the trees before I opened the barrel and helped Shadow out; even tough old Joe would have been horrified at the sight of a pale-skinned ghost. While I waited, I enjoyed a smug fantasy of Illuminus searching the house with a fine-toothed comb and grinding his teeth as he found nothing. What could have possessed him to betray our family by crystal-smuggling? Debts? Blackmail? A bet? I'd never thought of Illuminus as a particularly bad person, but then I'd never had much to do with him. He'd been too old to bother with Klea and me for good or ill when we'd been children. Once the ghost was gone, I would have to do the responsible thing and tell someone about him. But who? And how?

The ghost's pale skin had gone a greenish colour, like he wanted to puke. We sat under a bush, while he gasped in deep breaths of fresh air.

"My excrement was almost scared out of me," he slurred.

"Sorry," I said, trying not to laugh at his words. "It was too dangerous to come back and tell you what was happening. The saying is scared shitless by the way."

"Scared shitless," he repeated. "I am sure I will have

further reason to use that phrase. So what do we do now?"

"We walk. Marellason's hut is a few miles from here. Come on." I pulled him up off the ground. "The walk'll settle your belly."

"Oh, joy," muttered the ghost as he staggered to his feet. His irony made me smile. Who would have thought someone so foreign would have had the same sense of humour as me? I took his hand to steady him. It felt clammy, but how lovely and brown my skin looked against his paleness! A first time for everything.

"Are you drunk?" I asked. "You were over an hour in that barrel."

"Let us hope the walk sobers me up. Now listen, before we get to Klea, I have been thinking. How do you know if we can trust her? How do we know she is not in alliance with Illuminus?"

"Klea hates Flara and her children—that's Illuminus, Scintillant and Chatoyant. She refuses to even be in the same house with them. It's why she ran off to Crystalline and went on the stage. Lucky beast! Anyway, if she were on Illuminus' side, you'd be done for already. He'd know you were here, instead of suspecting it."

"That's true," said the ghost. "Why does Klea hate this Flara?"

"Oh, Flara used to be the Matriarch years ago; I think she used to beat Klea and Lucient all the time. And she sent away their favourite nurse. Then something happened to bring Flara down, some money scandal. There's always something with our family. Eff said she was aiming at the throne. A long shot. She's the second noble daughter, not the first, and she mostly has sons. The Council would never elect her. Glitter is the solid heir.

"Anyway, Uncle Radiant, who was her Avunculus, was exiled to some monastery in the Western Desert over the whole thing. And Uncle Batty, who was the only other noble man in that generation and should have taken over as the Avunculus after Radiant's fall, came here and refused to have anything to do with the other mages ever again. He was smoked out of his brain most of the time. When he wasn't sipping holy wine. That's how lazy old Great-Uncle Nate became the Avunculus. And how Impi Claritas, who is only a consort and should have no say in this family, runs everything. Makes me mad thinking about him. Come on, let's get going."

I tied a scarf round our faces. This wasn't just to disguise Shadow in the unlikely event that we met one of the peasants on this Blessing morning; the deep forest was full of puffballs, a giant fungus that released hallucinatory spores. If you got a face full of such a release, which was very likely if you accidently stepped on one, you'd fall into a vision-filled sleep for the next half day—unless you were eaten by a wildcat or a grunter in the meantime. Another reason to stay on the path.

Even if one just happened to release naturally nearby, your sense of reality could be dangerously affected. The peasants made holy wine from puffballs and used it in their own nature-worship rituals. Uncle Batty had drunk quite a bit, till the visions of bats attacking him got too much. Bright and I had tried it too, but only the once. It was savage stuff.

After warning Shadow about puffballs, I presented him with the cat spear. Since we had no hunting cat with us and he was following behind me, it was his duty to discourage wildcats from jumping down from the trees onto his back. He blanched at that; apparently it wasn't a problem on the other side of the Bone Mountains. I should have known. So, of course, I had to show him how to carry it properly tucked up over his shoulder with the heel resting on his belt and the point shielding his neck.

"Wildcats mostly sleep during the day, but you never can tell," I said. "You might strike a sick one, or one with hungry cubs to feed. So it's best to be careful. Don't leave Klea's side if you can help it—and if you do get separated from her, don't leave the path. Hundreds of years ago when Willow was built, this was a huge crystal mining site. After it was worked out, it wasn't good for much else, so they left it and the forest grew back. Unfortunately they didn't fill in the mineshafts, so the forest is full of them. When the mages come up here hunting, they fly, but the rest of us just have to be careful where we tread."

We crossed the bridge into the forest proper and took the small hunting trail up into the hills. After walking a short time we passed a tree that was tied all over with little pieces of ribbon and cloth: prayers to the nature spirits. I said a silent prayer as we passed. Beneath the tree was one of the many Mooncat altars that dotted our district. As usual it was loaded with fruit and flowers. I made a mental note to stop and say another prayer on the way back.

After that, the forest got wilder. The tall, white-trunked trees were like pillars among the riot of smaller, mossy trees, flowering shrubs, cycads and ferns all bound together by a tangle of vines. The air smelled rich and earthy and birds were chattering away everywhere. I had fond memories of whizzing through here in Bright's chariot, ducking round tree trunks and chasing light-footed deer through the underbrush. We'd even come at night sometimes. Moonlight was best. You could see the animals moving below and sometimes even catch sight of a wildcat hunting.

"Are they big, these wildcats?" asked Shadow nervously

"There's a couple of sorts. The big ones are twice Katti's size." I thought of the Mooncat, who'd been three times as big as Katti, but decided not to make Shadow any more nervous than he obviously was. With its size and eerie glow it was clearly magical, and therefore not normal.

"Another thing you should keep an eye out for is grunters," I said. "They're a kind of big pig. They travel in family groups and the adults can be vicious, but at least they don't come looking for you. Though they will eat you if they find you passed out from puff ball spores."

"*Wow*," said the ghost. "Such a friendly forest. Anything else I should be careful of?"

"Well, there's still a lot of crystal dust in the soil. It gets in the water. Some of the animals and plants out here, especially the night ones, have magical powers. Some fly, some get very big. Some look extremely odd. Some glow. Sometimes you get fish in our stream with two heads or three eyes."

"So if I drink the water I could start to glow?"

"Depends on if you've got some magical ability."

"If you had a crystal, would you have magical powers?"

I felt a shock go down my spine. The pain was still there. I pulled myself back from it.

"The crystal only enhances what's there. It can't give you what you don't have." I said, keeping my voice as steady as I could and trying not to clench my jaw.

"You've been tested, though?"

"We're all tested, when we come to mating age. A team of mages tours the country looking for candidates. Those who respond to the crystal are taken away to College to train and have a crystal implanted in their foreheads."

"Why foreheads?"

"Hell, I don't know." I swiped a stick though some fern heads breaking them off. "Always burns me up when I see a flying mouse. To think a stupid mouse could have more magical power than me. Me—with my lineage."

I still remembered that day so clearly—curse it. How I'd started out so certain; my mother was a mage, so why would I doubt myself? How I couldn't move even the smallest coin. My chest still hurt remembering the stern look on the face of the testing mage when I begged him to let me keep trying.

Eff had met me in the hallway afterwards hugging me and saying, *At least I get to keep you with me,* even though I could tell she was disappointed for me. I didn't know which I hated remembering more, the pain of failing the test or how I'd thrown Eff's comforting words back in her face. I'd told her I hated it at Willow and I didn't want to share her stupid exile, before running off to my room to weep and wail.

I must have let something show. Shadow said tentatively, "It must have been hard, failing that test."

I swallowed hard.

"We survive. I'll never be a noble, but at least I'm well born. I live in a good house that mostly doesn't leak. I read and write, I have a lineage. I just... It's just I get so *bored*. Every day is the same."

"You will get out of here," said Shadow. "Wanting to can take you."

"No, I won't. I'm not going to leave Eff alone. She's been like a mother to me, and she needs me. This place was falling apart before I took over. Eff was giving all her time to educating the peasants, but because she's no good with figures: there wasn't much work and no improvements. Made it hard for them to buy food in winter. Even—"

"That's not the real reason, is it?" said Shadow. Amazing how much he understood things.

"No," I said and I told him all about Eff's illness.

"Sounds like what we call broken nerves," said Shadow.

"If I were a mage it would be different," I said. "I couldn't go on the Spice Road, because that would mean leaving Eff, but at least I could live in Elayison. A mage can do the two-day journey to Elayison in half a day. Bright used to come down to visit us all the time, before the scandal.

"And I'd own this estate. I'd be able to reform how we do things here instead of going on in the same old broken way. Build a water wheel to irrigate the high fields. Pay wages instead of relying on labour duties. Really make a difference. And do... I don't know what. Interesting things, like... I could go to the theatre every night, and parties, and wear silk and meet people who don't talk about crops all the time and maybe..."

I stopped myself. I wasn't going to let Shadow know about the tall slim handsome artist or writer or actor or scientist I was going to meet one day, the sort of man who I could laugh with over dinner and love myself stupid with in bed later.

"But none of this is going to happen. Things will go on in the same old way. I'll never meet anyone interesting out here. The family will come every year and call me Aurora's Mistake and Ghostie, and make snide remarks because I can't afford new clothes. And Impi will keep on saying there's no money to pay me for the work I do even though I've started to make this place pay. Even a 'thank you' would be nice. I won't even be given an allowance out of my mother's estate, because no one knows if my mother is still alive or not. I'll waste my life here and never do anything."

I'd broken my stick into little pieces. I threw it away with a huff of disgust

"Hey," said the ghost. He put his hand on my back. "Hey, I am sorry I upset you. I should have thought. I am trying to learn how things work here." He rubbed my back. I do love having a man with nice strong hands rub my back.

"Oh, stop it," I said, blinking my eyes. They were suddenly full of tears, curse it. "Sympathy makes me go all gushy."

He let out a huff of laughter and squeezed me round the shoulder. "Yeah, I know how that works. Do not worry. I will find your mother for you."

Thinking about my mother put some fire back into my belly.

"I've done perfectly well without *her* all these years," I said. "If you don't find out what happened, it will hardly matter."

"You said you would get some money if I found out what happened to her."

"I suppose an allowance would come in useful. Even stuck out here."

MARELLASON'S HUT WAS a split-shingle building at the top of a steep rise called Marella's Pinch. We were panting hard by the time the trees thinned out. The hut was surrounded by a fence of wooden stakes about head height, pointed at the top and silver with age, designed to keep out the wildcats. The hut's shutters were closed, but smoke rose from the stove pipe in the roof.

As we came up to the fence I could see through the slats to where Klea was sitting on an old log outside with her back to us. Something about her hunched posture spoke of sadness. I called out her name.

She glanced briefly at us over her shoulder, stood and ran into the hut, slamming the door behind her.

"Klea?" I shouted. I flung open the gate, rushed over to the hut door and, finding it barred, banged on it. "Klea, are you all right?"

"Yes, yes, Just a moment! Wait there," came the voice from inside.

"What is the matter?" asked Shadow

"Klea, I brought some food," I called into the hut, for lack of anything better to say. "You want some?"

After a moment she called back. "Thanks. Back in a moment. You start without me."

"Was she crying?" whispered the ghost. I wondered that too.

"That's none of our business," I told him firmly, although my own brain was agog with curiosity. He shrugged and sat down on the log, taking off his gloves and scarf but leaving on his hooded robes. I sat down beside him and offered him some bread and cheese from my bundle. We admired the hut and I pointed out the fine old apple tree that I'd taken some cuttings from. We were filling up air—both of us wondering what was wrong with Klea.

When she finally came out of the hut, I was pleased to see that Shadow stood up and bowed in a very mannerly way, and waited till he was asked before he sat down again. Quick on the uptake, this ghost.

Klea's eyes looked suspiciously red, but otherwise she was all smiles and lightness. I judged it best not to press for an explanation

"What's the news? Find the letter?"

Had she been crying about the letter? Was it that serious? Surely not. I wished she'd tell me what it was so I could comfort her, but I didn't feel able to ask.

"I took a look in Chatoyant's room, but I got interrupted. She has one of those mage-proof chests. I don't suppose you know the combination."

"Curse it, I wonder who would? Probably no one, knowing Toy. But you'll keep trying, won't you?" asked Klea.

"Oh, yes. But in the meantime, I had a problem with Shadow and I thought you could look after him for me."

"Problem?" Klea winked at the ghost. "Is he too virile for you?"

"Illuminus is after him, for some reason," I said. "Shadow says he wants to kill him."

"He does," said Shadow.

"Why would he want to do that, little Shadow?" asked Klea.

Shadow dropped his gaze. "I'm an illegal ghost. Isn't that enough of a reason?"

"Illy's ruthless, but not like that. I'm guessing there's something more here."

"You might as well tell her," I said.

He shrugged and told her most of what he'd told me about the crystal mine.

"That's quite a story. Are you sure it was Illy?" asked Klea as he finished.

"I saw his face. Both times. And his voice is very distinctive."

"True. What was he doing at a mining camp in the mountains, I wonder?"

I was surprised that she'd believed Shadow so quickly. "Why would he do such a terrible thing?" I asked.

"Flara's get are capable of anything. That's how she brought them up. And all of us are short of money."

"You don't dress like it," I said, before I could stop myself.

Klea laughed. "You dear little country mouse," she said, not unkindly. She struck a pose with her nose in the air. "One simply *must* dress!" She dropped the pose and said, "My couturier was my biggest creditor when I lived in Elayison, and it's probably true for half the other nobles. I think I still owe him a hundred lumins." She nudged my arm. "So what's this one like as a lover? Much different to our men? I assume he's got a prick and balls. Are they a good size?"

I opened my mouth to correct her misconception, but Shadow interrupted. "Do you mind?" he snapped, red faced. "I'm a person, not a piece of meat."

Klea stared at him. "He's gone a funny colour."

"He does that when you talk about pleasuring," I said. "Embarrassment. Apparently it's a taboo for ghosts."

"But how do they get baby ghosts? They're not really undead, are they?"

"We do it. We just don't *talk* about it all the time," snapped the ghost through gritted teeth. "It's a private matter between the... the..."

"The people pleasuring," I finished helpfully.

He stared at us and blew out a breath. *"Dhrtyh wilkjhh!"*

"I've not pleasured with him," I told Klea. "And I don't plan to. The last thing I need is to bring another little half-breed into this world."

"Really? Is it that bad? I never thought... I'm sorry, I guess you don't like being called Ghostie."

"Nor half breed, nor blood pollution, nor Aurora's Mistake. And I don't like everyone telling me I look sick all the time, either."

"So are you trying to avoid breeding?"

"I'm not eating meat, if that's what you mean. But who knows how ghost spurt works? Maybe it's stronger than man spurt. I'm pretty sure my mother didn't plan me."

"Wilkjythith dyrhury," said the ghost. "Listen. I'm going to go in here and look at the arrangements. And you can have a lovely chat about my prick and my spurt and my hose and my nozzle and the length of my fingers if you like. Call me when you've got it out of your system."

"Wow! Passionate." Klea gazed after him.

"Klea, promise me you won't try to make love to him unless he wants it. Things are obviously very different in ghost land."

"Clearly."

"He must be afraid. He's got no one but us, and Illuminus does seem to be after him. Think of him like some child we have to care for. Or your brother. Klea?"

"I was curious."

"Well, don't go undressing him either. He's really shy. His prick's quite normal."

"The same colour as the rest...?"

"Yes. Klea? Promise you won't upset him."

My impression had always been that Klea was a kind person, but power seems to make mages insensitive to other people's feelings and you can never be too sure.

She reached out and pinched my cheek. "I know how to handle mundanes. No, I really do. And I've no interest in a reluctant prick. That's just awful. So about this search? How far did you get?"

"Only as far as Toy's treasure chest."

"Damn. She takes herself seriously, doesn't she? I mean, what would she have to hide that was so imp—Hey! I wonder if she and Illy are in the smuggling together."

I tried to cast my mind back, but couldn't remember whether Toy and Illuminus had been especially friendly the night before. "I thought they hated each other."

"Money has a way of bringing people together."

"Would Scintillant be involved?" I asked. As far as I could tell, he and Illuminus didn't speak. Everyone said so.

"Oh, him. Does he think of anything but his prick? You're not hoping for anything in that area, are you? Because you won't get anything but a disease from him."

I felt my face go red. I hadn't expected Klea to be so perceptive.

"He's a mage. He heals himself," I protested.

"He's a dirty little ride rat, is what he is. Sorry," She put her hand on my arm. "I shouldn't be so blunt. I thought he cared about me once upon a time but... it was all empty charm. He can't keep it in his pants."

"That's him," I said. I pulled a face and Klea pulled a face and we both found ourselves grinning.

"I usually make love with Scinty once during the Blessing," I said. "I don't get a lot of loving here."

"What? But all the hunky peasants...."

"When I was younger and hot blooded, yes, I did that; but now I manage the place, it causes trouble between everyone. Anyway, at my age I'd like someone special, not just a quick pleasuring. What are you doing?"

"Looking for grey hairs. You're speaking like an oldie."

"Stop it. Life is serious out here."

Klea let out a derisive-sounding snort so I tried to push her off her log. She laughed and pushed me back. It was like being with Bright again.

"Well I hope you're not looking to Scintillant for a true love."

I suppressed a guilty twinge. "Nobody would be that stupid," I said, too heartily.

"Lumina is," said Klea. "I know she's asked him to be her consort."

"Bright Lady! She's welcome to him," I said, in a voice which sounded fake to me. Klea pulled a face, and I decided to change the topic before I made a complete idiot of myself. "Do you know a Hagen Stellason?"

"Who's he? Handsome?" She grinned.

I laughed. "No. Pleasant looking, but not memorable. He's some new servant of Great-Uncle Nate's."

"What? Nate hasn't got rid of Bundle, has he?"

"No, Bundle's still stalking about the place. This Hagen claims to be a secretary."

"Oooh!" said Klea.

"What do you mean, 'Oooh'?"

"He must be some kind of intelligencer. I wonder who for. Blazeann, perhaps. Though I can't see Nate... Oh, blackened hell! It might be Lucient."

"What? Your brother?"

"No. Great-Uncle Lucient."

"What, Lucient the Premier? The Empress's Lucient?"

"It's sure to be him. He was very annoyed over how that scandal over Bright came out of nowhere. He might have a spy in the household now."

"Well, this Hagen Stellason seems to be everywhere I go. Sneaking about checking people's rooms. Interrupting me when I'm sneaking about checking people's rooms."

"He mustn't find my letter!" She jumped up and seized my arm, her face all serious now. "You have to go back right now and check the rest of Toy's room. Now. Get into that box. He could be searching the room as we speak. Quick, go. Go. Now!"

"Klea, what's in this letter? What have you done?"

"Not now. Go and get it. Please. Go on."

She pushed me toward the path.

"You'll look after Shadow?"

"I'll look after him. I promise not to harass him. Go find that letter, Shine. This is serious."

CHAPTER ELEVEN

Such was the panic in Klea's voice that I started back towards the house at a run. But I slowed to a walk soon enough. If Hagen was going to search Chatoyant's room, he'd have done it by now. I was really beginning to feel uneasy about this letter. What if it was something serious and I got caught up in a fight between mages? Despite Shola's Pact, a mundane like me who got entangled in their plots would be disposable in such a struggle and likely to come to serious harm.

Also I didn't like the idea of Klea crying alone. It seemed so lonely. I must find that letter for her.

I'd kept a wizened apple and some cheese separate from Klea's supplies and when I came to the prayer tree, I ducked in under the low branches and crunched through the fallen leaves. Feeling slightly embarrassed (Eff would have told me I was being superstitious), I glanced around to see make sure I was alone before placing my small offering on the Mooncat altar. I crossed my arms over my chest and bowed to the altar, whispering the prayers that I heard the peasants say to the nature spirits that inhabited their world.

"And thank you for not eating me last night," I added, in case it was all true.

"You're welcome," said a voice behind me. I almost jumped out of my skin.

Spinning round I saw a grinning man leaning against a rock. He was so shaggy-haired and dishevelled, it took me a moment to recognise him. But I knew his voice and his grin hadn't changed.

"Dannel? Dannel Graceson? Bless! You scared the life out of me. What are you doing here? I thought you were in the army."

I felt such a rush of pleasure to see my old playmate and lover that I lunged towards him before I thought it might not be appropriate and stopped.

He was wearing long Blessing robes.

"A man can come home on a visit. How are you, Shiney? Or are you all grown up and proper now and only called Marm?"

"No not really." I wasn't sure what to say. "You sod! You scared the life out of me. Hey, your brother was just here."

"I saw him last night. He visited our mother. Not the happiest of visits. She's still mad at him. Not lucky in her children, poor Ma. No girls and both her sons away, I mean," he said, almost as an afterthought. He got up from the rock and started moving toward the path, and I followed, and soon we were walking down the little hunting trail towards the road.

Being me, I wanted to know all about where he'd been. He was just a soldier, but anywhere was more exciting than here. I peppered Dannel with questions about where he'd been stationed. In Elayison? In Crystalline? He'd been briefly in both those places, but he'd quickly been stationed in Parratee on the border with the Sultanate. What were the people like there, I asked? Were they really covered with blue markings and had he seen the great temples of the ancients?

He laughed and told me common soldiers didn't get to go sightseeing; they kept to camp, they patrolled lonely stretches of border and he could tell me all the different ways to serve beans if I liked. Though it was different if you were gentry and an officer. Then you had more freedom.

That made me uncomfortable, even though he said it with a lopsided grin. I felt certain he had said it to shut me up, as a way of telling me he didn't want to talk about his life in the army. In the silence that followed, I noticed that Dannel's feet were bare and he didn't seem to be wearing much under his robe. He had a musky smell about him, like someone who hadn't washed for a while. Like someone who was sleeping rough. I began to have the feeling that perhaps he had left the army, that perhaps he was even a deserter. Which didn't shock me, because he was my dear old friend and probably had his reasons. You heard bad things about the life of ordinary soldiers in the army.

So we talked of old times, how we'd ranged through this forest and hidden in old mine pits and fallen out of trees and off horses and accidentally burned down two haystacks one year. The usual country childhood. The only thing we didn't talk of was the two summer nights we'd spent together at our old tree house where we both first discovered the pleasures of making love— the fumbling uncomfortable ecstasy of it. A few nights later, I waited and waited, and he didn't come; and then I heard he'd run off to join the army.

"Here's where we part again," he said as we reached the road. He turned, and as if he'd been reading my mind, he said, "I'm sorry I ran off all that time ago without telling you. There were a lot of problems at home and I had to go."

"Stefan said you had a big fight with Old Grumpy," I said helpfully. I'd forgiven him a long time ago, accepted that our loving had been more curiosity and hot-bloodied youth than passion. Anyway, since then I'd found much bigger things to be angry about.

"Yes, that was it. It wasn't you. You were lovely." He took my hand and kissed it.

"Oh, look at you, you smooth fellow. You've made me blush. And you've probably got a truelove somewhere."

He laughed and gave me back my hand. "Dozens," he said. "A woman in every town."

I wanted to offer to help him, but there seemed

no proper way to broach the subject without being patronising, so we bid each other farewell. I went off down the road feeling bad about not saying anything. I decided to call on his mother, Grace, after Blessing time and tell her I had work for Dannel on the farm. So I'd got quite some way before I noticed how Dannel's touch had made my hand oily. Some kind of grease. I lifted it to my nose and smelled animal fat of some sort, and noticed something glinting in the sunlight. Little specks of crystal.

Rogues. They said that rogues often powered their magic covering by themselves in grease full of ground crystal. Was my old friend something worse than a deserter?

My spine went cold and I whirled around to look back at Dannel. There was no sign of him. He must have gone back into the forest.

MIDDAY HAD PASSED when I reached the house. I was famished and wished I'd eaten more of the food I'd brought Klea. I stopped in to check on Katti, who was asleep on the stableman's bed and seemed comfortable. As I crossed the stable yard to the house, I came upon Hagen Stellason on a bench with his feet up on an overturned bucket. Men! They seem to have nothing better to do than hang around making a nuisance of themselves.

"Did you have a nice walk?"

I considered him for a moment. He was so ordinary looking that he'd make a good intelligencer. Yet that twinkle in his eye made his face come alive.

"Shameful how servants laze about when their betters' backs are turned," I said pointedly. "Surely you have some work to be at."

"But I was longing to see your lovely face again," he said.

"Of course you were," I said, trying not to smile at his cheekiness.

"So why was Lord Illuminus searching your room?"

If he thought to startle me, he failed. "I really couldn't say. Family politics, I expect. I try to stay out of it," I said. I added for good effect. "It's always someone."

The moment I said that, I knew it was a mistake.

"I've been travelling with your uncle for the whole Blessing period and there's been more room searching here in one day than I've seen in the last three weeks. Still, I guess your aunt being a known radical must make a difference. No doubt the Matriarch wants to see what she's at, eh?"

All my amusement disappeared. I'd always worried that Eff's writings would get her into more trouble with the family Elders, and now here was an intelligencer, possibly from the heart of the government, asking questions about her.

"Which is nothing," I said, far too quickly. And going into the house, I would have walked firmly away from him, had he not caught up and kept pace with me the whole way.

* * *

AFTER ALL THAT, when we got back to the kitchen, he seemed to lose interest in me and started flirting with Toy's maid, who was washing out something silky in the scullery. I ate some bread and cheese and ignored them. I was only happy that he didn't seem to notice when I slipped away and hurried up into the Eyrie. Certainly he didn't follow me.

This time the tower was completely deserted and I managed to do a thorough search of Toy's room. In the little hiding place under the floorboards, I was surprised to find a couple of bundles of smokeweed and four little papers of potion powder. Toy had always struck me as too scarily focused to be a smoke rat, but some people hide their vices well.

I felt petty because I couldn't help being annoyed to see that there was no dust under Toy's bed. Clearly people had swept up properly in here. You might think your staff care about you, but they know who really needs to be pleased.

The room searched, I could think of nothing more to do until I managed to get hold of the combination to Toy's treasure box. I should really return to the Blessing party so as to blend in as much as possible, but the ceremony would be almost over by the time I trudged out to the fields. My feet were tired enough as it was. So I gave into temptation and paid a little visit to the women's retiring room instead.

During a family visit, the top floor of the Eyrie was customarily the preserve of the noblewomen, retainers and family. We slung a silken canopy from the stone roof and furnished it with carpets. Day beds were set out and hung with soft linen drapes so that the ladies could be private while they enjoyed massages or dallied with lovers.

The view from the windows was beautiful—deep green forest stretching away to the tall, snow-tipped mountains. But I'd seen that view. I was more interested in what the mages had brought to decorate their eyrie. The day beds had been re-hung with heavy silk drapes more suitable for the cool days of early spring and loaded with bright silk cushions. All kinds of delicious-looking massage oils were arranged on a little table. I love nice smells. They seem to hold the promise of far-off places.

I was taking a sniff at a bottle when I heard a rustling behind me. With a soft glow of crystal light, the curtains on one of the massage beds floated open, revealing my cousin Scintillant lolling on his side among the pillows. He was wearing his tight Blessing breeches and a big white shirt left open to the waist. His dishevelled curls made him look even more loin-meltingly handsome than usual. Curse him.

"Shine, sweetie. How nice to see you. I was hoping we could have a little chat. I hate being on bad terms with you."

"Are we on bad terms? I'm sorry. I'm so busy at the moment, I'd forgotten."

"Spiky, spiky," he laughed.

Verbal fencing was one of the pleasures of being with Scinty. I always tried to hold off with him as long as I could. It had never been very long.

152

He came over and leaned against the wall beside me. "Are you really mad about the belt? It's just a bit of fun. I'd be horrified if you were hurt by it."

"It was the way Lady Lumina told me that annoyed me." Lumi's face had been so satisfied. She seemed to know how attached I got to Scintillant, how much I'd wanted his attention back after he'd strayed off, how much I thought about him after he'd gone. I was so angry that I had a weak spot for her to get at, I'd sworn to get over Scintillant immediately. And the only way to do that seemed to be to avoid him completely.

"Oh, Lumi's such a prick. Don't let her stop you doing what you really want to do. Madness lies there."

"What makes you think I have?" I said. "One tires of doing the same old thing every year."

He tossed back his head and laughed. "You are such a treat!" he cried. "And so pretty. I love your delicate skin." He slid my sleeve up my arm till he reached the point where I'd stopped darkening my hands. "I do wish you'd stop colouring yourself. Your natural colour is so attractive."

He dropped a soft kiss in the crook of my elbow. The softness of his lips sent a shiver of electricity down my spine. Despite myself my body leaned into the warmth of him. Scinty was the one who had first showed me how to really make love. Men are easy to please, but it's fun to really make them swoon.

"Haven't you got new conquests to win?" I said.

"I always look forward to loving you. You are the Queen of Lovers, my beautiful Shine."

I laughed. "You say that to all the women. I've heard you do it."

He grinned and squeezed my arm.

"Lady Chatoyant isn't going to like you fooling about with her Spring Flora perfume," he said.

"I'll have to live with that," I said calmly, opening another bottle and sniffing it.

"I think this will suit you much better," he said. He held out the stopper of a bottle for me to sniff.

"Oh, no. Too fruity."

"That's right! You like musky, don't you?"

As if he really remembered what I liked. Maybe he did.

"How about this?" He sniffed the stopper and then pressed his nose gently against my neck as if enjoying my scent. "Mmm, yes. This would be perfect on you."

I reached forward to take the stopper from him, but instead he held it under my nose and when I gave a smile of pleasure, he traced the scent down my neck.

"Oh, yes, delicious." He traced a warm finger down the scent trail and further down my neck into the hollow of my shoulder. He pressed his lips firmly into the hollow.

I tried not to arch into him, but something melted in my belly and tightened between my legs. His arm was round my shoulders and his big hand lay snug across my stomach as he kissed and nuzzled my neck.

"Lovely Shine. I've been so looking forward to seeing you."

"Cheap words," I said, trying to break the spell. "How do you remember our names, I wonder?

I turned intending to break away, but somehow I

found myself facing him, squeezed against him, chest against chest, hip against hip

"It's true when I say it to you. I *have* been longing to make love to you." He traced my lip with his finger. His touch sent a jolt of desire though my belly.

His mouth came down on mine. I abandoned all my good intentions, slid my arms around him and opened my mouth to him.

As we kissed, I felt my robes slide off my shoulders and rustle to the floor. His knee slid between my legs and I slid myself on to it. His hand stroked down my back and cupped my buttocks very briefly, pushing me upwards so that I was riding his hard thigh. The pressure of it was delicious and I couldn't help rubbing myself against him. I slid a hand into his shirt and felt his firm chest and belly and sliding down, the hard jut of his erect cock straining against the cloth of his breeches. Still riding his thigh, I tried to undo his belt.

"Patience, patience, my darling," he murmured. He pulled away and I was lifted in his arms, and he was carrying me over to the day bed. "I want to enjoy your lovely body first."

He slid me down onto the bed and standing over me pulled off his shirt. I rubbed my hands over the lovely hard muscles of his chest and arms while he bent forward and began to undo my body shaper. Murmuring, "Lovely lovely," as if I was some wonderful gift, he released my breasts and began to lick and stroke the nipples. I tried to wriggle round so that I could return the favour, but he pushed me onto my back.

"Relax! Enjoy!" he crooned as he slid himself down my body. He ran his tongue down my belly. The feel of it sent tingles down into my crotch. Somehow my breeches were around my ankles. He was pulling them off. I sat up, hungry to ride him, and put my hands on his breeches, but he batted them gently away.

"What's the hurry, my beauty?" He kissed me hard and deep and his fingers slid in between my legs, tickling, teasing my pleasure bud.

"Oh, Scinty, I want to ride you," I moaned. I was slick with juice and my flower wanted to open and be filled.

He slid two fingers inside me, sending a jolt of pleasure deep into me.

"Such an impatient little Shine. Always have to hold you back, don't I?"

I moaned, rubbing myself against those teasing fingers, and felt his tongue stroke down my belly again. This time he tickled it across my pleasure bud, teasing it with the tip. I moaned with desire begging him to let me ride, but he kept teasing and tickling and filling me with his fingers till I was in a fugue of pleasure, writhing and bucking against his hand. The pleasure of his touch was unbearably delicious. I was climaxing. I was completely out of control.

Only then did I feel him sliding his cock into me. For a moment I was startled out of my pleasure haze. I was used to being on top. But the feeling of his hard cock filling my flower sent such waves of pleasure up though my body that I abandoned myself to another climax.

CHAPTER TWELVE

I WAS ALONE when I awoke later. I lay under the crisp sheet for a few moments, remembering his warm strong hands, the delicious fullness of him inside me, the deep damp feeling of satisfaction between my legs. So much for my good intentions. I felt slightly ashamed of myself, especially after my conversation with Klea. But only slightly. One delicious pleasuring was better than none. *Life is long and Blessing time is brief,* as the old poem says.

As I was considering getting up, I heard the door open and someone walked across the room outside the curtains. My spine froze. The colour of the daylight showed it to be late. Curse it. Had the Blessing party come home?

I could imagine one of my noble cousins finding me here.

"What are *you* doing here, Ghostie?" they'd say. "This room is for mages," they'd say. They'd probably complain to Impi that I was getting above myself.

If it was a maid, she'd be politer, thanks to my lineage; but she'd think I was getting above myself too, and there'd be talk, which would also get back to the mages.

When I heard the footsteps go away up the stairs to the rooftop above, I gathered up my clothes, slid out of the day bed and feverishly started to dress.

Another set of feet came stomping up the stairs below the room and someone else came crashing in at the door. As I ducked back against the wall behind the bed curtains, I glimpsed my cousin Blazeann. Since she didn't storm up and order me out, she clearly hadn't seen me.

"Toy!" she shrieked, thundering around the room throwing open the bed curtains. I slid under the end of my bed to join two pairs of sandals and some damp towels. No dust here either. "Toy, where in Hell's name are you? This is a complete mess!"

"Why?" Toy's voice came from the roof. Footsteps trod back down the stairs. She sounded utterly indifferent. As a mage, she could afford to ignore Blazeann's temper.

"She didn't do it," snarled Blazeann. "She's done it at every stop this season, she's hardly been sober the whole time, and now when there's someone here to see, she doesn't do it. Curse her."

"I think Impi may suspect Glisten's reasons for being here," said Chatoyant. "He's no fool."

"Curse him. Curse him, curse him, curse him!"

Crystal light flashed and something smashed on the ground.

"Will you kindly not wreck the place?" said Chatoyant. "No, don't throw anything else." Another crystal flashed through the linen spread and something clicked softly onto a table surface.

"'Call in the Elders,' you said," snarled Blazeann, through what sounded like clenched teeth. "'They'll see things for what they are,' you said. Well, they're not going to see anything, are they? And in the meantime, that mad old rat wrecks the place and that *man* raids the family's coffers and fills the house with his kin."

Mad old rat. Nice way to refer to your mother, I thought.

"So what other bright ideas do you have, cousin?"

"If she's not going to overindulge on purpose, she will have to be made to overindulge by mistake," said Toy. "Here..." There was a rustling of paper. "This is that ghost powder called Open. Slip all of it into tomorrow's smokeweed and Splen'll fall over during the next blessing."

The blood rushed to my head at her words. I almost yelled out a protest. How could they?

Blazeann let out a thoughtful huff. I could almost feel her shoulders relaxing.

"Lucient might notice," she said. "He often mixes Mama's pipes."

"That's why it's dust, and why tonight you mix it carefully into the rest of the smoke potion and give the whole thing a good shake," said Chatoyant, as if explaining to a child. "Honestly, darling, can't you work that out for yourself?"

"Hmm," said Blazeann.

I heard Chatoyant's feet gliding away towards the roof top stairs again. She was probably doing her Salute to the Setting Sun. Chatoyant was very assiduous in her religious observances, and believed in the discipline of mind and body. She went on about it often enough. "Oh, and by the way, you owe me twenty lumins for that Dew of Edilon you just broke," she added.

Blazeann was moving too, though she was going for the stairs.

"Twenty lumins?" she said, in a voice almost as nonchalant as Chatoyant's. "Don't be penny pinching, darling. When we get rid of Impi, all of us will be getting much bigger allowances. You'll be able to bathe in Dew of Edilon."

The moment Blazeann was out of the room, I saw the glow of magic again and heard a slushy crunching sound. When Chatoyant had gone back upstairs and I was able to climb out from under the bed, I saw that she had gathered up the broken bottle and spilled ointment and slopped the lot into a bowl on the perfume table. No doubt when she had finished her precious exercises, she would spend some time separating the skin lotion from the rubbish and put it in another bottle. I could imagine her having that level of magical control; and that level of thriftiness too. No doubt she'd still extract the twenty lumins from Blazeann as well. Rat. Child of a dog.

I was deeply tempted to knock the bowl back over—no, to steal it and toss it down the jacks. But I kept my hot red anger in check and scampered off as quickly and quietly as I could.

Curse those two rats for planning to ruin tomorrow's Blessing. Did they have no conscience, no sense of responsibility to the mundanes who relied on our family? Think of the omen if the Matriarch collapsed during the ceremony. The mundanes would be so shattered the harvest would probably fail.

And tomorrow Splendance would be blessing all the new babies. Bright Lady! Imagine what a blighted life such children would lead. They would be marked forever as unlucky children, and maybe their children, too. Damn the mages. Why did they have to involve the mundanes in their little political schemes? I had to put a stop to this. But how...?

Dusk was falling. Up here in the Eyrie, the candles had been lit and servants were rushing in and out of rooms carrying robes and buckets of hot water as everyone dressed for dinner. I could hear Lumina shrieking at some unfortunate. I wondered if any of our girls would be brave enough to take service with her this year, and if they would last or come trailing home after a couple of weeks with a black eye like the last brave one had.

As I hurried past Auntie Splendance's room, I heard Lucient's voice call out my name. I stopped and peered tentatively round the door frame. Splendance's bedchamber, the second biggest in the house, was hung with ivory and blue, and Auntie Splen was lounging on her bed, sharing a long dreamsmoke pipe with Great Uncle Nate. Lucient was packing another from a blue and white jar on the dressing table. The men were also wetting their throats with glasses of a gold-coloured alcohol. Honestly, the ability of my family to absorb befuddling substances never ceased to astonish me. Mixing drink and dreamsmoke would have left me dribbling, but to them it was merely a little pre-dinner nerve toner.

"Darling, we'll sit together at dinner, won't we? And you'll come and spend the evening with me again?" asked Lucient.

I smiled and nodded, though inwardly I sighed. How was I going to do something about Blazeann and Chatoyant if I sat in Lucient's room all night? My eye fell on the jar on Splen's dressing table, no doubt the very jar that Blazeann would later pollute with the ghost drug. The sight sparked something in my brain. I knew how to foil the plot. And Lucient would be the perfect ally.

"Of course, Lord Lucient," I cried, giving him a big hug and a kiss on the cheek as if we really were having a Blessing affair.

By the time I'd washed, dressed, fussed over Katti— who was curled up on my bed and seemed to be healing well—resolved a heated dispute between Hilly and Tane over whether we needed to cook ten or fifty extra rissoles after the feast ("What about the late night snackers?" wailed Tane, as if the mages might die of hunger over the lack of a few rissoles) and scampered downstairs for dinner, I'd formulated a plan. Find out when Blazeann drugged Auntie Splen's smokeweed and replace it as quickly as possible with some clean weed. Splen would keep the weed close all night so the switch was most likely to take place when the women were assembled upstairs for the Blessing prayers.

My biggest problem had been getting some clean smokeweed to replace the polluted stuff. Smokeweed was way beyond the means of us at Willow-in-the-Mist. But as I had hoped, Lucient had plenty and when I whispered to him what I heard in the Retiring Room, he was furious and more than happy to supply me.

"Those rotten rats," he kept muttering. I don't think he cared much about the failure of the Blessing, but he was clearly excited to thwart Toy.

The other benefit of confiding in Lucient was that after dinner, he sent his extremely efficient valet, Busy, to watch Auntie Splen's room. Instead of ducking round the balcony trying to avoid being seen, I was able to relax in Lucient's room, drink a delicious after-dinner digestive and listen to the singing and playing of his heavily pregnant little maid, who had a divine voice and was clearly the apple of Lucy's eye.

"If only I was mundane and could pair-bond with Sharlee," sighed Lucient into my ear, leaving me in little doubt that they were lovers. I wondered cynically if Sharlee would have wanted to pair-bond with a mere mundane, but she seemed fond of my cousin.

"Lady Blazeann has gone into her mother's room," said Busy, appearing at the door and bowing. "Does my Lord have instructions?"

"No, Busy, take yourself down to the party now. I won't be needing you again tonight. Sharlee, go get me some of those nice spiced nuts we had at dinner, will you? I find myself a little peckish."

Once the servants were out of the way, Lucy gave me his blue and white porcelain jar of smokeweed.

"Mother bought these jars as a pair," he said fondly, explaining why the jars looked so similar. "Thanks so much for doing this, Shine. I know Mother isn't the best Matriarch in the world, but believe me, Blazeann would be a lot worse. At least Lord Impavidus pays the servants."

I thought I did a very good job of slipping into Splendance's room without being seen, though since most of the mages in the house were at evening prayers or off looking for the night's lover, it wasn't very hard. The smug feeling lasted until I tip-toed up to Auntie Splen's dressing table and realised that she'd locked her smokeweed jar into another of those cursed mage-proof strong boxes. Did no one in this cursed family trust anyone else? And what was the point when untrustworthy people like Blazeann knew the code?

Lucient would probably know it, because someone as vague as Auntie Splen could not be expected to remember it without help. I tiptoed back to the door and opened it.

Hagen Stellason stood in the hallway, hand poised to turn the door knob.

This time his reaction was different. Fast as lightning, he thrust me back into the room, slamming the door behind him. He pushed me back against the wall so violently, I lost my hold of Lucient's drug jar.

"What are you doing here?" he hissed as the drug jar slammed to the floor and shattered.

"Hell!" I cried before a hand was shoved over my mouth.

"Quiet," hissed Hagen. Such was the authority in his voice that I stood passive while he held his hand over my mouth and stood listening. I was beginning to think about struggling when he relaxed and looked down into my face.

"What are you doing here? Are you going to scream if I take my hand off your mouth?"

I shook my head and he took his hand away.

"As if I'd scream over some stupid mundane like you," I hissed at him. "What are you doing here?"

"This and that," he said. He looked at the mess on the floor. "Are you stealing Lady Splendance's drug jar? Why?"

"It's not hers. It just looks like hers."

"Why are you in here with an identical drug jar?"

"This and that," I said, pointedly

"I wouldn't have thought you were so friendly with Lady Blazeann. Did she offer to send you to university?"

"Blazeann. No! She wouldn't help me." I saw where his questions led. "And I'm not helping her. Never."

He sighed and seemed to come to some decision.

"So you know Lady Blazeann has drugged Lady Splendance's smokeweed."

"Maybe," I said.

"You can't steal the smokeweed. There'd be an outcry."

"I'm not," I snapped. "And now thanks to you there's going to be an outcry anyway." I crouched down and started collecting the pieces of the jar.

"So you're stealing Lady Splendance's weed and replacing it with another identical jar. That's very good. You're quite the intriguer, aren't you?" Patronising sod, but at least he looked impressed.

"But I haven't managed to do it yet," I snapped. "And we're going to have to get a mage in here to clean up this mess. Hundreds of lumins worth of weed wasted."

"Brush it under the carpet for now. The maids are going to be in any minute to put in the warming pans. So you haven't made the exchange yet?"

"Not yet," I said. I looked at the box. "I don't have the combination."

He smiled, but it was an understanding smile. "Don't worry. I've got it."

He stepped to the chest, spun the little wheels till he was happy and opened it. He took a package out of his pocket and unwrapped that.

"Curse it," he said. "I need something to put the fouled stuff in. Have you a handkerchief?"

I pulled it out. It was clean, if ragged.

"How'd you get the combination?"

He grinned. "All the mages know it, and most of the servants too."

He spread the handkerchief out, tipped the contents of Splendance's drug jar into it, ran his fingers round the inside of the jar to check it was clean and poured the contents of his package into the empty jar.

I picked up the handkerchief and tied it securely.

There were voices in the corridor outside.

"Someone's coming," I hissed.

"Quick! Under the bed."

He seized my elbow and I didn't think twice about following him.

One of the maids who came in was very quiet and serious and went quickly about her business. The other two, local girls here for the Blessing festival, hovered in the doorway chattering and laughing about the coming party and speculating as to whether they could both give a rose to Lord Scintillant that night.

I was very aware of Hagen Stellason's body leaning against my side. His hand was on my shoulder. Halfway through the maid's conversation, his fingers began stroking my neck. My favourite touch. The delicious feel of it flowed all the way down into my belly. He pressed his lips against my temple. I turned my head to glare at him and he kissed me on the lips. I suppose I should have pushed him away, but he was a lovely kisser. I only shoved him away when I noticed that the room was quiet again. I shot out from under the bed.

"You'd better get out of here," I snapped. He smiled up at me from the floor, a slumberous smile full of offers.

"Yes, I enjoyed it too," he said, holding out his hand. "Here, give me the weed."

"No. It has to go back to the person who lent me that stuff we spilt."

"They'd be very unwise to smoke it."

"That's up to them," I said, dancing backwards as he made a grab for my ankle and darting out the door before he could get any more ideas.

As I WAS scuttling along the landing with the bundle of smokeweed clutched to my chest, an imperious voice called "Marm Shine! Come here."

My Great Aunt, Lady Glisten, was standing at the end of the balcony beckoning to me, while the rest of the women who had attended family prayers on the roof of the Eyrie filed down the stairs behind her. Had she seen me come out of Splen's room? I couldn't be sure. Maybe I should confide in her about Blazeann's plot. Lady Glisten? She was clearly close to Blazeann. A doubtful prospect, and one not to be tried unless desperate.

I followed her into her room and stood before her as she arrayed herself in her chair. Her current consort, a tall, white-haired retainer with overly regular features, made to leave, but Glisten held up her hand and he relaxed back into his chair by the fire. She had left the door open, too. So this was not to be a private conversation.

This chamber had originally been earmarked for Splendance, as it was the best one in the house. When she had arrived, Lady Glisten had greeted Eff with an airy, "Don't worry about me. Put me in any room," but as a member of the Council of Family Elders (among many other things) and an older generation, Lady

Glisten outranked Lady Splendance, so Eff bumped Splendance down to the second best bedroom and put Glisten in here.

Lady Glisten was not only an important member of our family council. She was a major player in the Great Council that shared power with the Empress. The mages appointed the Empress and voted on her policies. Politics was a major pastime for them and Glisten was deep into it.

"If you don't show Great Aunt Glisten all possible respect, she sulks, and then there's all kinds of trouble," Eff had once told me. One thing Eff was good at was understanding family politics.

With this in mind I bowed as low as I could to my great aunt.

"What's that lump in your robes?" said Lady Glisten, pointing to the smokeweed, which I'd stuck haphazardly into my body shaper.

"It's smokeweed. For Lord Lucient."

"Oh, yes, just what I meant to talk to you about, child."

The 'child' made me blink. Though clearly meant to put me at my ease, the tone in which it was said chilled me.

"Lady Lumina tells me you are not eating meat. She says that you refuse to start breeding."

A knockout blow from Rat Queen Lumina. I felt breathless from the sheer gall of it. And from the fact that Lumi was obviously watching me closely.

"What is the point of Lord Lucient wasting his time and his seed on infertile ground? It's wasteful and most improper of you to give him your flower. You should be wearing the long robes. Or better still, eating meat and breeding daughters for this family, Marm Shine. That is your family duty."

Suddenly I was furious. To tell me who to give my flower to was a blatant breach of Blessing etiquette. And the rest of it was blatantly unfair. All my frustrations came out.

"How can I breed children with a clear conscience when I have no income? I have no profession and no chance to get one. I work hard all day for this family and am paid no wage. And no one will allow me to draw the allowance that is my right under my mother's estate. Why should I do my duty when this family does no duty to me?"

"How dare you!"

Lady Glisten's eyes had widened almost to bursting. The sight of her shocked face made me falter. I had lost my temper with a noble and in front of witnesses. Bright Lady!

"You wretched, ungrateful creature. How dare you talk like this? We feed you and clothe you."

The anger rose up again.

"My mother's estate feeds and clothes me!" I shouted. "This family does nothing for me except turn up every year and eat us out of house and—"

"Shine! Stop." Eff's voice rang out from the open doorway.

"And who, may I ask," resumed Lady Glisten, "allows you to live on this estate? May I remind you, mundane, this is not *your* estate? This is your mother's estate, to be inherited by a mage. You live here only on the good graces of the family. If you wish to make another choice, you are perfectly welcome to leave."

Too late, I saw the precipice I was heading for.

"Yes, I thought so," she said. "You gentry. Always talking of your 'rights.' You are just mundanes. Be grateful that we do anything for you, Marm Shine."

It came into my head to assert my right to an allowance again, but I quashed the thought. I had no mage to support me in claiming my allowance and I knew it. So did Lady Glisten.

Eff came forward and took my wrist in a vicelike grip.

"I apologise for my foster child's manner, Lady Glisten. She's young and foolish and she does not mean to be disrespectful."

"She seems a most ungrateful girl," snapped Lady Glisten.

"The young," said Eff. "You deal with them so often, my lady, and you know what they are like."

"Yes, well. She clearly has little sense."

"But she is a hard worker. And clever. She is making this place pay. You would not get such good work out of a paid servant."

"That is true."

Eff turned and took me by the forearms, placing herself between me and Lady Glisten.

"Apologise to your noble Great Aunt for your disrespect." This from radical Eff, who believed everyone was equal. How had we come to this point?

We had come here because I had opened my big mouth, of course. As always.

"Do it," mouthed Eff, her face sharp, her fingers digging into my flesh.

"I apologise, Lady Glisten. I spoke out of turn."

As Eff let me go and turned back to Lady Glisten, I made a low bow.

"Very well," said Lady Glisten. "We shall say no more of it. You may go. But I wish to see you eating meat tomorrow, girl. This family needs daughters, strong magical daughters. There will always be money for *them*."

So now she was implying to me that I would be paid for breeding children. It was rubbish. The children would come and I would have nothing. We would live on Eff's small allowance as we always had, eat the produce of the farm and wear cast-off clothes and shoes from the Great House. Until they finally decided who would inherit my mother's estate and we were cast out or exiled somewhere worse.

"You may go, girl," repeated Lady Glisten irritably. Eff took my arm and gently led me to the door.

"Shine is a clever girl," she said to Lady Glisten as she did so. "She would like to study to be a lawyer or an assistant. And having grown up in poverty, she dreads bringing up children in similar poverty. And I dread it also."

"Oh, Eff, not you too. Do you know what struggles this family has faced since that dreadful business with Flara and Radiant? We're all on short rations. And you two must do your part. Though if Bright and Shine are the results of your mothering, Eff, I wonder if we should not bring Shine's children up to Elayison after they are weaned."

I turned, shocked at such an awful thing said so casually, and saw Eff's face in the doorway behind me. It was set and calm.

"Indeed, Lady Glisten?" she said. And closed the door in my face.

I stood there starring at the door, appalled at what had happened, at what I had exposed Eff to. I wanted to storm in and tell Lady Glisten what a wonderful mother Eff had been and how much better she was than any of them.

"You really told her, didn't you, Ghostie?" sneered a voice nearby. Lumina was leaning against the stair rail at look of triumph on her face. She bought me to my senses, which would probably have annoyed her had she known it.

"Lady Lumina," I said giving her the barest of nods. I turned and stalked away along the balcony and didn't even stop when Lumina started sniggering. Rat Queen!

CHAPTER THIRTEEN

I FELT SO wretched that I almost ran back to my room to hide. But I had things to finish. I ran down to Lucient's room.

One look at my cousin told me that here was not the place to unload my feelings. He was leaning on his side with his head in Sharlee's lap, smoking his pipe. He was so smoked, I had to glare at him for a couple of moments before he sent her away to get some wine.

"Someone came in and startled me and I dropped your jar. I'm sorry. It broke. You'll have to go in and pick it up."

He didn't seem overly upset about the loss of his smoke jar—or about Hagen, when I told him what happened.

"I should have known someone else had the situation under control."

"So is it true, what I hear? That this Hagen is the Premier's intelligencer?"

"I hadn't thought about it," said Lucient vaguely. He sat up and held out his hand for the cloth bundle. "Maybe. I thought he was just keeping an eye on things for Uncle Nate. This family does get itself into trouble a lot." He untied the cloth and shook the weed inside gently. "Interesting. You can't tell there's any Open."

He took some smokeweed dust on the tip of his finger and dabbed it on his tongue.

"Yes, I can taste something funny, now I'm looking for it."

"I don't think you should smoke that. Lady only knows what it will do to you."

"True," said Lucy. "Someone should give that Blazeann a good thrashing. What are you doing, darling?"

"I'm going back to my room. You'll be quite safe from Toy tonight, and it's been a busy day. Far too busy," I said, pulling open his window. "Come on. Lower me down, will you?"

"Oh, you want to make a discreet exit. I get it." He touched the side of his nose. "Got to keep up the pretence. But you'll stay with me tomorrow night, won't you?"

"Of course I will, darling." I wondered what Lady Glisten would do when I ignored her advice. It was none of her business. But best not to tell Lucient what she'd said. He'd only worry himself into a state.

By the time Lucient had deposited me gently on the flower bed four storeys beneath his window, depression had settled on my chest. The garden was cold, but it would be just as cold in my room. I missed my ghost; I could have told him all about everything. But he was Klea's ghost now. He would probably go up to Elayison with her, and I would stay here as was sensible. And I'd never managed to find out anything about Ghostland from him.

Perhaps Great Aunt was right. I had to stay here with Eff anyway, now. Perhaps this year I'd try and get pregnant and get on with my life as it was always going to be. And never go anywhere, nor meet anyone interesting, nor find anyone to love me.

Katti came bursting out of the bushes and leapt up on me, her feet on my chest, her mind full of joy.

Come, come! It's hunting time. Her thoughts exploded into my mind.

She pushed off me, almost knocking me over, and loped away into the garden. What could I do but laugh and run after her?

The garden was silver in the moonlight. The limbs of the freshly budding trees were stark black. Tree mice were busy scrabbling and hissing along those limbs. Perhaps it was Blessing time for them also. The young males kept dashing down the tree trunks and scampering across the grass ahead of us in a way that smacked of bravado. Katti knew they were playing with her, but she could not resist chasing them, hunter instincts all aquiver. She bounded from tree trunk to tree trunk, ignoring her bandaged paw and missing them every time. I was caught up in the excitement, wanting them to escape and wanting her to have the pleasure of a capture at the same time and laughing at myself and at all of them. Nature is a thing of beauty and joy even as its teeth and claws are cruel and red with blood. Being out among the trees with Katti always lifted my spirits and filled me with gratitude. But after a while the cold became too much.

You need fur, Katti told me.

"Sometimes I wish I was a cat," I said to her.

Only sometimes?

She could be so smug.

I looked up at the house. No sign of light in Eff's room, so no point in going up there to commiserate with her. She would probably be curled up with Auntie Four in the little guest room in the attic arguing about peasants' rights the way they always did.

I could see the glow of a stove in the winterhouse. This was a kind of doorless shed overlooking the stream, built by an ancestor who wanted a shelter from the rain during winter picnics. I ran over and was glad to find no one in it, which meant I could pull up a bench near the stove and get warm.

But as I headed for the bench, a dark hooded shape rose out of the corner and came at me, reaching out with ghostly pale hands

I squeaked.

"It's me," hissed Shadow. He put his finger to my lips.

"What are you doing here?"

"Klea came to check about her letter."

"Why'd she bring you?"

"I did not want to stay at the hut alone. You were right. It is very strange out there. All these flying mice, glowing and nipping."

Katti put her head in the door and gave an enquiring chirrup, before seeing that I was unharmed and going away again.

I was so pleased to see him I put my arms around him and hugged him. I could feel him hesitating in my grasp.

"Oh, you're so nice and warm," I said, to hide the soppy moment. I pulled him over to the bench by the fire. "How have you been getting on with Klea?"

"Fine," he said, sounding as if he meant it. "She's been very good to me."

"Really?" I said.

"No, not in that way." He laughed. "No she's not going to do that. She's got too much else on her mind."

"Did she tell you what was in the letter?"

"No," he said.

"Are you telling the truth?" I felt a sense of being left out. Or maybe it was jealousy at not being the centre of his story any more.

"Yes. But I have an idea, now, of what it might be, and we do need to find it."

"So, come on," I said after a little silence. "Tell me what it is." I was dying to find out what was in this all-important letter. What could Klea have done?

"I cannot. Because I am not sure."

I whacked him on the arm.

"You are mad at me?" asked Shadow.

I already felt ashamed for hitting him. Childish to be jealous like that.

"I'll get over it," I said.

He put his hand through my arm and squeezed my elbow.

"I understand, Shine, I do. Do not worry. I will not let Klea go up to town without you."

The way he read my mind made me feel happy.

"She's a mage. You've got no say in it."

"But I think she will keep a promise. You were right about her. She is a good person at heart. Have you got any way of contacting her? She is waiting in your room for you."

"I'd best go up and get her. Already spent most of the evening running round after mages." I sighed and stretched out my legs, unwilling the leave the warmth and comfort.

"I begin to understand what you mean," he said wryly. "Tell me what's been happening."

Strangely enough, now he was here I didn't want to ruin my good mood by whining about Glisten, so I told him about Blazeann's plot. Halfway through the story, there came a rustle of leaves and a glow of magic. Shadow threw himself back into the dark corner, but it was only Klea dropping down through the trees into the winterhouse. She had her hat pulled down well over her head, but her crystal still gleamed through the felt.

"Any sign of my letter?" she asked as Shadow got up and dusted himself off again. "What are you doing down there, Ghost?"

"He was scared you were Illuminus, and I don't blame him. Why on earth did you bring him back here?"

That was no way to be talking to a mage, but I was feeling testy.

"Did you find my letter?" she asked again.

Always the letter. What was in that letter? What could possibly be so important?

"No. Blazeann tried to poison your mother and I've been busy trying to sort that out."

Her eyes widened. "Really? Do tell!"

"Well, not poison exactly. More like drug."

But, of course, I had to tell her everything.

"That was a narrow escape," she said, when I'd finished. "Toy's a real rat. And Blazeann is just plain stupid."

"You know Toy wants to take Lucient as her consort?"

"Lady of light, poor old Lucy. Why on earth must she torment him like that? Now what about my letter?"

She seemed much more anxious than she had been before. She kept rubbing her hands as if she were washing them. What could it be? Something as serious as crystal-smuggling. What else could be that serious? Curiosity was eating me up.

"We need the combination to Toy's treasure box," I said.

"Does it need to be the right number, or can you try a few on the chance?" asked Shadow.

"No. Those things are built to be touchy," said Klea "It's the right number or nothing. Sometimes you set them off even with the right numbers. Maybe Lucy would know the combination. Ask him, will you? And search Toy's maid's room. Toy sometimes gives her things to mind."

"Very well," I said, irritated at being ordered about so heedlessly. Elders are one thing, but your cousins... That's annoying. "But you need to keep your side of the bargain. This is no place for Shadow. What if Illuminus had let his hunting cats into the garden?"

"I'll put him on the roof next time, if you like. There's lots of places to hide here. There were all these weird mice at the hut. They gave us the shivers."

"You didn't think to kill them?"

"Yes, I did, but there might have been more. Those woods are scary. There's a tree that moves, just by the clearing. And something is talking. I'm not sure what. It didn't actually make any sense."

"It's probably a night spirit. You know, those tree-climbing things with the big ears. They make a sound like talking."

"It's not fair on Shadow to leave him there alone. He wanted to come."

It seemed so ridiculous that a mage like Klea should be scared of the woods, but I thought of the Mooncat that might still be out there and decided to stop being difficult.

"Well, you might be best to go back to the hut now," I said.

"I guess. I wish I could help poor old Lucy."

"Maybe you should get him to come and live with you."

"Not unless he's willing to lose his allowance. Impi insists everyone lives under the same roof. He says it keeps us respectable. As if."

"So why hasn't he cut your allowance?"

"He did. And Mother let him, too, damn her. But my dear friend Fabi Trudison got me work as a singer at the Golden Bubble in Crystalline. So I don't need my allowance."

"Do they pay a lot?" I asked. Her boots were the very finest leather.

She laughed. "Not much but, oh, darling, it's lovely in Crystalline. Everyone's so excited to meet a member of the Imperial Family. And be seen out at the best eating houses with one. And have her wear their clothing. And as for loving... The place is full of rich merchants who would adore to have it whispered that they're my favourite, and if I bloom because of it...?" She threw out her hands. "Think of the kudos for them."

The lucky beast. Magic, looks and all this too.

"Oh, look at you, all envious," she cried, surprising me with her perception. She pinched my cheek lightly. "Come down to Crystalline and join in. You're a member of the Imperial Family too. A ghostie girl like you would be a big hit there. Everyone's crazy for ghostie things at the moment."

"Small problem of how I'd eat," I said.

"Oh, nonsense. We'd find you something to do in the theatre and my friends'll pay for your food." She patted my cheek. I didn't believe a word she said, but I couldn't help smiling at her. "Come on. We'd have lots of fun. I'll take care of you. I promise."

"I can't leave Eff," I said. "This place would go back to rack and ruin."

A door slammed and people started laughing on the other side of the garden.

"We should go back to the hut," said Shadow.

"I know, I know. Don't worry, little Shadow. I'll look after you," said Klea.

She put her arm round Shadow's waist and pulled her hat down low over her head to dim her crystal light. "Shine, find that letter or I'll be unable to help you. Let us return to our elegant abode, Sirrah Shadow!"

With a rustle of leaves they shot up into the air and very quickly her light was gone.

I called Katti a couple of times, but in typical cat fashion she had got interested in something else and gone off. I knew I should go and talk to Eff, or at the very least go to bed, but it was hard to leave the warm fire. I lay down on the bench feeling drowsy and cosy, thinking I'd lie here and get really warm before going up to my chill room.

It only seemed like a moment later that I was woken up by someone shaking my arm.

"You should go to bed," said Hagen Stellason. "Preferably with me."

"Oh, don't be such a pepper groin," I said, rubbing my

eyes. I thought about Klea and the ghost, and scanned the winter house for any sign that they'd been there. No sign. It looked like Hagen had safely missed them.

He sat down on the bench and offered me a drink from a flask, which I declined. I didn't need to feel any sleepier.

"So who put you up to changing your aunt's smokeweed this evening?" He'd taken hold of my arm.

"No one!" I cried. "This is not your business. Will you unhand me, man?" I slapped his hands away.

"Now come," he said. "Tell me who. And why."

This was getting annoying.

"Nobody. Do you think I can't think for myself? I overheard... some people talking and decided to do something about it."

"Why not tell Lord Impavidus?"

"You're joking. He doesn't like me. And how do I know he's not involved? I've no time for the mages' petty politics. The only thing I care about is the Blessing. If Splendance had been taken ill... It would be a nightmare. No crops for the next year at least."

"Nothing to you. You'd eat."

"That's a selfish attitude. You're a town dweller, aren't you? Here, people go hungry when the crop fails."

"Yes I've heard you radicals are very close to the peasants."

"All good estates are run with the peasants in mind," I retorted.

"So no one put you up to it? I'm not sure I believe you."

"Believe what you like. It's hardly any of your business."

He stroked his chin thoughtfully.

"You are a remarkably clever little person," he said. "So what's going on with you and Illuminus? He's spending so much time in your room I'm beginning to think you are having a Blessing affair with him as well."

I couldn't help laughing. "Illuminus! I'm not doing anything with that stupid dog. Hey, I've heard a rumour that he's a crystal smuggler."

Looking back, I don't know why I said that. At the time, it seemed like a good idea to tell someone who might be able to do something useful with the information.

His face thinned to seriousness. "Who told you that? Your cousin Bright?"

"Perhaps," I said, suddenly realising I might have got myself into trouble. What if Hagen was Illuminus' man? Or if I had betrayed the ghost?

"Did Bright bring you something?" asked Hagen.

"Some books," I said casually. "Nothing else. I guess Illuminus thinks he left something else, though. I figure that's why he's been searching my room."

"You *are* a clever little person, aren't you? Why is the family keeping such a clever little person holed up here in the country?"

"Lady Glisten has just been telling me they're too poor to do anything else. And I'm damn good at running my mother's estate. And cheap. Apparently."

"Which will be the real reason they keep you here," said Hagen. "You should be careful of Illuminus. Try not to be alone with him."

"And how would I prevent that?" I said. "Well, I guess if I took you to my bed I'd be safer, wouldn't I?"

He grinned. "It's one way. "

I laughed and he leaned forward.

"I could get you out of here," he said. "My master has a need for clever people to serve him."

Another pointless lure; I was here at Willow for as long as Eff was. But that didn't mean I couldn't pretend to be interested. And I wondered if he knew the combination to Toy's treasure box. How to ask him?

"So who is your master? I thought it was Great Uncle Igniate. And he's only interested in cooks. Which I'm not. A cook, I mean."

"I've other connect... Holy Mother, what's that?" breathed Hagen.

I swung round and saw it—the huge shining white Mooncat from the night before, standing on the other side of the stream. He was looking away from us down the stream, probably unable to hear us over the sound of the water.

He lowered his face to the stream and began to lap it delicately. The beauty of him—his shining fur, his huge velvet paws, the soft pink tongue lapping so neatly at the water—made me tingle all over.

Then his head jerked up. He looked straight into my eyes, and at the same moment a clap of thunder sounded in my ear.

I slammed my hands over my ears and whirled around. Hagen was standing up behind me pointing a smoking metal tube towards the Mooncat. Even over the sound of the stream, I could hear the creature crashing away through the undergrowth.

"What in hell's name are you doing?"

"What do you mean? It could have killed us."

"It was the other side of the stream."

"It was huge."

"The forest creatures never cross that stream."

"It was a rogue, you stupid thing."

I saw red, then; no one likes being called stupid. He yelped as I grabbed that silly little firework out of his hand and I yelped in my turn as it burnt me. I dropped it.

"You idiot. Don't do that." He pushed me away so I pushed him back.

"You almost deafened me with it," I shouted. "You stupid man. It didn't see us. We could have watched it."

"It was dangerous, you fool. A damned shape shifter. Not some little pussy cat."

Derision came off him like a bad smell.

Sometimes my temper...

Ignoring its heat, I scooped up his stupid metal tube, threw it into the stream and stalked away.

As I reached the house, Katti came loping through the trees toward me, all concern over the loud noise. Hilly and Tane were peering out of the back door, but no one else in the house seemed to have heard the explosion.

"Don't worry. It was just some idiot with a firework," I told them.

Upstairs, everyone went on laughing and dancing.

CHAPTER FOURTEEN

GREY DAWN LIGHT. I was awake. Someone was in the room, and it wasn't Katti.

I sat bolt upright.

"Oh, sweetie," said a man's voice. "I woke you. So sorry."

"Scintillant? What are you doing here?"

"I wanted to watch you sleep. You looked so pretty."

"Really? Since when did you care about watching people sleep? You haven't got a sentimental bone in your body."

He laughed his warm sexy laugh and the bed shifted as he sat down beside me.

"You have such a cynical view of me, sweetie, and really I'm a terrible softheart." His hand cupped my face and as always I felt beautiful and my heart turned to syrup. He kissed my cheek lingeringly. I felt myself start to open to him and let him push me down. Magic glowed dimly and his boots thudded to the floor. He stretched out beside me, slid his arm round my waist and nuzzled his head into my neck.

He smelled of sweat and salt and someone else's scented oil. The smell brought me back to myself.

"Scintillant, may I remind you that I didn't invite you in?"

"Oooh, getting all haughty, are you? I know it was naughty of me. I'm not taking you for granted. I was passing by your window on the way to my room and had an overwhelming urge to see you. Such a lovely pale little thing, shining in the darkness." He nuzzled my cheek. "I'm sorry I woke you. It wasn't my intention. I was going to do a quick in-and-out."

I couldn't help laughing at the double entendre.

"That did sound bad, didn't it?" He laughed. "As if anyone would want to love you like that." His hand slid over my breast, the thumb grazing the nipple. He kissed my neck in the perfect spot and my lips once and again—a deeper kiss, this time. Somehow his hand had got in under the quilt and begun stroking my belly. The feeling was delicious.

I slid my hand onto his prick. Nothing.

"Sorry, sweetie," he said quite easily. "Old fellow's a bit tired."

"No doubt," I said.

"Don't be disappointed. Why don't you let me tickle

you sweet instead? I do love watching a woman enjoy herself."

I wasn't going to accept the offer of a tickle no matter how much he insisted he liked it. I get self-conscious when I'm enjoying myself and my partner isn't.

"It's nice like this," I said. Lying in bed with a man you've already made love to has a certain relaxing innocence.

"It is, isn't it?" he said, nuzzling me. "Just holding you. Those maids... they only want my seed. It's nice to be with someone who likes me for myself."

I should have been meltingly happy to hear this, but I felt uneasy.

All this soft cuddliness. That wasn't Scintillant. I pushed away my doubts and relaxed into his arms as he kissed my hair.

I must have fallen asleep, because I woke to a thump against the door and remembered. It was Blessing time and I had duties!

"Ladybless, what time is it?"

"I think I heard the maid putting the hot water outside your door," said Scintillant. He was standing over by the window opening the curtains. Bright light flooded into the room.

I jumped out of bed and rushed to the door. I'd have been astonished if there'd been a can of hot water there; the maids were too busy waiting on the lords and ladies. Katti had made the noise, thumping against the door. Scintillant must have closed the window. She stalked into the room, tail lashing, clearly annoyed at being locked out, and crouched and hissed at Scintillant.

What is this tom cat doing here?

"Oooh dear. Your pussy cat doesn't seem to like me." Scintillant smirked, stretched out on the bed again and put his hands behind his head.

"She doesn't care much for mages. I'd better get a wriggle on, Scintillant. I want to go out for the ceremony today."

"You didn't go out yesterday, did you?"

"Too much to do looking after you lot." I'd worked out my lies the day before. I hadn't expected to be testing them on Scintillant.

"You weren't secretly visiting Bright in the forest, were you? I thought he might still be out in one of the huts."

"No, he's long gone," I said firmly. I started collecting my clothes into a basket so that I could go down to the bath house.

"I wasn't going to tell on him, sweetie. I know you love him like a brother. Just curious. When I heard about his escaping with a woman, I hoped he'd found his way back to the right path. If he has—the family would be sure to have him back. I could shoot out there and tell him, if you like."

"Nowhere to shoot to," I said. "Bright's gone, honestly."

"So who was the woman?"

"I don't know," I said. "Maybe someone from his regiment?"

He paused and said, "This old place. I love it here. So

quaint. All dark passages and mysterious rooms and... Hey, didn't old Uncle Batty build a hidey hole here somewhere? For when the bats got too bad?"

My neck tingled with fright. Fortunately I wasn't looking at Scintillant.

"Do you know where it is?" asked Scintillant. He leapt out of the bed and started tapping the walls.

"Don't do that!" I cried.

"Why not? Come on. It must be here somewhere. Ah-ha, Got it." He said, hearing a hollow sound. "So, how do you get it open? Come on, sweetie, show me."

He pulled me to the wall and I touched the panel without thinking. Once it opened and the ghost wasn't there huddled in the wall, I realised why I'd been anxious about it and relaxed.

"Marvellous!" cried Scintillant. "A secret little hidey hole. I love this old place." He climbed into the gap.

"We've got a lover's cupboard, too," I said helpfully.

"Oh, but everyone's got—what's this?" He picked up something from under his feet. "What a strange colour!"

A small bright orange square dangled from his fingers. The moment I saw it, I knew it was the ghost's. My mind went blank with panic.

"What odd fabric. Like satin, only hard. And something sewn inside it. How do you get it out, I wonder?" He pulled the square of metal dangling at one end, but it didn't open. "What *is* it?"

The orange square was the same sort of material as the little blue backpack the ghost carried everywhere with him. I could feel some sort of padding inside it. I almost pulled the dangly square sideways the way the ghost did to open his pack, but stopped myself in time.

"I've never seen it before," I said quite truthfully. "I guess... It could belong to one of Auntie Eff's visitors," I added quickly. "Some of them have been in here. I wonder how long it's been there."

"Auntie Eff's visitors? Lady of light, does she have a string of radicals through here?"

"Not a string. But I know she does sometimes show her guests this little hole. In case the Imperial police raid the place. As if! Please, Scintillant, you won't go telling Im... Lord Impavidus will you?"

Scintillant laughed. "Oh, sweetie, I never tell him anything. That's why, if Bright were hanging around, you'd be safe to confide in me."

"Well, he's not," I said firmly. His endless questioning, his interest in Bright, was so unlike him. He was up to something, possibly to Bright's disadvantage. I'd actually thought for a moment that he'd come into the room for me. I was annoyed at myself—and at him because I was disappointed.

"And I don't know why you're so interested. I'd better take this and give it to Eff." I put it in the basket with my clothes.

"You leaving me?" cried Scintillant

"I'd really like a bath before today's ceremony," I said.

"Wouldn't you rather make love to me?"

I couldn't help laughing. "Are you a machine, Scintillant? I thought you didn't have any left."

He waved a little folded paper at me. "I've got

Rampant." He jumped out of the wall, put his arm round my waist and nuzzled my neck. "Take a moment or two."

Rampant! He'd have an erection, but he probably wouldn't climax. It didn't appeal.

"Why don't you rest?" I said, wriggling out of his arms.

He looked shocked.

"You're knocking me back?" he cried.

"I must to go to the ceremony," I said, blowing him a kiss and running out the door. Anxiety fluttered in my stomach as I ran away. When I analysed it later, as I took my bath, I realised I was scared. What if he did care about me and I had put him off? No! There was no way. He was just using me to get at Bright, for some reason. How easily I could come to believe in his care! And what a trap it would be—I knew it couldn't be the case.

Almost certainly not the case.

I WAS VERY glad to be able to attend the Blessing Ceremony that morning. After my conversation with Glisten last night, I really needed to feel that sense of connectedness and celebration, and to repeat the beautiful traditional prayers lead by the Matriarch. I'd sought out Eff at breakfast to find out what had happened between her and Glisten. She was deep in an argument with Cousin Two and Auntie Four about the morality of strike action by the stone masons working on the Elayison Sunspire.

All she did was pat my cheek and tell me not to worry. Her vague smile left me no way to commiserate over the awful thing Lady Glisten had said to her, and I felt like a weed.

To top it all off, Old Man Jenkal, one of the peasant elders, took me aside as our procession started and told me that one of Lord Impavidus' servants had been round asking him about the newly drained fields. Curse Impi; why did he have to be so efficient? I'd been hoping to make a little money for me and Eff out of growing vegetables on those fields. I figured I was entitled to something for draining the fields in the first place. I'd even helped dig the ditches myself. Curse it. All the other estate managers in the neighbourhood diddled their employers out of huge sums of money, yet I couldn't even get away with a tiny skim like this. No wonder Impi has accused Eff of skimming yesterday.

"What did you tell him?"

"I said as I dun't know nothin' about no drained fields," said old Man Jenkal, putting on the dumb hayseed face and accent that was the peasant's main defence against questioning superiors.

I thanked him warmly and shook his calloused old hand, but I had a sinking feeling there were going to be some ugly questions when Impi and I had our business meeting on the final Blessing day.

A SLIGHT MIST rose from the ploughed fields in the golden morning sun and dew sparkled on the grass. Beautiful sunny mornings like this were one small consolation for being stuck in the country.

Once again Auntie Splendance floated before us in a shining light with her pink robes flowing out behind her, Impi at her side and the female mages of the family clustered around her. Was it my imagination or did Blazeann seem to be leaning very close? The peasants followed behind in their long robes, singing Blessing hymns with only slightly less vigour than they had the day before. Priest Zostre kept time for them.

As Lucient and I followed the other worshippers from field to field, he told me all about his struggles with Chatoyant, which made it hard to feel any sense of holiness. Twice she had drugged him with Rampant and, using a man's inability to control his own prick, had mounted him and later claimed on the strength of these two successful couplings that he adored her. Blazeann had laughed when Lucient told her he'd been forced, and Impi had told him to show some backbone.

"She blindfolded me, stuffed a scarf in my mouth and treated me as if I was just a prick," he whispered. "She feels like rubber to touch."

He seemed obsessed with the idea that Blazeann would force him to become Chatoyant's consort. I told him that I couldn't see why Chatoyant would want that.

When Lucient became Blazeann's Avunculus, as seemed inevitable as the only male mage Splendance had birthed, he was likely to obey Blazeann without question and without needing a second woman to manage him.

As for Chatoyant having only managed to get one child so far, and that a mere boy—while pair bonding with a cousin might give her a better chance of birthing a mage, it wouldn't improve her fertility any.

"She's a big bully. You need to stand up to her," I said, knowing full well as I said it that Lucient would never be able to. The horribleness of his story gave me a dull ache in the gut. As a mage he wasn't protected by Shola's pact, and as a mere man he could not hope to overpower and drive away a woman mage. Toy would always be the stronger in terms of sheer brute magic.

"She'll be after me tonight, you wait and see," he whispered, voice trembling. "Promise you'll stay in my room tonight."

"Of course I will," I said, squeezing his hand. I was protected by Shola's pact, and it was bad manners and bad luck to disrupt a Blessing affair. Manners are an oddly powerful shield in our civilised world.

"Look how put out Blazeann looks at how well our Matriarch is doing," I said, to distract him.

"She does, doesn't she? And I've already seen Glisten saying something nasty to Toy about spreading baseless gossip," he said in a more cheerful voice.

He didn't know the combination to Toy's treasure box, or anyone who might know, so I concentrated on wheedling some information about Klea out of him. He and Klea were only a year apart and had been close as children. I'd hoped he could give me some hint about what Klea's letter related to, but he didn't know anything about her life in Crystalline. They'd hardly communicated at all since she'd left home. He missed her.

"But she would go," he said sadly. "Terrified that Auntie Flara would regain control of the family and that Radiant would come back. They treated her dreadfully."

"How?" I prompted when he stopped talking.

"Flara's way. Toy's way, too. Always forcing people to do things they don't want. Best not to talk about it. Wish Klea would come back. She'd fix Toy."

And he went back to dwelling on his own situation. I was hard pressed to cheer him up again.

Lady Splendance was in excellent form the whole day, blessing the farm animals and the village babies with great spirituality and focus. At the end of the day, we finished our tour of the estate in one of the more distant villages—not the one where the inn had been burned down, I noticed. We watched children wreathed in garlands made from last year's grain harvest dancing their funny little jumping dance to make the crops grow. Lady Splendance cooed loudly over their sweetness. Then it was into the carriages and back to the house to change into our best robes for the great Blessing Feast.

THE BOTTOM OF the Eyrie had been cleared and tables set out for everyone, villagers included. Blessing night was the night when mages and mundanes mingled most freely. Many mages felt that breeding with the mundanes refreshed the bloodlines of the great families. Smug mages would accept as many flowers as they could from enthusiastic mundanes, who were always eager to impress with their love skills in the hope of being whisked away to service in the city, or to achieve the blessing of a child. A child who turned out to be a mage would become the Ward of the Empress, to be taken into paid Imperial service when they came of age. A mage could win all kinds of further patronage by sitting in the Great Council that approved the Empress's policies—or becoming the consort of a great lady, as Impi had. Even a mage from a very humble lineage would be able to keep her mother and family in comfort for the rest of their days.

A fire had been built on the lawn in front of the Eyrie, and a bullock and a pig were being spit-roasted under the anxious supervision of Tane. Later the fire would be built up into a huge blaze. Everyone would dance round it to celebrate the renewal of Shola's Pact. The villagers would blow grain alcohol from their mouths into the fire, creating huge plumes of flame; this was actually an offering to Grain Boy from the old peasant religion, but the nobles always pretended not to know.

Given the tremendous difference in power, there was always the potential for things to turn nasty between mage and mundane. You heard horrible stories of rape and abuse. But never here: here, Elder mages such as Splendance, Glisten and Impi took good care to make sure no mundane was mistreated by a mage. Lord Impavidus was the result of a Blessing Feast mating between a mundane and mage, and he seemed to have some sympathy for the limitations mundanes faced.

Sadly I would again be sleeping alone, though it looked like I would be doing it on the hard couch in Lucient's room. Perhaps we could play some checkers and make a really wild night of it.

Since this was the Blessing feast, it was all meat, meat, meat. Quite apart from the risk of pregnancy, if the truth be told I'd never been that fond of red meat. It always sat heavy on my stomach. Give me a spinach-and-cheese pastry any time. But I made a show of piling my plate with plenty of roast beef, nibbling a little whenever Lumina or Glisten was looking and slipping the rest under the table to Katti and a couple of her offspring. The only other thing to eat was bread and butter. So I drank wine, and on my not very full stomach, it went right to my head. Soon I was trying to drag Lucient outside to dance around the fire. Lucient refused. He was deep in a conversation about the local newts with Uncle Five. Apparently they had a fascinating vestigial fourth toe. I ask you!

I had to content myself with singing and clapping.

"Not dancing?" The voice of Hagen Stellason came suavely in my ear. "Perhaps you'd let me remedy that."

"You surprise me," I said, going for an equally suave tone. "You seemed a little displeased with me last night. And I was not thrilled to be called a fool."

"My deepest apologies. I'm not as brave as you in the face of large animals and I fear I lost my head." Hagen sat down beside me and crossed his legs. "I thought to partner you in a dance by way of a peace offering, but perhaps the conversation is too exciting. Hmm, yes, newts. Uncle Five is always so enthralling. So much to know about them, don't you think? How could I possibly dare to think you might be enticed away?"

I couldn't help laughing.

"Should you be wasting your time with mere gentry?"

His eyes twinkled. "My dear Marm, I've been travelling with the Blessing party for three weeks now. The mages aren't interested in me anymore. And dare I say vice versa?"

Across the fire, I saw Scintillant being kissed and nuzzled by a group of pretty peasant girls. He caught my eye and winked. I was annoyed to be caught staring. I was not having him thinking I was lovelorn.

"Fair enough," I said, taking Hagen's hand "Let's dance."

I'm not a good dancer, but I was enthusiastic; and Hagen knew the steps very well. His hand felt warm and delicious in the small of my back—that pleasant tingle of attraction before it becomes too intense.

But wouldn't you know it, after our first dance together, the band stopped playing to have a drink. I took a surreptitious glance round after Scintillant. He'd already slipped away with his peasant girls. Lucient waved me over. I checked for Lady Chatoyant; she was talking to Michael, the village blacksmith, who like all such tradesmen had a wonderful body. Surely with Michael on offer, she wouldn't go after Lucient? But tonight I was at my cousin's service, so I went back and sat down beside him. At least Uncle Five had taken himself off to the stream to catch wrigglers for the newts he'd already captured. Tonight he would be tripping over loving couples in the bushes until the early hours of the morning, but he probably wouldn't pay much attention.

To my surprise, Hagen came and sat beside me. He clearly knew Lucient very well; they began sharing theatre gossip, stories about who was feuding with whom and which leading man threw a tantrum over not being allowed to take his little dog on stage. I loved this kind of talk, even if I had no idea of the people involved. Hagen was being delicious, smiling at me as if to check that I wasn't feeling left out.

The Eyrie was loud with talk and laughter. Through the wide open doors I watched people dancing round the huge bonfire and the gigantic plumes of flaming grain alcohol spurting from the mouths of the peasants. The sensuous movements, the way people touched and kissed and broke away in couples or threesomes to disappear into the bushes, made me feel warm in the pit of my belly. The way Hagen kept stroking my arm made the feeling grow until I felt as if honey were sliding glistening though my loins. Watching the whirling figures, the sensual touches on faces, the smoothing of hands over limbs and chest, the brush of hip against hip—how I wished I had someone to take part with! Someone with velvet skin to press my mouth against and ride hard into the dawn.

"There goes Lady Chatoyant," murmured Hagen in my ear, nodding at the door. "Perhaps Lord Lucient will be able to spare you tonight after all." He smiled at me in a way that made my belly melt.

"That's for him to say," I said, opening my eyes wide and innocent. "Really, Sirrah Hagen, I begin to think you are trying to break up a Blessing affair. Surely that cannot be so."

"You really are too delightful to rot here in the country," he said. He lifted my hand and kissed it.

"Shine, darling, would you get me another jug of wine?" asked Lucient over his shoulder. He gave me a grin that said he knew how Hagen was making me feel.

I took the pitcher and went out into the hallway towards the kitchen, aware all the time of Hagen behind me. As we reached the servants' door, he put his hand on my shoulder.

"Are you sure you wouldn't like to sneak away later when Lucient is asleep and meet me somewhere?"

"Perhaps I might need to return to my room for one or two things later," I murmured, reaching for the door handle

He took advantage of my stillness to kiss me on the back of the neck. How did he know the right place to do it, the place that sent shivers down my spine and made my back arch towards him? His strong arm slid round my waist and his slim hand caressed my throat and smoothed down to my breast sending heat all the way down into my belly. I steered him into a shadowy corner and pressed my mouth on his. His mouth opened beneath mine and we kissed deep and hard.

He leaned back against the wall and pulled me against him and I felt the exciting hardness at his groin against my belly. I pressed my hips against it. I like a slow man but tonight...

"Marm, Marm, where are you?" called a voice and Lucient's valet, Busy, was at my elbow. "My lord needs you. Lady Chatoyant..."

"Curse it. I'd thought we were free of her."

I pulled myself away from Hagen.

Hagen caught my arm and said something in my ear, but I was too intent upon getting back to Lucient to listen.

Back in the great hall, Toy was on the bench beside Lucient, almost sitting in his lap with her hand on his thigh. No sign of Michael the blacksmith.

"Oh, Shine, darling, there you are," Lucient jumped up, flung his arm round my neck and drew me to his shoulder. "Let us retire, sweetheart," he said. "Cousin, you must excuse us. Shine becomes very heated after dancing, and I promised not to disappoint her."

With a flash of crystal light, he scooped me up and leapt into the air, knocking over his chair in his haste. The effect of manly passion was undermined by his trembling, but Chatoyant wasn't to know that. As he flew up through Eyrie carrying me in his arms, I pressed my face into his neck. Over his shoulder I caught sight of Chatoyant's face. She was grinning—I was certain she was enjoying Lucient's fearful retreat. Was she bullying him for the pleasure of it? Ladybless, she was mean.

"Thank the Lady you came. That woman's hand was heading straight for my prick," jittered Lucient.

"Why don't you just tell her no? She can't force you in front of everyone."

"I couldn't, darling. She's awful when she's upset, and she sets Blazeann and Lumina off."

Poor old Lucient. No spine at all.

CHAPTER FIFTEEN

HE WAS SO full of jitters that he insisted on smoking several pipes of smokeweed laced with his favourite potion, which he called Bliss. Soon enough, he was lying smoked flat out on his bed with his little mundane maid snuggled up beside him.

I sat on the windowseat reading one of his travel books, trying not to feel disappointed at how my Blessing evening had ended. My flesh was still singing with the memory of Hagen's strong body against mine and the feel of his lips. I wished I could sneak away. He'd said something about a meeting. But I knew I had to stay here. Toy might well have a servant watching the room, as she'd clearly had someone watching the feast earlier.

Katti was curled up at my feet.

Are you on heat? she sniffed, eyeing me. *Your thoughts are as gooey as mud.* She curled round with her back to me and wrapped her tail tightly around herself, indicating that she refused to listen anymore.

A little while later, she lifted her head and looked at the window. I heard a light tapping on the glass.

Scintillant! I thought, pathetic creature that I was, and twitched back the curtain.

Klea was hovering outside.

"Open up," she mouthed at me. With a quick glance over my shoulder to check that Lucient—and, more importantly, his little maid Sharlee—were fast asleep, I did so and, climbing outside, sat on the chill stone parapet to speak with her. She steadied me with her hand.

"Did you find my letter?" she hissed.

The letter! I felt guilty. I'd completely forgotten.

"No! I told you. I've got no idea how to get into Toy's strongbox. I asked Lucy and he doesn't know and I can't think of who else to ask. Is Shadow safe?"

"Yes, he's in your room."

"You brought him back here again?"

"I couldn't leave him out there alone. I could have sworn I saw a huge glowing cat last night. Now look, friend Shadow has come up with the brainiest plan to get us into Toy's strong box, but I need your help. Come on back to your room and we can talk about it."

"Very well. But you'll have to bring me back later. I'm protecting Lucient from Toy, and she may have someone watching."

Klea pulled a face. "Poor old Lucy." But she wasn't really interested. It was all about the letter. What could be in it? She was a female mage, top of the heap. What in the world could be worrying her so much? Some shady financial dealing? Some unsuitable consort? Had she... killed someone?

"We have a problem," was the first thing Shadow said to me when I climbed over the window sill; and sure enough, we did. A familiar figure sat on the bed, its hands tied around my bedpost and one of my best kerchiefs shoved in its mouth.

"Who's that?" asked Klea

"Hagen Stellason. Curse it!"

"Uncle Lucient's intelligencer?" Klea seized me and dragged me back out the window. "He mustn't find out about the letter," she hissed as we hovered outside in the chill night. She insisted I promise to keep quiet before she would let me back into the bedroom.

"Are you going to shout for help if I pull out this scarf?" I asked, returning to stand before Hagen. Something in his glare spoke of outrage rather than terror, so I took the risk, seized the end of the scarf and drew it out of his mouth.

"What the benighted hell is that?" was the first thing he said, pointing to Shadow.

"*He's* not a 'that,'" I retorted

No one expects to see a ghost in an Imperial Family House sixty miles out of Elayison, but his tone wasn't very polite.

"'What the hell are you doing here?' is the question,

Sirrah Hagen," snapped Klea. This was the first time she'd put on her haughty mage's look, and it was impressive.

"I was waiting for Marm Shine."

"I said *perhaps* I'd come back later," I protested.

"You were hiding," accused Klea. "I didn't see you when I came in, and I *did* look."

"Of course I was. Someone comes in the window, it's not going to be Marm Shine. I'm under the bed, very disappointed but planning to leave discreetly later. Then this"—he pointed at Shadow—"tried to get under the bed with me. What's a ghost doing here? Has he got permission to be out here? Is he even registered? He doesn't look like anyone I've ever seen before."

"Hagen works for my great uncle, the Premier. I think he's an intelligencer," I explained to Shadow's questioning look

"Oh, great!" said the ghost sarcastically. "I suppose it's out of the question to keep him prisoner for the next two days."

Klea was looking at Hagen speculatively.

"Of course it's out of the question," snapped Hagen. "I will be missed."

"We better tell him everything." Shadow sighed. "At least the Premier is sympathetic to us."

"I'm sure there are limits," snapped Hagen.

"You tell him all about yourself," said Klea. "I need to have a word with Shine."

She dragged me into the corner of the room and started whispering her plan to get into Toy's strong box into my ear. It wasn't a bad plan. I could see how it could fail, but no one was likely to be exposed if it did, so I didn't protest. Klea's hands were shaking and there was an edge of hysteria to her voice that worried me. When we'd played together as kids, Klea had always been very cool-headed, not one to fuss about nothing. Clearly what was in this letter was really serious.

"It'll be fine," I said, squeezing her hands.

"If Great-Uncle finds out, everything's ruined," she hissed. "Please, please don't tell Hagen."

When we turned back to the bed, the ghost and Hagen sitting together very companionably chatting about, of all things, the qualities of the local beers. Men can be such frivols.

"Come on, let me loose," said Hagen. "My lord's interests are not going to be served by my arresting this fellow. You'd best go on as you were. Your plan seems adequate. Though make sure you take him straight back to the Capital. Honestly, he couldn't have fetched up in a worse place at a worse time. Lady Glisten is a leader of the anti-ghost faction in the Great Council, and his being here would just give her more ammunition against them. They already claim the outlanders can't be trusted. Aah, better," he said rubbing his unbound wrists. "So for Lady's sake try not to involve anyone else. You, Sirrah Shadow, have put the government's goodwill at serious risk by your actions, and I hope you know it."

"But possibly the information about Lord Illuminus is useful," I pointed out. "Possibly telling someone like Auntie Glisten or Lord Impavidus about Illuminus might get him off our back and prevent Shadow being exposed."

"Yes that had occurred to me," said Hagen, shooting me a look that had a hint of eyeroll in it. "Any other instructions for me, while you're at it?"

"Lady Klea doesn't want anyone to know she's here," I said, thinking that for Klea's sake, it might be best to get this out into the open.

"Of course. You may rely on my discretion, Lady," said Hagen. He rose and bowed to Klea and gave her a look that I couldn't read. What was it? Solemn, kindly? I couldn't read the glance Klea gave him back either, but I knew they understood something I didn't and I was annoyed. Why was I always on the outside?

"Oh, and—Here," said Hagen, picking something off the top of my chest of drawers and handing it to me. "This is for you, Marm Shine. A small token."

A little bundle of sweetmeats wrapped in cloth and charmingly tied up with a red ribbon.

"Oh, I do love a man who brings sweetmeats," I quipped, to hide the fact that I was thrilled at his thoughtfulness. Had I ever had received sweetmeats from an admirer before? If I had, I couldn't remember it.

"I'll let Lord Scintillant know that, will I?" he said, and slid out the door so quickly that the sweetmeat bundle I threw at him hit the closed door.

Klea magicked them up into her hand, and sniffed the bundle. "Mmmm, rosewater chocolates," she said. "Nice. Sorry to ruin your fun, coz. He had rather a nice bottom, didn't he?"

The ghost groaned and put his head in his hands. "This is rapidly becoming a diplomatic nightmare. I am about to go down in history as the man who ruined all hopes of a trading relationship between our two peoples. And all you two can think about is bottoms."

"I think 'diplomatic nightmare' is a bit strong," said Klea. "I'm sure as long as the conservatives don't find out about you, Great Uncle Lucient will be understanding." She sat down beside him and put her arm around his shoulders. "Come on, Sirrah Shadow. Cheer up."

She offered him one of my sweetmeats.

LATE NIGHT HAD become early morning, and in a couple of hours the servants and I would be dragging ourselves out of bed to prepare the hunting breakfast.

Shadow suggested I give up on Lucient and get some rest in my own bed, but I'd promised to stay all night and I didn't like to let my cousin down. Klea didn't offer to take me back. She was intent on preparing for her plan, and I didn't like to bother her. Anyway, the mages decided to hold a wrestling match on the lawn, making it impossible for anyone to go out of my window unseen—or, for that matter, to get any sleep, on this side of the house. Scintillant and a couple of the retainers were staggering round half-dressed and reeling drunk, each with a half-naked servant mounted on his or her shoulders. Apparently the idea was for the servants to try and knock each other off their mounts' shoulders. I hoped for the servants' sake the grass was soft. Everyone was shouting, shrieking and laughing at the tops of their voices.

As I was watching them, annoyed but a little bit envious—they did seem to be having fun—a window opened in the Eyrie and a pair of boots flew out and hit Scintillant on the head. Scinty spun round and roared furious insults at the person in the window, who turned out to be Illuminus. Illuminus shouted at him to shut up because people were trying to sleep, and compared him to an inelegant part of the body. Scintillant shouted back and flew up at the window with a poor unfortunate maidservant still mounted on his shoulders. She screamed hysterically and clutched his head like a terrified hat, while he took a swing at Illuminus through the window, all the while yelling abuse. Things might had gone badly—for the maid especially—but luckily a window opened at the top of the Eyrie and Impi shot out. I'd heard he was extremely strong for a male mage; certainly, he broke up the fight between Illuminus and Scintillant quickly enough, with just a few choice words and magical blows. More importantly, he plucked the servant girl off Scintillant's head and lowered her gently to the ground, tonguelashing the mages as he did so.

With all this excitement outside, I decided it would be best to sneak back through the house.

"I'll try and get her to sleep," Shadow told me, nodding at Klea, bent over her task.

"Good idea. Perhaps a glass or two of that brandy," I suggested, pointing to a bottle our household had received as a Blessing gift from a local feed merchant.

I'd hoped to trade it on for something more practical, but I was getting worried about Klea's state of mind.

The inside of the house was quiet. Most people had clearly settled into a post-loving slumber, while the party around the bonfire outside the Eyrie seemed to have reached the point of drunken sleeping or the maudlin singing of broken-hearted ballads.

One of the maids was sitting on the stairs up to the second level and weeping, but when I stopped to check on her, she was simply drunk and overwrought. A couple was having an enjoyably noisy time in one of the bedrooms on level three, and Michael the blacksmith was stretched out naked and asleep in the fourth-level corridor. I suppressed a niggle of envy. I was off to the back-breaking couch in Lucient's room while Klea slept in my comfortable bed with my ghost. Typical. At least Lucient's room would be warm.

With everyone so distracted by pleasuring, there seemed no reason to sneak about; I'd stopped being careful about who saw me and was pattering along, longing for sleep. So I bear some responsibility for what happened next.

Just as I was reaching for Lucient's door knob, I heard a shriek from above. "You! Mundane! Get away from it."

Blazeann was leaning over the opposite balcony of the floor above, resplendent in a red silk dressing gown. Screeching like a mad parrot, she launched herself over the railings and swooped at me.

Hot panic filled me. I pushed open the door and fled into the room, screaming Lucient's name. I had enough presence of mind to slam the door shut behind me. By the time Blazeann had flung it open again, Lucient was sitting bolt upright on the bed, a mage light burning in his hand and Sharlee had slid off and underneath the bed with a speed that bespoke of long practice.

Blazeann stood in the doorway, swaying, fury writ large on her face. She was very drunk.

"You!" she shrieked, pointing at me where I crouched on the bedside carpet. Hitting the floor is the logical reaction when faced with a drunk and angry mage; you don't fall as far, that way. "Get out of here before I throw you out. My brother has more important women to pleasure."

"B... Blazeann. What are you doing?" stammered Lucy, looking like a frightened rabbit.

"You crapulous little smoke rat," screamed Blazeann, advancing into the bedroom. "What did I tell you about Toy?"

"But I hate her."

"You useless little... You and she could breed true together. Had you thought of that? Make some mages for this family. We're drowning in hell-cursed mundanes. What the hell are you still doing here, mundane?" She snarled at me. "Get out. I said now!"

Her force hit me and I slid across the floor, hurtling towards the doorway. All I could think of was the balcony beyond the door, with nothing but the wooden balustrade between me and four long storeys of stairwell down through the Eyrie.

"Stop!" shouted Lucient and I slowed, as if I had

run into a bank of mud. I managed to seize the door frame and stop myself even though the original force of magic was still pulling at me and sucking my body away towards that stairwell.

Then, suddenly, the force was gone.

Lucient was standing up on the bed. "You can't treat Shine like that. She's Fam—"

"I don't care what she is. She's no substitute for Toy in your bed."

"I hate Toy," shouted Lucient. "I don't want her to mount me again. I can't."

"A bit less weed would fix your prick," snarled Blazeann. She lunged out and slapped Lucient's smoke pipe and mixing bowl off his bedside table. "You're a man, aren't you? Take some Rampant and shut your eyes. Light knows you take everything else."

"Who do you think you are?" shouted Lucient. "I can mate with whoever I like."

"I'm your older sister and soon enough I'll be the Matriarch of this family. Then I'll make *sure* you do as you're told."

As I clung to the door frame, I saw Lucient's mouth open and held my breath in case he told about the polluted smokeweed.

But instead he said with soft venom, "Not everyone has your taste for incest, sister dear."

Blazeann screamed and flung up her arm, and Lucient was thrown back against the wall behind his bed, stopping himself just before he hit. I threw myself out of the doorway and wriggled round with my back against the wall as Blazeann came shooting out of the room. Fortunately, she streamed back up to her room without seeing me.

"You scrofulous muckeater!" yelled Lucient from the bedroom, when Blazeann was too far away to hear him. I couldn't blame him for putting discretion before valour. She was so much more powerful than he was.

"Oh, my lord, my lord, are you all right?" cried Sharlee, creeping out from under the bed.

He wasn't the one who'd almost gone over the balcony rail. I patted the nice strong door frame with shaking hands.

"Are you hurt, Shine?" asked Lucient. He was standing by the bed, shaking, his jaw clenched.

"No," I said, though my knees seemed to have turned to jelly and parts of me were badly grazed. I staggered back into his room. I'd never had a mage handle me like that before, though I'd seen it happen to others. I'd always thought I was immune, at least inside the family. But I was just some little mundane. A door to possibility had opened, and the draft chilled me to the core.

"I am not—I am never—going to become Chatoyant's consort," snarled Lucient. He ruined the whole stalwart effect by picking up his smoke pipe and checking to see if there was any smokeweed in it. Sharlee seemed to know the drill, for she had already scraped up some of the spilled weed and was tucking it into another pipe. He lit it with his finger and took a deep suck on it, breathing out long and slow before sitting down on the side of the bed. Sharlee packed the bowl of another pipe.

I found I wanted to cry. But Lucient was absorbed in his own dilemmas

"Blazeann gets like this. Hell of a temper. I will complain to Impi... to Mother tomorrow. She had no business tossing you around like that. And if it had been Sharlee..."

He stroked his maid's hair and Sharlee patted her belly protectively.

I closed the bedroom door against the outside.

"What are you going to do?" I asked Lucient.

"Hold firm as best I can. And hope she doesn't become Matriarch. Once she controls my purse, I'll have to do as she says. Fortunately Mother's young yet, and Toy may lose interest if she manages to get pregnant some other way. Curse the prick."

"You might be wise to tell your mother about the smokeweed."

"Yes. And I better make sure I pack all her pipes in future too. Would you like one?"

I nodded. My hands were shaking.

DREAMSMOKE WAS ONE way to get to sleep after shock, but it put Klea's task out of my mind. Luckily I was awoken at dawn by Katti demanding to be let in at Lucient's window and as she crawled up onto Lucient's couch beside me, something sparked in my brain. I threw on my clothes and ran back to my room, sucking the grazes that skidding across the carpet had made on my hands.

CHAPTER SIXTEEN

THE MAGES ALWAYS hunted for the last two days of their stay at Willow-in-the-Mist. Traditionally the hunt had been to clear dangerous animals and rogues out of the home forest, but these days the mages seldom caught anything—or anyone—more dangerous than a few deer.

The tradition was to go on horseback. Horse riding was a skill that all children of noble families, myself included, learned. Gentry sometimes mounted their horses and joined in too, but I never bothered; the mages used their powers to lift their horses over obstacles and through the dangerous trackless undergrowth, and you soon got left behind. Also I felt cruel chasing frightened animals till they were exhausted. A hunting party of mages is a formidable threat. I hoped that Dannel

Graceson had taken himself away by now and that the Mooncat was hiding in a safe burrow.

Though we didn't join them, custom decreed that as hosts Eff and I should see off the hunting party from the steps of the Eyrie. Eff always gave a small speech thanking them for keeping our forest clear of danger, and silver cups of mulled wine were offered to warm the hunters against the morning chill. Despite the partying of the night before, most of the family and all of the magely entourage were there. I suspected many of the mages had not bothered to go to bed at all, but were using various means—Revive potions being the most popular—to extend their energy.

The horses, which had been brought up from Elayison by mundane grooms and who had been stuffing their faces in our stables at our expense for the last week, were of the very finest stock and had been brushed to a silken sheen. Sleek hunting cats crouched beside their masters, jewelled collars around their necks. According to the stable boys, the cats would all out hunting today, so there was no chance of them sniffing through the house after Shadow.

Even Great Uncle Nate was there on his floating commode chair with Cousin Two hanging on to the back of it as she always did. They would follow the action from a distance and enjoy the forest picnic.

Only Auntie Splendance, Lucient and Scintillant were missing.

Klea's plan had been to cover everyone's hands with the blue powder used in mage-proof boxes. To this end, she had drawn some blue powder out of an old treasure box of Uncle Batty's and mixed it with a little face cream. I'd stolen the carefully polished silver stirrup cups from the pantry last night and Klea had brushed the mixture on the inside edges of the handles. This morning I'd taken them back down to the pantry and arrayed them on their trays so all the servants needed to do was fill the cups with mulled wine. When the servants offered round the trays of cups, the mages would take the cups by their handles and get blue powder on their fingers. The plan was that those with secrets in their treasure boxes would instantly get worried and rush upstairs to check them. Hopefully one of these would be Toy. She would find her treasure box sprinkled with powder put there by Klea, who would be hiding in her room. When Toy opened the box to check the contents, Klea should be able to see the box's combination.

The first part of this plan went very well. I felt a rising glow of satisfaction as I saw the mages brushing their hands against their legs and looking at their riding gloves in surprise, while they listened to Eff's speech.

"Someone's been at a treasure box," murmured a man's voice from somewhere on my left.

"Must I do everything myself?" snapped Lord Impavidus to Eff as she bowed at the end of her speech. "Now I find I will have to speak to the steward about dishwashing." He held up a glove smeared with blue powder. "What on earth is this?"

"It looks like treasure box powder," I ventured loudly, in case anyone had missed the implications.

Lord Impavidus harrumphed and rolled his eyes at me for speaking out of turn as he waved at the huntsman to blow his horn. He didn't bother me as much as usual. Being attacked by Blazeann had one advantage. Now there was someone I hated more than him. Perhaps I could get through our accounts meeting tomorrow without answering him back.

"Wait a minute," Blazeann called.

"Yes, wait for me too," called Lumina and both of them flew off their horses in a flurry of bright hunting robes. I noticed Toy and Auntie Glisten had already made more discreet exits.

"Bloody women. Expect the whole world to wait for them," muttered Lord Impavidus under his breath.

My shoulders were tensed, ready for the sound of shouting that would come if Klea was caught spying on Chatoyant. Nothing. A few minutes later all four mages floated calmly back down the stairs.

"Perhaps if we could get going before lunchtime," snapped Lord Impavidus, nodding the party into motion. "And you," he pointed his riding crop at Eff, "see those cups are cleaned properly."

WHEN EVERYONE WAS safely gone and after a brief meeting with Hilly on the stairs where I cut her off impatiently (and I'm ashamed to say, with a curt remark about the state of the floor under my bed) as she was settling in to tell me all of Tane's sins, I ran quickly upstairs to my room and knocked on the door. The first thing I saw when it was opened to me was Klea sitting on the bed weeping.

"Apparently Lady Toy took everything out of the box, put it in her jacket and took it with her," explained the ghost.

"That rat!" screamed Klea. She hit out at the air, knocking over my bedside table. "That thrice-cursed devil. I should have broken open that box when I first came here and stolen everything."

"Ssh, Klea! Keep it down!"

"No, I will not keep it down. She has no business prying into my affairs. I'll show her." She leapt off the bed, fists clenched.

"No," cried the ghost and I together, but it was too late. Klea went out the window, throwing it open so hard it hit the wall beyond.

"*Arskthyel Blithech*," said Shadow, putting his hand on his forehead. "What's she going to do?"

"I pray to the Lady she doesn't confront Toy. Surely she wouldn't with all the others there?"

To be honest I was fed up with Klea's fireworks. She refused to tell me what was in the letter and what sort of trouble she was in. She'd knocked over my bedside table in her rampage and broken a little vase that Bright had given me. Now there was a big crack in my window pane too. My palms and knees were skinned from my slide across the carpet last night and I kept thinking about the Eyrie stairwell. Nightcursed Mages! What was the good of them?

"I'd better go back in the hidey hole," sighed the ghost.

"I don't think there's any point of you using it anymore. Scinty found it yesterday. Oh, and he found this too." I pulled out the satiny orange bag and threw it at him.

"*Datrh*. Then he'll know I was here. Scinty. He's the one you've got a crush on, right?"

"I have not got a crush on Scinty. It's just physical."

"He's Lord Illuminus' brother, isn't he? So he'll probably tell him."

"That's not certain at all. They hate each other. That was them fighting last night. But he's a chatty soul. So you might as well hide under the bed. Did Hilly clean under it, I wonder? I chewed her ear... Nope. As dusty as ever."

"Isn't there somewhere else you can hide me? How about that Hagen? Has he got a room?"

"He's in with Great Uncle Nate's valet. Look, Illuminus has searched this room several times already; surely by now he must have decided there's nobody here. Anyway he's gone out hunting with all his cats, so you're probably safe for the day." I wondered what to do if we did indeed lose Klea's protection. Perhaps Hagen could—

"Hey!" said Shadow, taking my hands and turning them up to look at the carpet burns. "These are nasty. How did this happen?"

He was angry when I told him about Blazeann, which did my heart good to see.

"Your cousin should be reported for throwing you around like that. Is not that breaking Shola's Pact?"

"Only if I'm hurt," I said. In truth I didn't want to think about it anymore. My chest felt too heavy.

"Come on, report her. Who would you tell? You have a right to—"

"You sound like Eff," I said. "I bet you two would get on like a house on fire. In fact, maybe you should go in with her. She's next door. I feel sort of guilty for not telling her about you. She'd love to meet a ghost."

"Why not expose me to *everybody* and be done with it?"

"Don't be like that. Eff's a bit of a flutterbrain, but she knows how to be discreet, and no one could call her a conservative. And they wouldn't be looking for you in her room. The only problem is that she'll probably drill you about ghost politics. What do you think?"

Before he could answer, the window flew open and Klea burst back in.

"I've lost them. You'll have to come and show me the way," was all she said as she seized me around the waist.

"Wait, we have to take him," I cried, gripping Shadow's arm.

"Can't manage both of you," snapped Klea. "He stays here."

She jerked me away from the ghost and we were away before I knew it. I glimpsed his pale frightened face briefly in the window behind us as we shot up over the house. Klea could go fast.

"You rotten dog," I shouted at her through the whistle of the air around us. "It's not safe for him there."

"Illuminus and his lackeys are out with the hunting

party," she snapped. "Now stop fussing. I need that letter. Which way do I take?"

She could have taken to the sky and found the hunting party easily, but she would have risked being seen. So she had tried flying low along the forest paths, sticking as much as she could to the cover of the trees. Of course she'd got lost.

There's not much you can do when a mage gets an idea into her head, and Klea could clearly think of nothing but this letter. I comforted myself that since Illuminus was out hunting, Shadow should be safe enough for the moment, and helped her find her way to the hunting party even with anger sitting in my belly like a hot ember. But there was pity too.

You could hear the hunting horns all through the forest. By mid-morning, we had found a path to the mages and were following them while staying discreetly in cover. The hunting cats ranged around at the front of the party picking up scents. The mages and horse riders behind them were completely focused on what was going on ahead. As we followed, the group chased and took down two deer, and caught a wild cat and a litter of kittens. I tried not to feel sad about their deaths. They would have played havoc with the peasant's poultry had they lived.

"Good to see mages doing something useful," I muttered in Klea's ear, as the party turned toward the luncheon ground.

"Shut up," snapped Klea. "I couldn't have brought you both and still had strength for Toy."

"What are you going to do to her anyway?" I hissed.

"She'll need to piss eventually. When she does I'll jump her."

"You're joking. That's your plan? They bring chamber pots for the mages. And a little shelter for privacy. You're never going to get her alone."

"Well, you suggest something, if you're so clever."

"We should go home and try again tonight while she's at dinner."

"I must have that letter," she said, through clenched teeth. "I must. No, shut up. If you speak again I'll drop you."

I was almost certain this was an idle threat, but I shut up anyway. I could feel her arms shaking with strain or emotion, or simple exhaustion. Her distress was starting to affect me. I was afraid too. What had I got myself involved in? Was I going to find myself in a battle between mages? Or something illegal?

By the time we got to the luncheon site and found a good spying place in the fork of a tree, the servants had set up canvas shelters for the mages to relieve themselves. As I'd expected, Toy availed herself of one of these instead of going off into the bushes alone. In fact, Blazeann was standing outside the shelter, talking to her the whole time she was inside. My one consolation was that Illuminus, his servant and his three cats were all there enjoying the marvellous pies, pasties, cakes, cold meats and breads set out on rugs on the ground. My stomach rumbled enviously.

"Go down there," hissed Klea. "Put something in her

food so that she has to go home early, or get someone to offer her a pleasuring, or—"

"No I won't." I snapped, holding on tightly to the tree branch we were perched on. "I've got nothing to put in her food. Do you think I carry laxatives around with me? And they'll all wonder where I've came from, and Toy's suspicious enough already, and —"

"We have to do *something,*" she cried. Her voice broke on the last word and she started to sob silently.

My heart went all soft. Fear was replaced by tenderness. I put my arms around her and rubbed her back and called her a poor old thing while she wept uncontrollably on my shoulder.

"What on earth is in that letter?" I asked her, as the first weeping fit passed.

"I have been a terrible, terrible fool. I lost my nerve and I ruined everything. *Everything.*" And she started to weep again.

"Oh, Klea," I said, sensing exhaustion in her weeping. "When did you last eat? Or rest? You can't go on like this. I know it seems bad, but we can still recover. There's another day of chances. I know where there might be some food. Let's get out of here."

She didn't say anything, but she took some deep breaths, dried her eyes, picked me up and followed my directions.

A mile or so away there was another shrine to the Mooncat near a small lake. As I had hoped, someone had made a recent offering: an entire cheese, still safely sealed in its wax coating. The forest animals had nibbled at the fruit left on the altar, but there were some apples still untouched. A little washing in the lake and they were fine to eat. Now Klea had wept, she seemed tired; but she had also relaxed at little. I could still sense underlying tension but she wasn't panicking anymore.

It was midday and the pale spring sun had some warmth in it at last. We stretched out on the grass near the lake.

"I guess you're right. There is still tonight. Till then I should try and rest. Thanks for calming me down. I wish I had you living with me in Crystalline." She bit appreciatively into an apple. "Want to come and manage my affairs? The pay's lousy, but you'd get to spend time in my delightful company."

"I think that would be far too great an honour for humble little me," I quipped.

"True," she quipped back. "The great and the good are lining up do my accounts."

"What's in that letter?" I asked, thinking she might be softened now.

"Full of questions, aren't you? You'd hate me if you knew, so it's better that you don't."

"Have you harmed someone one?" I asked, too afraid to say *killed*.

"No, nothing like that. I promise," said Klea.

I felt my shoulders relax, as relief rushed into me.

"The only person I've harmed is myself. Almost," she continued.

"I can't imagine you would have done anything really bad," I said.

"You are a sweetie," she said. She sighed. "It's so much harder than I thought it would be."

"What?" I said.

"Nothing. Thanks, Shine. You've been great. Sorry about the hysterics."

It was odd to be the strong one here. Mages have the power, not mundanes. Odd to be the one giving help instead of receiving it.

"It was nothing. I understand, even if you won't tell me what it's about."

That was a supportive lie. I was dying to know what was in the letter. If I got it, I wouldn't be able to resist reading it. If only she would stop being so secretive, maybe I could suggest something to help. A new perspective, something she wouldn't have thought of.

"Thanks," she said.

I was starting to feel embarrassed.

"Anyway," I said, to lighten the mood. "I've always been grateful to you for letting me out of that cupboard."

"The cupboard? Oh, back at the house in Elayison! Bless, weren't Blazeann and Lumi pigs? All those names they called you. Why did they pick on us, anyway? They were already mages by then. Should have just ignored us. Lumi always was a mean rat, though. Hey, did we do anything to get them back? Was that when I put a frog in their beds?"

"No, we stole every left shoe from Lumina's wardrobe and every right one from Blazeann's. Do you remember?"

"And locked them in the cupboard they left you in! That was a brainy idea. That was yours, wasn't it?"

"I thought it was yours."

"Clearly we're both geniuses."

I laughed. We were silent then—a comfortable silence. I thought if I stayed quiet, Klea would fall asleep. She needed the rest.

Something splashed in the lake. I sat up in fright but it was only a duck landing on the water.

"Don't worry," said Klea. Her eyes were closed. "They're nowhere near. I'd bet on it."

"No, it's not that."

"What, then?"

"You'll laugh at me."

"I promise I won't "

"I'm a bit scared of this lake. Once... Well, Bright and I used to come here a lot. It's so pretty. One day we stole some Holy Wine from the priest, you know the stuff that they make out of puffballs, and brought it out here to drink. It was for a dare."

She laughed "So what does this stuff do?"

"It's fascinating. Everything seems to glow, then it turns different colours. Anyway we were lying here soaking up the sunshine, enjoying seeing the purple clouds in the orange sky. Then a woman came out of the water."

"What?"

"There was a kind of shushing, rustling noise and I looked up and there she was, a woman-shaped column of water rising out of the lake." I traced a rough shape with my hands. "As if a wave had reared up out of the pool. She came up taller than a human and you could see through her and she swirled around with a sound like a stream and she looked at us."

"Ladybless!" breathed Klea.

"She started to slide towards us," I said, enjoying her reaction. "She seemed... sort of curious. Her head was turned slightly on one side. And we stared at her, we were too surprised to do anything else. Anyway, I think she must have got between us and the sun. I felt so cold all of a sudden. And I got scared—or Bright did—anyway, we yelled and she just collapsed. Slid back into the water."

"Lady," breathed Klea again. "What do you think...? Was it really...?"

"Hilly said it was real. The Spirit of the Lake. Of course, the peasants believe these things. They take the Holy Wine as part of a religious ritual. They say it helps you see spirits."

"But you both saw it."

"Yes. We never came here again. But I figure that I'm safe enough with you."

"I wonder if I'd be any use against a spirit."

"At least we could run away quickly."

Klea gave a little humph. "That's all I seem to do these days."

"I don't blame you for wanting to be free of the family."

"Why don't you...?"

"I can't leave Eff."

"She's a grown up," said Klea. "She'd manage."

"Not after what happened to Bright." I told Klea about Eff's broken nerves and she made suitably sympathetic noises. "If things had gone as normal and Bright was still in Elayison, he'd be able to come down for visits. And there was some hope that he'd be able to sponsor her back out of exile. Now she has no hope, and Bright's in the army and a long way away. And it's very lonely for her out here. She's clever, interested in ideas. At least I can give her some of that."

"She's like a mother to you, isn't she?" said Klea.

I nodded. "I can't go off and leave her."

We fell silent again and I thought she'd fallen asleep. I was beginning to drift off myself when she spoke again.

"Do you mind that she isn't your real mother?"

"Not really. When I see some people's real mothers, I realise how lucky I've been."

"Mine, for instance," sighed Klea.

"I didn't mean that," I said uncomfortably, because I had meant exactly that.

"I know. Mother was never much interested in us. Well, I mean, she's always been so smoked up."

"You had Flara."

She shuddered, and I patted her shoulder; I'd met Flara a few times when I was a child. A cold, hard woman.

"My nurse was lovely when I was little," said Klea. "Flara sent her away when I was twelve. That was about money and…" She shook her head. "Curse it, why must I think of that?"

"Don't," I said. "She's long gone, and from what I hear, they're never coming back."

"Never say never," she said. "I think Toy will be much the same if she gets control of the family. As she will, if Blazeann becomes Matriarch. But I'm never going back. Not if I have to sleep on the streets. Don't let your children be brought up in the Family House. It's a recipe for neglect and mistreatment."

"Was it really so bad? I remember Radiant being rather nice. He gave me—"

She sat up straight. "Him? No, he was vile. Vile! A beast of a man."

I stared at her. I remembered him as a friendly man with nice books who liked to stroke my hair.

"Was he? I guess it was different when you knew him well."

She stood up.

"Yes," she said. "Very different."

"How?" I asked.

"I'm not going to talk about him." The growl in her voice warned me not to press her further. She really did hate him.

She was brushing herself down. I sat on the ground watching her, certain she was going to tell me something more, but she just stood there brushing and brushing herself long after there was not a leaf anywhere on her body.

"But he isn't going to win," was all she finally said. "Come on. Let's get back to the house."

When she put her arm round me, her shaking was gone.

CHAPTER SEVENTEEN

BACK AT THE house, my room was empty. No sign of the little blue backpack. Even Uncle Batty's hidey hole was empty.

"I told you we shouldn't have left him alone," I hissed furiously at Klea. Something had clearly happened. A pail of water had been upturned on the floor of my room and a mop and broom lay askew beside it.

"I'm sorry. I was certain he'd be safe," snapped Klea. "Look, I'll go check Illy's room."

"Wait," I said. I opened my door. No one was in the hall, but I almost fell over a bowl of water, a loaf of bread and five lit candles sitting on the floor in front of the doorway. A garland of flowers and a ratty-looking sheaf of last year's wheat had been tied over the door.

"Oh, Dear Lady!" I cried.

"What on earth's this?" Klea peered out over my shoulder.

"The room's being exorcised. Someone's seen our ghost." The thought sent a chill down my spine. You heard terrible stories of mobs of peasants attacking ghosts with pitchforks when they ventured outside Elayison. That was one reason they were limited to the city. And hadn't some peasants in the west tried to burn a ghost when they'd first seen him? Terrible visions of the ghost trussed up and thrown on a fire filled my head. Where would they throw him? We had a range in the kitchen. Into the boiler?

I shook myself.

"I'll get up to Illy's—"

"It won't be Illy. It'll be the servants."

I ran down the hallway, yelling for Thomas, but as I reached the top of the stairs I heard a voice calling behind me.

Auntie Eff was standing in her doorway beckoning me, and something about the way she was smiling told me she knew everything. I ran to her faster than I've ever run anywhere.

The ghost was standing behind her door. I flung my arms around him, crying that I was sorry, and was he harmed?

The ghost laughed and squeezed me. "Someone tried to clean under the bed. Would you believe? After all your grumbling, someone must have listened. *Wstts akstriuchg*, but she screamed! So did I, to be honest.

After she ran off, I knew I was not safe. So I came in here hoping it was empty and came face to face with Marm Eff. She screamed too, but she got over it very quickly."

Eff shook her finger at me. "Weren't you going to share this wonderful fellow with me? Shame on you."

"I was going to wait till everyone was gone."

"Well, I'm most displeased with you."

But she wasn't really, she was thrilled. Almost before I'd stopped fussing over the ghost, she was sitting back at her desk, patting the chair behind her. She'd piled the books and papers that covered the desktop on the floor, where they joined countless other piles of books and papers. "Now, let's get back to this," she said, picking up her pen. "Tell me how this universal suffrage works? You must have to keep voter lists, yes?"

"Did you tell her about Klea?" I murmured in the ghost's ear, as he turned to join her.

He grinned and shook his head. "No chance," he murmured.

"And Illuminus?"

"And everyone votes, even the lowliest peasants? Sirrah Shadow?" called Eff.

"Your aunt is very interested in political organisation," said Shadow. "We have talked of little else." He turned and smiled at Eff. "I hope I can satisfy her curiosity. I do not know much about such things. I've never voted."

"What?" cried my Aunt. "When you have the right? Sirrah Shadow, I'm shocked. Do you know the Imperial Guard rained fireballs on a group of cloth workers demanding the right to be heard in the Great Council? People died that day. For the right to have a say. And you've never voted. Shame on you! I hope you will start immediately you get back to Ghostland."

And she smacked him on the leg in a startlingly flirtatious way.

Shadow smiled sheepishly and said he would, and Eff decided to forgive him. Not that there was any chance she wouldn't. Soon they were sitting side by side at her desk with him drawing a diagram showing how the ghosts' Great Council was divided into two houses.

"I'm going for a sleep," I said. "Wake me if you need me."

She waved absently in my direction as I went out the door, and the ghost didn't even look up from his diagram. I didn't mind. My Aunt was the happiest I'd seen her in a long, long time. I would have envied her the chance to find out more about Ghostland, but I was too tired.

"She's already planning an article about the workings of universal suffrage in Ghostland," I told Klea back in my room. My magely cousin must have worked out that everything was fine, because she was relaxing on my bed with a glass of brandy in her hand.

"Won't this expose the ghost?"

"The journals Eff writes for spend most of their time shut down by the Imperial Police. It'll be months before the article comes out, and by then he'll be safely back in his own country. Whew I'm exhausted! I'm going to lie down and have a rest. In this supposedly haunted room, we should be safe from any intruders, but I'm locking the door just in case. Why don't you have a sleep too? That brandy should make you nice and relaxed."

"Yes, mother!" She grinned, tossed back the rest of the glass and lay down.

I spread my cloak over her.

"Shine, how do you feel about your real mother?" she asked, as I was drifting off.

"Aurora? I don't feel much at all. Sometimes I'm annoyed at her. If only she'd made some financial arrangements for me."

"Is that all?" Klea sounded shocked.

"It's impossible for me to feel very much. She was gone before I knew her. I'm curious about her. I'd like to know what sort of person she was. But I hardly think of her. Sometimes when I was younger I was upset that she left me. But Eff used to say she'd have come back if she could. Eff thinks she's gone. Dead, I mean. I think so too. It's Eff who's my mother, Klea."

"Yes, I see that," said Klea. She let out a sigh and was quiet and I must have fallen asleep, because the next thing I knew it was dusk and the house was all a-bustle. The mages must have returned from the hunt.

I dragged myself out of bed and slipped quickly into clean clothes. Klea slept on—the sleep of the exhausted, or rather the sleep of one who had consumed half a bottle of brandy. I wondered again what must be in that letter, and it occurred to me how I might find out for myself. There was a lead Klea had suggested, but which we had forgotten about in all the excitement.

Taking care not to be seen leaving my 'haunted' room, since that might mean that I too would need to be exorcised, I slipped down the hall and climbed up the winding staircase into the servant's quarters in the attic. What if the letter had never been in Toy's possession, but had been given to her maid for safekeeping as Klea had suggested?

As I'd hoped, all the servants were away, running around after the returning mages, leaving the servant's quarters deserted. Having helped with the organising, I had a good idea which room Lady Chatoyant's maid was lodged in. I crept up to her door and, emboldened by the silence of the attic, opened it without listening first.

Hagen Stellason was sitting on the small bed, with only his trousers on; his feet and chest were bare. Nice hard body, I thought, before it occurred to me what he must be doing there. A bit of *delight in the afternoon* as the old saying goes. I'd seen him flirting with Chatoyant's maid on a number of occasions.

We stared at one another.

He smiled, and I felt the outrage rise in me.

"You ride rat!" I said, before I thought not to.

He shrugged.

"It's Blessing time," he said. "And Drusa is a lovely woman. And keener than some."

That last slighting remark bought me back to myself.

"True," I snapped, and managed to shrug in what I hoped was an uncaring fashion, before slamming the door and striding away with very firm steps. Nothing to show the dark disappointed feeling in the bottom of my stomach. I felt miserable for some time after, all through the bustle of getting ready for dinner, which included a battle of Imperial proportions between Hilly, Tane, and Thomas in the kitchen, and an awkward conversation with the unfortunate maid servant who'd discovered the ghost in my room.

The poor woman, who seemed to be the first cause of the battle between Tane and Hilly, was sitting in the corner of the busy kitchen, pale, covered with Holy amulets and being fed garlic soup by Hilly to protect her from being permanently haunted.

"It was horrible, horrible," she kept saying. "A dead thing under your bed. All horrible and white and pale. Oh, Marm Shine, I fear for you. 'Tis some ill-omen, for sure." She and a couple of the other servants pressed Holy amulets into my hand. I thanked them for their kindly thoughts and tucked them into my body shaper, where they stuck into me uncomfortably. It was nice of them to care.

I spent most of that night sitting in Lucient's room, watching him play cards with Great-Uncle Nate and some of the retainer mages. He hated cards, but had decided that this was better protection against Blazeann and Chatoyant than me. It seemed to work. Both women stuck their heads in at the door and went away quickly.

Out on the lawn, Scintillant had organised a game of blind man's bluff which seemed to end very early with everyone disappearing into the bushes. The only excitement occurred when Great Uncle Five wandered into the midst of it and spilled his bucket of river sludge.

He called Scintillant an over-sexed rotifer, which had a certain ring to it.

The boredom of watching cards (I mean honestly, who wants to *watch* when they can *do?*) gave me time to think over the scene with Hagen. It occurred to me that he'd been in the perfect position to search Chatoyant's maid's room (and indeed her person) for things she might be keeping safe for her mistress. Was I misremembering, or had one of his hands been hidden under the bedclothes—a hand that could have been holding, for instance, a letter? Since Lucient didn't need me, I excused myself quite early in the evening and went off and searched the room Hagen shared with Great Uncle Nate's valet. To no avail, of course. If Hagen had the letter, he must be carrying it on his person.

When I looked in at Eff's room to check on Shadow, he and she were deep in argument over whether adopting ghost inventions meant we had to adopt their mindset.

"Your Empire needs to open itself more to outsiders," the ghost insisted.

"Not at the price of outside interference in our polity," came back Eff.

There was no chance of getting a word in edgeways, so I left them to it.

Hilly had told me my own room should be safe for me now, as long as I kept the amulets with me. I still had to step over the bread and bowl of water to get in through the door, but the candles had burned down to their stubs, so there was no chance of my setting myself alight in a thoughtless movement. Klea was gone, leaving only a tumbled bedspread behind. No doubt she was off stalking Chatoyant.

Lucky me. I had the evening free to spend time checking that my accounts were in order—a suitably anticlimactic finish to another tiresome Blessing Festival. Now all I had to look forward to was the inevitable interview with Lord Impi. He always stayed home from the hunt on the last day of the festival and looked over my books, querying every expenditure, complaining that we were wasting too much money on frivolous items such as wages and fence building and suggesting that if only I'd try harder, I could get a better price for our mangel-wurzels. Or mangel-wurzels for a better price. It never seemed to matter if I was buying or selling.

As I WAS dressing in a workmanlike outfit next morning, trying to find a nice balance between practical and fit for an audience with a nobleman, Klea came in the window. She was calmer than she had been the previous morning, but her news was no better. I put a quilt round her shoulders and rubbed her back. Through chattering teeth she told me that Lady Chatoyant had once again spent the night awake, drinking Nightowl and pleasuring and playing cards with a couple of young village men.

"She must suspect I'm here," she said. "Curse her. I must have... Do you think Lucient would be willing to act as a diversion?"

"Maybe. Listen Klea, we may have another... Wait! What's that?"

Someone was pounding on Eff's door and now I could hear raised and urgent voices.

Fearful for Shadow, I popped my head out of the doorway. Thomas was whispering to Eff in the doorway of her room.

"I swear to you it's something wrong," he was saying. "Something's going on in the Eyrie," he explained to me as I approached.

"It's just another family spat," said Eff.

"No it's more than that," said Thomas. "Lady Splendance is the one screaming."

"Splen? That's new. We'd better... I'll get some clothes on. Shine dear, would you...?"

I agreed with a sigh, thinking Auntie Splen was probably fussing over a mouse in her smokeweed jar or some similar thing. But as Thomas and I entered the Eyrie, there was something about the sounds of the screams echoing down the tower that made us both break into a run. We arrived panting on the fifth floor to find the sound of hysterical weeping coming out of Blazeann's room. A hubbub of people blocked our route to the door. One of them was Hagen.

"What's happening?" I asked, tugging his arm.

The look on his face chilled me.

"Lady Blazeann is dead," he said.

THOMAS AND I were still clutching each other in disbelief when Impi appeared in the doorway of the room.

"Get out of the way, you useless pack of rodents!" He

flapped his arms and people shrank back. "Come on, you!" he barked back into the room behind him.

Something long, wrapped in a sheet, came floating out of the door. A body. A man's body from the shape of it through the thin sheet. A pale-faced retainer walked slowly behind the floating body, his hand under its head, clearly using his magic to carry it. A couple of damp-eyed women retainers followed behind, arms round each other's shoulders.

I huddled back against the wall to let them pass.

"One of the retainers. Rapheal Angelus. Her bed mate," whispered Hagen. "They were both found dead this morning. Too much dreamsmoke, apparently. Mixed with alcohol, most likely."

"But she doesn't smoke."

"That could have been the problem. They say that you have to build up a tolerance for it. Maybe they started too strong." His voice was surprisingly detached, but then he muttered with more feeling. "This is a disaster."

"Poor Auntie Splen." I could hear my aunt wailing inside. I wasn't sure who the other voice belonged to. It sounded like a man.

"Poor *us*," muttered Hagen. Only then did it occur to me who the next Matriarch-in-waiting would be now Blazeann was dead.

Impi was shouting at the hovering servants and mages. At least something was normal.

"You! Why aren't you seeing to the carriages? And you! Get the bags packed! We're going back to Elayison as soon as we can. And you! No one wants to see your ugly face round here! You people have got work to do. Go and do it!"

The protective barrier of people between me and Impi broke apart and scurried away

"You! Get Marm Eff," shouted Impi at Thomas, and his mouth twisted sourly as he looked right at me. I made to leave.

"No, you don't. You get in here, Ghostie!" he shouted. "See if you can sort out Lucient. He's making a spectacle of himself as usual."

Under his glare I crept into the room

Blazeann's room stank. She lay on her back on one side of the bed, eyes closed, horribly pale and still. Yellow lumps of vomit stuck on her cheek and lips. Her pale hand dangled off the edge of the bed.

I'd seen dead people before, but the sight still chilled me. Such a strange absence of person.

As I watched, Auntie Splen's maid tried to wipe the vomit away from Blazeann's cheek with a cloth. Auntie Splen smacked her hand away.

"Don't touch her," she screamed. Her face was wet and red and puffy from weeping. She was kneeling beside the bed keening. She started shaking Blazeann and calling her name.

Glisten, Lumina and Chatoyant were huddled by the door, but my eye was drawn to Lucient, who was leaning against the bed post, white-faced and shivering, his fist in his mouth, choking back sobs.

Seeing him so distressed, I felt genuinely sad for the first time since I'd heard the news. I went and put my arms around him, but he didn't respond so I leaned against his back, murmuring soothing noises at him.

"You! Get out of here!" shouted Impi behind me. I turned my head thinking he was talking to me or Lucient, but he was confronting Lumina.

"You can't talk to me like that anymore, consort," snarled Lumina. "I'm Matriarch-in-waiting now." The look on her face spoke of triumph and the horribleness of that emotion at this time sent a shiver running down my spine. Mean old Lumina as Mater. Lady of Light! Let Splendance live for ever.

Glisten was glaring at Lumina. Chatoyant snatched Lumina's arm.

"Lady Lumina. A word, if you would be so kind?" she said.

"Huh!" said Lumina. "Do you think you're going to run me like you ran Blazeann. Not a chance."

But she must have seen Glisten's glare, because she let Chatoyant coax her out of the room.

"My dear," crooned Impi, leaning over Auntie Splen and taking her by the shoulders. "My poor dear! Let the maid clean her up. You don't want people to be seeing her in this mess."

Auntie Splen protested, but she let Impi pull her away from the bed and manoeuvre her gently over to a couch by the wall, where he sat down beside her and cradled her head on his shoulder.

He really liked her, I thought with surprise, having always previously accepted the family consensus that he was only after the position Splen could give him.

"Splendance, pull yourself together. Think of the family's honour. You are behaving like a peasant," snapped Auntie Glisten, clearly deeply uncomfortable with all this emotion.

Impi gave Auntie Glisten the kind of glare that would have done my heart good had it not meant that she turned her attention to me.

Scowling, she jerked her head towards the door.

I took a firm hold on my cousin.

"Come on, Lu... my lord," I said. "Let's get you back to your room. A nice smoke will—"

"No!" screamed Lucient. "I will never smoke again." And he burst into loud sobs. I was astonished at how upset he was. Yesterday he'd hated Blazeann.

"No, my dear, never, never again!" wailed Splen.

"Hush, my dear. Hush," said Impi, this time glaring at me.

"My lord. This is no place for you. Please allow me to help you," said a voice beside us. Hagen took a firm grip on Lucient's shoulder. Between the two of us, we managed to manoeuvre the weeping Lucient out of the room and down the stairs to his own room where his servants were hovering anxiously

"My poor lord," cried Sharlee, putting her arms around Lucient.

"Oh, Sharlee, Sharlee," cried Lucient. "What have I done?"

"Get my lord a cup of tea," Hagen ordered Lucient's valet. As Busy goggled in outrage at being ordered about by another mere servant, I said, "Oh, please get it, Busy.

He needs something," and he went. Hagen slammed the door after him.

Turning the key in the lock, Hagen stepped over to the bed where Lucient was sitting with his head cradled on Sharlee's breast. He took Lucient's arm and shook it.

"My lord! My lord! *My lord!*" The last was almost a shout.

Startled, Sharlee and Lucient stopped their murmuring together and looked up at him.

"Did you give the smokeweed meant for Splendance to Blazeann?" asked Hagen sternly.

"Oh, Lady!" Lucient clutched his cheeks "Do you...? How do you...? Does everyone know?"

"No," said Hagen grimly. "I've simply put two and two together. Did you tell anyone else?"

"I meant it for a joke, to teach her a lesson, for revenge. She was being such a dog. I never meant... I never meant to kill.... And poor Rafie. He never did anyone any harm. Oh, Lady of Light." He burst into tears again.

"Did you tell anyone else?"

"Only Rafie. He was supposed to suggest a pipe to her after they pleasured last night. He knew it had been spiked, but neither of us.... He thought it would be funny if she was too smoked to... He must have been curious and tried it himself and... And he's dead too and it's my fault..."

He burst into tears again.

"A joke. A stupid joke. I never meant..."

I stared at Hagen. My thoughts were struggling with two and two as well but they couldn't seem to find the equals sign.

"I believe you," Hagen told Lucient. "That weed's obviously more dangerous than any of us knew. Where's the rest of it? Is this it?" He picked up a smokeweed jar.

"No, Sirrah Hagen, this is it," said Sharlee. "I cleaned out the jar and put the tainted stuff in here." She put a little painted box into Hagen's hand.

"And Lord Lucient didn't have any?"

"No!" gulped Lucient, moping his face

Hagen huffed decisively. "Right. Well. We need to keep this news secret for the moment. For your own sake, don't tell anyone about your 'joke,' Lord Lucient. Especially not Chatoyant."

"What are you saying? Why not Chatoyant?" asked Lucient.

"Think about it," said Hagen. "Chatoyant gave that smokeweed to Blazeann. It's possible Blazeann's accident was actually meant for your mother."

We all stared at him, faces frozen at the horror of it all. Did he really mean someone in our family had deliberately tried to *kill* another member of their own family? Someone we had once shared a nursery with had tried to kill her own aunt? The household Matriarch, no less?

"Lady of Light!" I cried. "You think Toy meant to...?"

Chatoyant had always seemed very ruthless. She'd seemed so confused this morning, not in control of things at all. But if she'd been expecting a death, it wouldn't have been Blazeann's. Not after all the effort she had put into befriending her.

"We can't know. She might be innocent in this. It could be Flara. Or Lumina. Maybe even Blazeann herself. They would all benefit from Lady Splendance's death."

"They'd never have Flara back!" cried Lucient.

"Or it could just have been a mixture of alcohol and smokeweed mixed with Open. That's why you all have to keep quiet. You especially," he said to Sharlee. "You now know too much and if it comes out, things could go badly for you. And your little one."

Was that a threat or a warning? I couldn't tell.

Sharlee looked up at Hagen with wide scared eyes, her hands clutching at her belly.

"I will not let that happen, my dear," said Lucient, squeezing Sharlee's shoulder.

"You'd best take care of what your mother smokes in future," Hagen told him. "And everything she eats or drinks."

He turned to me "And you..."

"My mouth is sealed," I said. "But I really hope you're wrong, because... It doesn't bear thinking about."

"I will have the smoke weed tested by an alchemist," he said. "If the Lady blesses us, I will be wrong. But I don't think I am."

CHAPTER EIGHTEEN

WHO COULD HAVE blamed Lucient for wanting to take revenge on Blazeann? But for such a prank to end like this... Fate had played a very cruel trick.

Lucient and I sat together for most of the morning, stunned to quiet murmuring by the events which were still raging outside the door.

True to his word, Lucient did not smoke, but he did drink most of a bottle of wine. Frozen Hell, I even joined him in a glass, though technically it was still before breakfast for me. The thought that someone might have plotted to kill Auntie Splen sent a horrible shivery feeling creeping along the back of my neck. I mean, we weren't the most harmonious family, but this...

Despite what Hagen had told me, I really wanted to confide in Eff when she poked her head in at the door to check on us. The idea that the mages had taken to poisoning each other was so frightening. Where might it stop?

But Auntie Glisten's stentorian tones called Eff away to some kind of hostly duty, and I thought better of sharing the secret before she returned. I'd tell her when everyone was gone.

The idea comforted me. I felt able to leave Lucient with only Sharlee for company and go and see if there was anything I could do to help. Going down the stairs, I saw Hagen leaning against the bannisters on the third floor chatting to one of the local maidservants. I remembered that I had unfinished business with him. Thinking of Klea and her letter, such a nice, predictable, unsinister problem, lifted my spirits. No doubt Klea would have been most unimpressed to know that. I wondered if she had any idea what was going on up here.

To my surprise, Hagen left the maid and joined me on the stairs.

"Don't let me interrupt you," I said. "You looked to be doing so well with her."

"Jealous?"

"Oh, searingly," I said, pleased to discover I'd got the sarcastic tone of voice right. Now how to get the truth out of him?

As we reached the bottom of the Eyrie stairs, I was comforted to see that the tables had already been set for luncheon. Someone was keeping things running in an orderly fashion, even though the world was turned upside down. Probably Thomas. He took comfort in such things. Habit made me stop and run my eye over the place settings.

"So will the family leave tonight as planned?"

"Yes," said Hagen. "Lady Splendance will not hear of salting or pickling Lady Blazeann's body, so they need to get back to Elayison quickly for her funeral."

I must have shuddered, because he touched my arm and said kindly, "How are you?"

"Still having trouble comprehending."

He squeezed my arm. "I—"

"Hey! You! Ghostie!" shouted a voice from above. A distinctive husky male voice: Illuminus.

Fright seared down my spine. I would have run, but a force had seized me and I was pulled backwards into the air and up into the gallery.

Below, Hagen's face was wide eyed with shock. I opened my mouth to scream, but a hand was clamped over it before anything could come out. My ankle banged painfully against the banisters as I was yanked over them.

Illuminus gripped me against him, arm around my waist, and twisted my arm round behind my back. His stubble stung me as he thrust his mouth against my ear. He was hovering above the first floor balcony.

"Where is he, you little rat?" he snarled. I could smell the vinegar scent of wine on his breath.

"What are you talking—?"

The tendons in my shoulder cried out as he dragged on my twisted arm.

"I'm sick of your games! Tell me where he is. I know he's still here."

"I don't know—"

"You're determined to make life hard for yourself, aren't you?"

"No!" I screamed, but was silenced as his hand clamped back over my mouth. For a moment he was holding me up only by my twisted arm and the pain was awful. His other arm took me round the waist and we were gliding. The door between the Eyrie and our wing of the house flew open and slammed shut behind us, and then we were flowing down the hallway towards my room.

"You almost had me convinced that he'd gone with that woman, but even witless peasants don't believe in a haunting without reason. Someone saw a ghost in your room yesterday, and we both know who he is."

The hallway was empty of potential witnesses. Once we were inside my room he could do what he liked to me. Would Klea be there? And would she reveal herself and help me if she was?

He still had his hand clamped over my mouth. I tried to swerve into the wall or brace myself against some furniture, but he was using magic to move us and I could get no purchase.

"Stop struggling," he hissed as my door flew open before us. "I could pop this arm out of its socket in a snap; and I will, if you don't tell me where he is."

I heard the door slam behind us. The room was empty. Only an unmade bed. No Klea. Oh, no.

"Right. Show me where he is, or I'll break something. I want that ghost."

He wasn't going to take his hand off my mouth, so I couldn't scream. My mind ran around and around, trying to think of some way out of this.

"Come on, quickly! No, don't shake your head at me. I know he's here."

He yanked my arm back further. The tendons at my shoulder stretched like hot wires. It hurt so much I screamed into his hand.

"Stop that!" shouted a stern voice and Klea jumped up from the other side of the bed.

"What are *you* doing here?" snarled Illuminus.

"I said, let her *go!*" shouted Klea. Her crystal flashed and I felt the force of her magic shake Illuminus.

"Stay out of it, rat!" shouted Illuminus, but he dropped me. Luckily we were standing just above the floor; but even so, I fell flat on my face. As I lay there trying to will my stunned body to flee, magical force streamed past me.

With a creak, my huge old wooden bed tipped sideways and Klea disappeared behind it.

I scrabbled forward, not knowing where I was going, simply getting away from Illuminus. A dark shape loomed over me and the huge wooden bed leg thudded onto the floor beside my head. I think I may have screamed like a child.

Klea must have tipped the bed back into place, almost

braining me in the process. At least now I was safely underneath it.

"How dare you?" The low hiss of Klea's voice made my blood run cold. Air rushed and flesh slapped into flesh, and Illuminus started gagging. I could see Klea's boots on the other side of the bed, and Illuminus' feet dangling off the floor, kicking at the air.

Something smashed against a wall.

"No, you don't, you prick," snarled Klea. He must had thrown something at her. "You—"

The door slammed open.

"Lor—Stop that! Let him go." The room was full of the rushing of magic. I—hero that I was—huddled under the bed, my hands over my head.

"Who are you?" cried a woman. "How dare you attack one of the family? Are you harmed, Lord Illuminus?"

She didn't know who Klea was!

Two sets of feet by the door. More retainers, from the look of their boots. And from the way the air was tingling with magical force and full of crystal light, they must have a good hold on Klea. Her boots were still and she'd risen from the floor.

"Let me go," shouted Klea. "I'm... Ooof!"

It sounded like someone'd hit her in the stomach. Then came the sound of a slap.

"My lord, should you...?" said the woman.

"Hold the rat still, will you?" croaked Illuminus and there came another thudding body blow and a groan from Klea. And they were letting him hit her, because he was family and they were new family retainers and clearly had no idea who Klea was. I had to do something.

"*Nooo!*" I screamed, pushing myself out from under the bed and grabbing Illuminus' legs. "Stop him." And for want of anything better to do, I bit him on the calf. Dry mouthful of cloth.

"Argh, you rat!" shrieked Illuminus and I felt him grab my hair, felt his force gathering against my body and—

"What is going on here?"

For once I was actually glad to hear Impi's voice.

"Stop this disgraceful... Klea, what are you doing...? Let her go, you idiots—this is Lady Splendance's daughter, Lady Sparklea. Illuminus, what do you mean by this appalling behaviour?"

They must have pulled their magic back because Klea dropped to the floor. She was clutching her chest. A breast blow, the dirty pig!

I crawled over to her, murmuring anxious questions. Her eyes were screwed up in pain.

"Lord Illuminus! I demand an explanation as to why you would strike a fellow family member. And where is Shine? Why are you mistreating her?"

"I'm here, my lord," I called out. "She was protecting me. I think he's really hurt her. Can you sit up, Klea?"

Auntie Eff was there, helping us both up. Klea was still bent over in pain and we heaved her onto the bed. No help from the mages, who were too busy being shouted at by Impi.

"My dear, are you harmed?" cried Eff, clutching at me. I shrugged her off. I was too worried about Klea, who was lying curled up on the bed.

"Did he hurt you?" I whispered to her.

"Leave her quiet so that she can heal herself," hissed Eff.

Klea opened her eyes and gave me a twisted smile and a nod and closed her eyes again.

"Come," said Eff, putting her arms around me and drawing me towards the door.

"Hold him!" shouted Impi, and sure enough, there was Illuminus' crystal lit up, trying to get out of the window. "Lord Illuminus, you will explain this disgraceful behaviour to me. What do you mean by trying to harm a member of the family like this?"

"This is a private matter between these women and myself. I can only say that my anger against this creeping little rat was entirely justified."

"But striking her is not. Not in this house."

"Perhaps I allowed my temper to get the better of me, but if you knew—"

"Rubbish," I shouted. "He's a—"

To my astonishment, Eff clapped her hand over my mouth.

"I will speak for my brother," said a voice. Toy stood in the doorway in a swirl of gauzy green robes. I wondered if anyone else heard Klea's gasp. I turned back to look at her and thought I saw alarm in her eyes. She closed them and seemed to curl further up into herself. I guessed she hadn't found the letter, and was now giving up all hope. I tried to go to her, but Eff was drawing me slowly but surely out of the room.

"It is me that my brother is defending." Chatoyant

gestured at me as she stepped into the room. "This little beast is in the pay of this disgraceful creature here. I have a letter which shows the terrible shame that this creature has brought upon this family, and this mundane has been trying to steal it from me. My dear brother was merely trying to warn off the mundane and to find out where Klea is."

She was wearing her righteous avenging Goddess pose. A hateful pose. I tried to push Eff's hand away and set the record straight.

"Later," hissed Eff.

"Oh, wonderful," sneered Impi. "My lady has lost her first-born, her beloved Matriarch-in-waiting, and all you lot can do is make uproar in the house over some trifling falling-out. I am fed up with your little plottings."

"Oh, no, Lord Impavidus, this is no small matter. This is a scandal that eats at the very fabric of our society."

"Really," huffed Impi. "No doubt you can substantiate this claim, Lady Chatoyant? Perhaps you will tell—"

"In front of all these witnesses? This is family business. I think this requires the Matriarch's attention."

"You know the Matriarch is indisposed."

"But Lady Glisten is not. And what better than to take this creature before her?" Toy strode to the bed and hoicked Klea up.

"Klea!" I called.

She shook her drooping head.

"Very well," said Impi "My dear, are you well enough to travel?" he asked Klea with most un-Impi-like kindness. This was, after all, the man who had cut off her allowance just for living outside the Family House. "Let us go up to the Eyrie and have this out. And you!" He took my arm out of Eff's grasp and held me firmly but quite gently by the uninjured shoulder. "I think you had best come with us and give your witness."

He nodded at a couple of the retainers who were hovering by the door. "You two see that Lord Illuminus comes with us and gives us his side of the story."

Eff pulled a face at me, and for the first time I thought of the ghost.

"Get away as quick as you can. We need to take him up to the old mine," she breathed in my ear.

Then Impi and I were gliding down the hallway surrounded by the crystal lights and rustling silks of the noble folk. Ahead, Klea was being helped by one the retainers, who was clearly apologising for her rough treatment at Illuminus' hands. Chatoyant was a minty green shadow at Klea's other side. Her hand kept straying to Klea's shoulder and Klea kept flinching away.

"Lady Chatoyant, will you please stop that?" snapped Impi as the double doors opened to let us into the Eyrie. "I think Lady Sparklea has suffered enough at your family's hands, don't you?"

"You won't be this way when you know..."

But Impi brushed past her and we were streaming up the Eyrie as fast as ash up a chimney. Impi was almost as strong a mage as a woman. Instead of holding me by my limbs and dragging me round as Illuminus had, his magic held my whole body up. Which was a relief. My poor arm felt as if it was ready to drop out of its socket.

Only the woman helping Klea kept pace with him, and even so, Impi was first over the balcony. A shriek came from Auntie Splen's room and Splendance came rushing out, the crystal shining in her forehead. Her hair draggled down at one side like a curtain only half tied back, but she had already changed into dark mourning robes.

"Klea's here?" cried Splendance. She saw her daughter coming over the balcony and launched herself at her, arms out, meeting Klea in mid-air and wrapping herself about her in clinging black cloud of draperies.

"My poor wounded darling," cried Splendance. "My last precious child."

Klea's face took on a clenched look, and Impi cursed in my ear; Two, who was hovering in the door way of Splen's room, seemed to shrink under Impi's stern gaze. *Last precious child* seemed a bit rough coming from a woman who still had three other living children and Cousin Two as well.

"Splendance," roared Glisten, from the door of her room. "Let the child come to me. Stop smothering her. Chatoyant has a claim against—"

"Chatoyant!" cried Splendance. "You!" She dropped her hold on Klea and still hanging in mid-air rounded on Chatoyant. "Haven't Flara's get wounded me enough? Is there no limit to your ambition?"

Impi put me gently on the ground and took Auntie Splen firmly by the arm. In the back of my mind I knew I should take the opportunity to run off, but I could not bring myself to leave Klea before I found out what was going to happen to her. So instead I followed everyone into Auntie Glisten's room.

"All of you who are not family withdraw," said Glisten, with a wave of her hand as she sat down upon her chair with a stately spreading of robes. With pointed patience, she waited as people muddled around, retainers leaving and Cousin Two and Auntie Four coming in. There was no sign of Lucient or Scintillant, though in both cases that was hardly surprising. As for Great Uncle Nate, who should have been here, I could hear his snores echoing up the Eyrie. Nobody asked for the pointless old fellow to be woken.

Klea stood beside Glisten, head bowed, with Splendance hanging off her like a cobweb. She looked like different person, smaller, thinner, like a wounded captive, all her usual jauntiness quenched. Cousin Two and Auntie Four hovered anxiously near the door and Impi hovered at Splendance's back.

Chatoyant strode up and down in front of Glisten in a wild swirl of minty green silk draperies and when the last retainer had gone out of the door, she made it slam after him.

"Now!" she said.

But Glisten wasn't having Chatoyant running the show. She turned to Illuminus, who had draped himself with elegant nonchalance over one of the chairs. "So, my boy! I have been hearing very serious rumours about you, and now I find you mistreating a mundane, against all the rules of Shola's pact. What have you got to say for yourself?"

"I told you, Auntie, Illuminus was protecting me," cried Chatoyant.

Glisten cut her short. "I think not. Shine, tell us why Lord Illuminus was mistreating you. I believe you have some evidence of illegal moneymaking actives on his part."

I felt myself shrinking as everyone in the room turned to me. The direct attention of all these powerful people couldn't be a good thing.

"No, I... I don't. He thinks I do, but I don't," I stammered, completely unprepared for this question. "I, um..."

"Don't be frightened, child," said Glisten. "Illuminus is not going to hurt you anymore. He is coming back to Elayison under house arrest with me until his activities can be investigated more thoroughly. Tell us what he thinks you have."

Don't be frightened, she said, after how she had treated me last time! I couldn't tell the whole truth, and what if she caught me in a lie? I fought down the rising panic and took a deep breath. I had to avoid mentioning the ghost. With that one proviso in mind and no idea how deep the well I was standing in front of was, I decided I might as well leap in and see if I could stay afloat.

"Bright said that he'd discovered Illuminus was involved in crystal smuggling. He said he had evidence. I didn't really think it was possible, but Illuminus kept trying to search my room. I think he thought Bright had given me some evidence, but I don't have—"

"This is a lie," shouted Illuminus, over the gasps from the rest of the room.

"What travesty is this?" shouted Chatoyant. "You listen to the lies of a mundane and an... an invert—a disgraced piece of filth—against my noble brother?"

"Bright's not filth. You're filth," I shouted. "Raping Lucient and..." I was about to accuse her of poisoning Blazeann, but I stopped in time.

"How dare—?"

"Shut up, all of you," snapped Impi.

"Shine is not my only source of information, Lady Chatoyant," roared Glisten. "I have heard enough of a disturbing nature against your brother to wish to investigate further."

"And I tell you this is all lies. My brother was protecting me against this little sneak." Chatoyant turned on Klea. "How can you turn your back on my accusations against this woman? This woman has had a child. Examine her and you will see it." A new gasp rose from around the room, for a new baby in the family was big news. It was the last thing I had expected to hear. "But where is this child? I'll tell you where. This woman—this disgraceful creature—has done the unthinkable. She has given her own child, a *daughter*, a child of our family, up for adoption. And money has changed hands."

A stunned silence fell. The enormity of the accusation was so great that Splendance dropped her hand from Klea's shoulder and stared at her. Personally I didn't believe a word of it. Why on earth would Klea do such an awful thing? It was even more outrageous than crystal smuggling. I went to Klea's side and took her hand, and at that, Klea burst into tears.

"Is this true?" Glisten asked Klea.

Klea shook her head. Her hard choking sobs echoed loudly in the suddenly quiet room. I rubbed her shoulder.

"Liar!" screamed Chatoyant. "It's true, and may you be cursed forever for such a dreadful crime. That poor little girl—for it *is* a girl—I believe her to be in the hands of merchants."

"I hope you have proof of this outrageous accusation," roared Glisten.

"Indeed I do. I have a letter addressed to this... this creature, which reveals all. My maid has been holding it for me."

So Klea had been right. And maybe Hagen too. If only I'd looked earlier. But what could be in that letter? Not what Toy had said, that was certain. The accusation was too outrageous. I squeezed Klea's shaking shoulders.

Chatoyant had swept open the door.

"Drusa! Come in here!" she shouted.

As her maid appeared in the doorway, Chatoyant held out her hand.

"Give me the letter!"

The maid whispered something to Chatoyant. She was shrinking away even as she whispered in Chatoyant's ear.

"What?" screeched Chatoyant. "What!"

"I can't find it anywhere," stammered the maid, loud enough for everyone to hear her. "Someone's taken..."

Chatoyant slapped her across the face so hard she was knocked back against the door.

"You useless little rat!" she screamed. She went at the poor woman with a closed fist, but Glisten gestured and Chatoyant's closed fist slowed as if the air had suddenly thickened.

"Enough. Remember the pact!" shouted Glisten.

I noticed that Klea's shoulders had relaxed, although she was still sobbing.

Chatoyant turned from her poor trembling maid, who took the opportunity to run away. She rounded on Klea. "You have had a baby recently. Your body will show the marks. Where is it? What have you...?"

"It's dead. It's dead," wailed Klea, and she sank to the floor so quickly that she slid out of my grasp. "It's dead! Why must you remind me?"

"Oh, my poor darling," cried Splendance, throwing herself on Klea. "Oh, my poor, poor darling."

"You poor child! What happened?" cried Glisten, jumping out of her chair and gliding over to Klea's side. I found myself pushed back against the wall as the two of them bent over Klea, patting her and making soothing noises. Underneath all those silken robes, Klea was muttering things about a carriage accident, a nurse being crushed to death and a baby killed. I couldn't make out much more through the murmuring and the choking sobs.

At this moment the door opened, and Eff appeared in the doorway beckoning energetically at me.

I felt so sad at Klea's pain. Such a disaster—and

now this humiliating, outrageous accusation from Chatoyant. I wanted to pat her too, but there was no room for me to do so. I was a bit player in this play and here was Eff reminding me that I had a more important role in another drama. Someone else needed me far more than Klea did. With a heavy heart, I left them all to it.

Katti was out in the hallway with Eff. She almost knocked me over in her anxiety to check that I was in one piece. Her fur felt good under my fingers.

I shall bite that man till he bleeds, she muttered. I remembered that I too had been wronged and was still in danger, and for the first time I noticed my hands were shaking.

"Come on," hissed Eff, pulling me down the stairs. "We have to get you both out of the house. We can't know how much will come out. What sort of mess has Klea got herself into? Do you think it will distract them from Illuminus enough for him to get away and come looking for you again?"

It was a thought. Illuminus might well be able to slip away, and with Klea gone there was no mage to protect the ghost. I was it. And the traditional thing to do when a mage was after you and no other mage was available to protect you was to hide. Somewhere where there was plenty of cover.

The forest.

Taking care not to let anyone else overhear, I filled Eff in on the details of what had been revealed in Auntie Glisten's room as we rushed down the stairs.

"Ladybless!" cried Eff. "What a thing... Well I suppose it's to be expected that something like this would happen. Klea wouldn't want any child of hers exposed to Flara and her kin."

"Why not?"

"Some other time," she said, looking uncomfortable. "To lose a daughter in an accident like that. Poor Klea. Come on. We need to hurry." She seized my arm and pulled me down the stairs.

In the bottom of the Eyrie, the table was still set for lunch, but now servants were sitting on the floor by the door threading yellow silk petals into garlands. Decorations for the carriage that would carry Blazeann back to Elayison. Blazeann dead. Possibly murdered.

My head felt like a bubbling pot. So full of thoughts about Klea and her baby (that was why she'd been crying that day!), and Blazeann's death, and the memory of Illuminus' face pushed into my own, and the feel of his hand across my mouth, and the tendons in my shoulder screaming as he pulled them... What I really wanted was a nice sit down and a warm cup of tea so I could still my thoughts.

Eff dragged me through into the kitchen where Thomas met us. Hilly and Tane stopped mid-argument and stared at us as we rushed past. Was that a whole leg of lamb Hilly was brandishing at Tane?

"Quickly!" hissed Eff, as she and Thomas bundled me down the cellar stairs out of Hilly and Tane's earshot. Katti came so hard on my heels that she almost tripped us over.

"I've already sent our friend down into the cellars with Hagen," Thomas hissed. "We weren't sure how much would come out. They're just inside the tunnel. I've given him some food and blankets. Here!" He had my crossbow and a heavy sheaf of arrows, and of course a long cat spear.

"Oh, you are a gem!" said Eff.

As I shouldered the bow and arrows, she hissed instructions at me.

"Take him up to the old mine. Bright's hiding there. No, he didn't go back to the frontier. He didn't like to leave you unprotected. We've been keeping it a secret so that you'd have deniability, but now... He should be able to protect you from Illuminus. When there's no light in the Eyrie, you'll know it's safe to come back."

A pulley disguised as a meat hook opened a door in the cellar wall.

Eff hugged me. "Take care, my dear. And give my love to Bright. Tell him he's a good boy and I love him."

CHAPTER NINETEEN

HAGEN AND THE ghost were waiting inside. Hagen held a lantern. The ghost hugged me and plied me with anxious questions. Hagen merely said, "Good, you're still in one piece. Come on. Let's get going."

"You're coming with us?"

I didn't picture Hagen opting for a hike up a mountain. He seemed too suave for such activities.

"No. I've got to stay and help sort out this mess Lady Klea's got herself into."

Something in his tone of voice... thoughts of the still missing letter that had so obsessed Klea jumped into the front of my mind.

"Will Klea need your help? Her baby is dead and she has everyone's sympathy."

"Oh, I see!" said Hagen. "How sad! Well no need for us to worry about her, then. Worry about this fellow. He's the one in danger."

His *How sad* sounded insincere. As if he didn't care that Klea's baby had died. Or....

"What I am worried about is that Illuminus will be waiting for us at the end of this tunnel," said Shadow.

"I doubt it," said Hagen. "Aside from the fact that he may not know where the end is, I've put a word in Lady Glisten's ear about his suspected crystal-smuggling activities. I doubt she'll take her eye off him even with all this uproar about Lady Klea. Family prerogatives are something she gets very worried about."

I was starting to worry about the letter. Perhaps there was more to Klea's story than had come out. Perhaps it would still be a good thing if I got hold of this letter. I bent down and whispered in Katti's ear. I felt her consent—and her confusion—but she didn't question me, Ladybless her. She just nudged her cheek against my hand. I rubbed her absentmindedly in her sweet spot as I wondered why we had spent so much time and so many tears on a letter that didn't seem to be important after all.

We walked in silence, until Hagen started grumbling about the length of the walk and the damp earthy smell. It was only three-quarters of a mile, which I pointed out to Hagen and which he failed to appreciate. Little glow worms sparkled in the roof, which pleased the ghost but Hagen also failed to appreciate these. The man had no soul at all.

The tunnel curved to the left, so that if someone found the entrance in the house, they could not easily find the exit in the forest.

"At last!" Hagen muttered, as the lantern light fell on a door and the end of the tunnel. The bolt was stiff with age and underuse, and screeched as the ghost and I wrestled it open. I made a mental note to oil it sometime soon.

The old wooden door opened onto what looked like a horizontal mine shaft. Pale light flooded in from an overgrown opening a short distance beyond the door.

"Strike," I told Katti.

Katti jumped onto Hagen's back, knocking him face down in the dirt. The lantern rolled away and, as I'd expected, went out. But at this point we were able to see without it.

I was on Hagen the moment he hit the ground, seizing his arms and twisting them behind his back while he was still stunned from being knocked over.

"*Fkeusht wilthkic!*" yelled the ghost.

"Don't worry," I told him. "I'm not going to hurt him. I'm going to search him."

I tied Hagen's hands with my sash and sat astride him.

"You mad dog," snarled Hagen. "What are you doing?"

I pulled the front flaps of his robe round to the back and started patting them down.

"I put the evidence together. Two and two makes four, as you said. You've got something I want. Ah-ha!"

Sure enough I heard the rustle of paper in his robe,

but I couldn't find out how to open the pocket it was hidden in.

"It's a lining," said Hagen.

"Of course I believe you," I said. "That's why you have a lining on one side of your robe and not on the other. Have you got a knife?" I asked Shadow, who was leaning against the wall with the air of a man who had ceased trying to understand and had consigned his life to the Lady's mercy.

"Oh, very well. Don't ruin the robe. It opens in that seam. Not that one, the other... I don't know why you're bothering. I know everything now, which means my master will too, soon."

"But you don't have the proof, and neither will the Premier if I take this from you." I wasn't going to tell him that some of my reason for stealing the letter was that I couldn't work out how it fitted into the story. I was hoping that reading it would tell me what was missing.

I slid four letters out of his robe and started looking through them.

"No," shouted Hagen. "Don't read those, they're—"

One of them had a purple seal with a unicorn on it. I resisted a strong temptation to take a look at the other letters and shoved them back in his robe. My life was quite complicated enough for the moment.

"Good," I said, tucking the letter into my body shaper. "Toy will never be able to produce this evidence. Nor will you."

Hagen had relaxed back into his usual suave persona now his others letters were safe.

"What? Are you getting up? I was beginning to enjoy myself."

"Oh, stop it!" I poked him with my foot and laughed. His ability to flirt at the most inappropriate times appealed to me despite myself.

"Pity I wasn't there to enjoy Lady Chatoyant's discomfiture. That must have been quite something."

"It was," I agreed, undoing my sash from around his wrists. "Though I feel sorry for her poor maid. And so should you, since it's your fault."

"I did what was needed," said Hagen, and suddenly he was much less appealing.

Eff would have used this to start an argument about mundane rights, but I had more important things to worry about.

"Come on," I said to Shadow and we stumped up to the end of the tunnel and pushed through the overhanging vegetation. The tunnel entrance came out hidden in a copse of tree ferns. Years ago after I had failed the crystal test Hilly had shown me the safe route under the ferns to a nearby path. But I wasn't interested in that. As soon as we were outside the tunnel I found a place where the sun slanted brightly through the fern fronds, opened the letter and read it.

My dear,

Stop this, or you will bring us undone and we will all lose her.

Our family wants for nothing, neither worldly wealth nor tender care. You must know this. You have seen it for yourself. What can you offer in its place?

We have returned it because we wish you well and we are determined to keep our side of the bargain. Keep yours. You have not done the wrong thing. She is safe and well.

You must see that you will bring about the thing you most fear, if you continue.

Yours sincerely

R

As I finished I found Shadow behind me reading it over my shoulder.

"Hmm," he said.

"Curse it. What does it all mean?" How could I have gone to all this effort and still be none the wiser?

"Lady Klea has had a baby very recently," said Shadow. "I recognised the signs of *prthigutklye depnkhthen*."

"Yes. She told the family it had died."

Hagen snorted. "That makes her a liar."

He'd followed us up out of the tunnel.

"How dare you?" I snapped. What really annoyed me was that he was probably right. The 'she' in the letter was clearly the baby, which was safe and well. So why did she lie? A new baby, a baby girl would cause jubilation throughout the family. I didn't understand what was going on.

"I think she's given her baby to this R to bring up."

"Why would she do that?" I snapped. "What are you doing here anyway? Go back to the house."

He held up the quenched lantern. "Have you got a match? I haven't."

Shadow took a bundle of matches out of his pack and passed one to Hagen.

"In our country a parent alone without a settled income sometimes adopts the children out," offered Shadow. "Often the parent sees it as best for the children."

I stared at him. "The family would never let her or the child go hungry. Especially not a girl. You can't give a child to strangers, who might not care."

"I'll wager that's not what's happened here," said Hagen. "This R will be some wealthy merchant. She'll pass Lady Klea's daughter off as her own. She might even be a blood relation, if a brother is the sire. Since Lady Klea has been in Crystalline these past two years, that's quite possible. She was away on a cruise around the Islands last winter. No one saw her then. She could easily have hidden a pregnancy and given birth."

"But why?" This whole conversation was so shocking. I couldn't imagine why Klea would do such a thing. What possible reason could she have?

"When Lady's Klea's daughter is of age there's half a chance she will be a mage and that... Think of it. These merchants will have a noble in their family, one of their own to represent their interests in the Great Council. Political power. I've heard rumours of merchants buying the children of impoverished nobles, but I'd always thought they were myths."

"Buying?" I remembered how Toy had said money had changed hands, and what did the letter say?

"Look here. It says *we have returned it*. That's money, isn't it? Is that how she can afford to live outside the family? Was Toy right? This is awful. No, you must be wrong. Klea wouldn't do something like that. Would she?"

Hagen took my arm.

"Shine, I'm not saying she did the right thing, but I'm not saying she did the wrong thing either. She has good reasons for not wanting her child to be brought up in this family. Her experiences at the hands of Radiant and Flara were dreadful."

"Why? What happened?"

"It's Lady Sparklea's story. Not mine." Hagen struck the match on the side of his lantern and lit the wick.

I grabbed his arm. "Tell me. No one will tell me."

"No," said Hagen. "I've told you quite enough. More than I should have."

He pushed me firmly aside and went away down the tunnel. I stared after him.

It was all too much. I didn't know what to think.

"Do you think Klea could have done such a thing?" I asked the ghost. As if he would have any idea, poor outlander.

"How can I know? But it seems to me she truly regrets what she's done. Look at how she has been: the tears and terror."

"But if she told the family the truth, they would get the child back for her. There wouldn't even have to be a scandal. They're the Imperial Family."

"There is clearly much more to this than we know. We should go," he added gently.

"Yes, yes! Sorry," I said to the ghost. I gave him a pat on the shoulder. "You're right."

I didn't know what to think. Was Klea really the sort of person who would do such an awful thing? She must have had a reason. Suddenly thinking was too hard.

In a sense, it didn't matter what I thought anyway. We were well below Klea's level—mere mundanes.

Time to get back to the matter in hand. It wasn't safe to stay here. I crouched down and started crawling under the tree ferns towards the path.

SHORTLY AFTER WE came out into the open Katti stopped and sniffed the air.

Cat, she said.

"Keep a track on it," I said. I had given the spear to Shadow to carry and now I pulled my bow off my shoulder and put an arrow in it.

And why would I want to do that? said Katti, sticking her nose sarcastically in the air. She didn't like obvious advice.

"Oh, forgive me," I snapped at her. "I've had a bad day."

She flicked her tail at me and looked away.

"Yes, you have, so I see," said Shadow. "Your hands are shaking."

"Can't be helped," I said. "We have to keep going."

I wanted to scream at both of them, scream from frustration and shock. So I strode on as fast as I could, making them both run to keep up with me.

Still I couldn't stop my hands shaking. I knew it was fright over what had happened with Illuminus. And every time I thought of Klea... I tried not to think about her, but thoughts of her and this child kept coming back into my head unbidden. Klea crying and all that stuff she'd asked me about mothers last night. Lady of Light, it must be true. How could she? How could she? What an awful, awful thing to do. A hard core of dismay settled in the centre of my chest, as if a black hole had opened up full of echoing darkness. I wasn't sure I'd be able to forgive such an action. I wasn't even sure I should *try*. Had she really done it for money?

After I'd been stomping along for a while, I noticed the ghost was trying to talk to me.

"What?" I snapped.

"Um, So I gather you have to be a mage to be part of the Great Council," he said.

"That's right, you have to be noble."

"And the Empress and the Great Council make most of the decisions."

"All of them."

"I suppose they're the ones with the power, yes?"

"That's right."

"So what if you're rich or powerful in some other way?"

I turned on him. "How is it you've got so much breath for questions? Aren't we walking fast enough for you?"

"I'm trying to understand what happened back there. You and Hagen suspect Klea of selling her child to a family of rich merchants, right? So they will bring her up as one of their own, and if she turns out to be a mage, they will have someone to send to the Great Council to promote their interests. It seems a great risk to take."

"Merchants have been trying to get more power in the Great Council for a long time. They seem to feel that money should have some say in government—that nobility isn't enough. Eff would probably agree. She thinks everyone should have a say. Usually merchants sponsor mages. Or try and breed with them. A couple of mages have become consorts to merchants, though it's social death for the mages."

"What if this little girl does not turn out to be a mage?"

"Then they'll have wasted their money, won't they?"

I could imagine the life of such a child once she had failed the crystal test. The disappointment. Maybe the anger. How could Klea have done it? How could she? Why?

I found my eyes filling with tears and dashed them away.

Mage coming!

Katti's thoughts hit my mind with the warning.

Had Illuminus got away from them? I wasn't hanging about to find out.

I seized the ghost's arm and pulled him off the path and into the undergrowth. He had not heard Katti's warning, but he followed me with only the briefest protest. We dropped down behind some rocks and huddled there with Katti between us. For a short time, we could hear nothing but birdsong and the wind in the trees. Then I saw mage light, less visible in the light of day but still bright enough. A figure shot past us along the path and was gone. Illuminus!

Eff had been right about my family's priorities. They'd clearly let themselves get distracted by Klea's mess and given Illuminus the chance to escape. No thought of the damage he might do to people like me.

"What do we do?" hissed the ghost.

"I'm not sure," I said. I judged we'd come about two miles, less than a third of the way. I examined our options in my mind. There weren't many. Illuminus was moving round the forest between us and the old mine. If only I could get a message to Bright. But perhaps it was better not to expose him to Illuminus.

This was the only path up the hill and Illuminus could wait anywhere beside it and ambush us as we went past. And he would, too, when he got to the top and hadn't found us. Climbing up through the scrub would make a very difficult and probably dangerous journey and would be too noisy. Sitting tight seemed to be our only real option. I took the bolt out of my cross bow and slung it over my back.

"Best find a comfy place to hide and wait for him to go away."

"What? That's it?" said the ghost

"Can you think of better?"

The ghost shrugged.

*　*　*

286

WONDERING ALL THE time how we would work out when it was safe to go on, I began to consider how we might spend the night out here. We had Katti to tell us if any wildcats were in the vicinity and help us keep warm, but the sky was threatening rain sometime during the night and the surrounding shrubs wouldn't keep out that out. We needed some tree cover, and the closest one was some distance away through the scrubland.

Keeping low and testing every footstep carefully, and with Katti ahead sniffing, we crept through the prickly undergrowth till we reached the tree.

Its trunk was scrawny, but it had plenty of low hanging branches, and not so low that we couldn't stand up. The ghost and I stretched our backs up gratefully. The ground was remarkably clear of leaves, so we had no need to worry about snakes or creeping insects.

Yet something worried me about spending the night here. I wasn't sure why. The branches promised to give good cover from rain.

Katti licked the air, tasting it with her tongue and put my thoughts into words.

Something smells funny.

I stepped around the tree trunk and was brought up short. The tree was growing at the edge of a large pit, probably where the roof of a mine shaft had collapsed. The pit was choked with bushes and vines, but it looked deep enough to for an unlucky fall to break a neck or a leg. The carrion stench I could smell clearly on this side of the tree told of some poor animal that had done just that, lying dead at the bottom. I peered into it to see what was there. Corpse lily vines grew all over the side of the pit, making it hard to see.

Leaves crashed behind me as if in a high wind and suddenly I was engulfed. Something whacked me hard in the back and I lost my balance and stumbled forward.

There was nothing beneath me; I lost my balance and fell. My hands stung as I scrabbled to get a hold on something. For a moment I had a firm hold on a little bush and then it gave, torn out by the roots, and I was falling again and it was dark. With a crashing thud that jarred all my bones, I landed on my hands and knees and slid on something that clattered and was gooey and springy and filled my nostrils with a foul stench.

"Shine!" shouted Shadow. "Shi—" The same crashing of leaves drowned out his call. He screamed. I rolled sideways as he fell at me. He thudded down beside me and let out a yelp.

"Katti, run!" I cried. But she'd already gone safely out of range

"*Whahthafah!*" groaned the ghost. "Did that tree move?"

"Must be crystal shot. Cursed crystal. Never done me any good. You hurt?"

Up above us the tree was still thrashing about wildly as if a whirlwind had settled on it. Or as if it was doing a victory dance. Hilly always said the still hated the moving, just as the dead hated the living.

"I'm fine. But there's goo. *Juthekiytj!* That smell."

The smell of rotting carrion was so thick it seemed to choke me.

"We've landed on its last victim. Think it's a deer. Ladybless, I hope it's just a deer!"

I couldn't make out much in the dim light down here, but I thought I could feel some kind of hide as I rolled gingerly over.

Mage coming, came Katti's thoughts from above. Her furry face peered over the edge and was gone. I didn't need to tell her to hide.

Curse it. Illuminus must have heard us. Our screams had probably echoed for miles. Would he see where we had fallen in? I made for the wall of the pit, which was still covered by vines. As I clattered and slide down the pile of refuse, I remembered my crossbow was still slung over my back. Did I still have bolts? Praise the Lady! Yes.

I could stand up straight against the pit wall. The ghost was still sitting on the enormous pile of refuse in the middle. Belatedly I realised he wouldn't have heard Katti.

"Quick. Over here," I hissed. "He must have heard us. He's coming back."

As Shadow scrabbled to my side, I pulled the crossbow off my shoulder and loaded it.

Our falls had pulled down some of the vines at the lip of the hole, but here against the opposite wall, they still gave plenty of cover. Around to our right I could make out a darker patch in the pit wall that hinted the possibility of an opening—perhaps the remains of the mine shaft.

Typical. I'd chosen the wrong side. The old mine shaft would have offered a much better hiding place.

Or maybe not. I could see something white squirming in the darkness over there.

"Is something moving?" murmured Shadow in my ear. "Snakes?"

"It's under the tree. I think it might be its roots.

"Moving roots? That's horrible."

"All this carrion. Be full of goodness for the tree."

Stay still. He's here, came Katti's thoughts.

Beside me Shadow was scrabbling about in his bag.

"Sshh!" I hissed.

A glimmer of light hit the wall beyond us. Shadow and I crouched in the darkness like frightened rabbits while the light of Illuminus' crystal played back and forth across the wall above us; he must be peering down into the hole. Hopefully his vision would be obscured by the vines and shrubs. At this point any movement might give us away, so I couldn't even turn my head to see what he was doing up there. I held my crossbow ready for the moment when I would have to shoot and try and wound my cousin enough for us to get away.

He mustn't catch us.

The logical thing for him to do would be to lower himself down into the hole and check. Maybe I could get a shot at him then. On the other hand, he could fill the hole with fire to burn away the vegetation and burn us up too. That would be an easier solution, but exhausting. And he would already be quite used up after all his activity back at the house.

Waiting, waiting. Sweat began to drip down my face. The light circled round the side of the pit, dimly illuminating the rocky earthen wall, casting silhouettes of leaves and tangled vines all around us. I could see the shadowy alcove more clearly. It was indeed part of the old mine shaft and it was curtained with white roots that writhed and undulated like fat snakes.

Leaves crashed and something *whoomped*.

"Argh!" cried Illuminus and the light was gone. I heard him scrabbling amidst crashing leaves and a rush of air blew the vines back against us.

Illuminus was yelling.

"What hap—What? Crystal shot! Curse you, you stupid tree."

Light burst out and there was an explosion. Fire flickered and the air was full of smoke and bits of burning ash.

A large piece of tree trunk came crashing through the vines and shrubs above and smashed onto the rocks and bones in front of us.

Illy let out a laugh.

"That'll learn you to whack a mage, you stupid tree."

The pit was much brighter now and I could see Illuminus quite clearly as he stood, arms triumphantly on his hips at the lip of the hole above us. A group of bats and several large transparent winged insects were streaming up out of the pit and into the sky. From the sounds of it, they all flew into Illuminus' face. This was the moment. Under the cover of Illuminus' spluttering and cursing. I took aim with my crossbow and shot.

The arrow connected. I saw a spurt of blood, heard a thud. Illuminus grunted and half-staggered, half-fell backwards, disappearing from sight. Groaning, grunting and the sound of foliage crashing came from beyond the lip of the pit. Then silence.

"Oh, no! I hit him," I squeaked. The enormity of what I had just done gripped me.

"Didn't you mean to?"

"I never shot anyone before," I said. I had a breathless hollow feeling in my chest. "What if I've killed him?"

The ghost put his arm around me.

"It was him or you," he said.

"Yes. Yes, of course. Of course it was." I shook the ghost off, ashamed at being such a baby. "Come on! Let's get out of this hole before he recovers."

With some vines, the remains of the tree and each other, we managed to crawl up from the pit. Katti was crouched beyond the edge waiting for us.

My thoughts were full of questions about Illuminus.

He's not up yet, but he's not dead either. Katti sounded disapproving of the latter. I followed her glare and saw Illuminus' foot sticking out of the scrub. I couldn't resist. I ran over to check on him and started back in shock. There was blood everywhere. The cross bow bolt was sticking out of the side of his cheek. It'd gone right through his face. His mouth was open and his breath came in gasps. His eyes lids were mostly closed, though I could see the glitter of his eyes beneath.

"Wow! Some shot!" said the ghost. He leaned over and felt Illuminus' wrist. "He's still alive. Amazing. I thought there'd be more blood. Pulse is well enough, considering. I think you missed his tongue."

The word tongue made me squirm inside.

The ghost looked up at me.

"What do you want to do? Should we um... finish him off? I guess I can do it if you can't."

"Bright Lady, no! He's my cousin. Anyway, killing him would bring a world of trouble down on us."

"I can imagine. Do you want to go back to the house and get help and I'll go on with Katti?"

"There's no need," I said, even though that was precisely what I did want to do. "His magic will heal him. That's why he's not bleeding as much as you expect. When he's healed enough, he'll come to and be able to take himself home."

"Really?"

I shot him a look.

"Yes. That's how it works. It's the only advantage we mundanes have ever had against the mages. If you can shoot them without their being able to stop your missile and inflict a bad enough wound, their bodies force them to survive by closing down all other activities. They become unconscious until they are healed enough to go on. That's how mundanes held their own in the civil war and won Shola's Pact."

I didn't tell him that in the old days, people would definitely have inflicted a death blow on a helpless mage.

"How long is he likely to be out?"

"I don't know. Most of the rest of the day, I suspect. Lying helpless out here with..."

What if a wild animal came and ate him while he lay here? How would his body react?

"It was him or me," I reminded myself. "He almost strangled me this morning."

"What?" asked the ghost.

He's my cousin," I said. Family. An uncalled-for memory came to me, of Bright and me peering over the balconies of the Family House in Elayison. Down below stood Illuminus and Scintillant and Blazeann back from the college for the Winter Solstice feast all wearing their student uniforms. They'd looked so strong and proud—so lazily, effortlessly powerful— and I'd felt such a glow in my chest at the sight of them. Pride: pride at being a Lucheyart, one of the Imperial family, and connected to these mighty beings. In those days, I'd still believed I would become one of them. Now Blazeann was dead and here was Illuminus horribly wounded at my feet.

The ghost was peering closely at Illuminus' cheek.

"Hey! This arrow is moving." he said.

"Yes. His body is expelling it using magic. Once it comes out, he'll start to heal much faster."

"Amazing!"

"Let's cover him up." I pulled out my hunting knife and started hacking at the shrubs around me. "Come on, help me. It'll give him some defence if a cat or a grunter comes along while he's lying there."

"Shine, may I remind you he almost killed you earlier!"

"But he didn't actually *do* it. Look, I know, but he's my cousin. I can't leave him there like that." I thrust a handful of branches at him. "Come on, put these over him."

Do not try to reason with her. She is quite mad, said Katti. Pointlessly, since Shadow couldn't hear her.

I'd toss him in the pit if I were you, she added.

"No one asked you," I snapped at her.

For once, Shadow didn't ask me what she'd said.

COVERING ILLUMINUS DIDN'T take long, but with everything that had gone on, it was mid-afternoon before we picked our way back to the path. All the shocks of the day had left me feeling dark and heavy, as if I were bearing an immense burden on my back. I kept up a hard pace as best I could. Shadow kept asking me how I was.

"Fine," I would mutter, and keep on as fast as I could. We were both panting hard, but I wanted to reach the top of the mountain before dark. I was already feeling shaky and I didn't want to have to fight grunters or cats in the dark. I also didn't want to think too much.

I only called a break when we reached the top of the mountain. By then, twilight had put a velvety light over everything. The forest might be dangerous, but it was beautiful too. The creaking sound of crickets and tree frogs filled the air with a quiet murmur. The corpse lilies on the trunks of the tall trees shone with their unearthly light, and their slightly rotten scent had dispersed for the night. Beyond the sweep of velvety forest beneath us, we could see Willow-in-the-Mist, the tower of its Eyrie shining through the trees. The mages hadn't managed to leave yet.

I was once in the Temple of the Mother of Light in Elayison, rumoured to be the most magnificent temple in all of the Empire. Its pillared walkways were not half as awe-inspiring as the valley at the top of the mountain. Tall pale tree trunks glowed in the lily light and fireflies twinkled across the dark carpet of ferns. Someone—perhaps the miners, perhaps my mad old uncle Batty, who had spent many summers up here—had trained corpse lily vines all along the path.

The beauty of it all did something to lift the darkness off my shoulders.

"This is an old volcano," said the ghost. "Thousands and thousands of years ago, lava must have spewed down these hills. Probably accounts for your wonderful soil. I wonder if the crystal mine up here is part of that. The land round that other mine looked volcanic, too."

"I'd like to see a living volcano," I said, feeling almost chatty with the relief of being so close to safety. "There's one a few days' ride from Crystalline, and the nobles often go down to view it."

"You are on your way," said the ghost. "Maybe Klea will take you."

"I'm not sure Klea will be taking us anywhere," I muttered. Surely she couldn't have done it just for the money? But why, then? I was still finding it so hard to accept.

"What's all that white over there?"

"Ladybless, that's Uncle Batty's puffball field."

"Who is this Uncle Batty person I keep hearing about?" asked the ghost.

"Eff's brother, and the closest thing I ever had to a proper uncle. He was a funny old man. He spent all day doing drawings he never finished, and couldn't remember to eat half the time. But every summer he'd come up here to live and get himself together enough to make a batch of Holy Wine. That's fermented puffball juice. Very rough. The peasants use it in religious ceremonies. He sold it to them and bought smokeweed. It's hard to grow puffballs. You have to clear the tree ferns away—something about them poisons puffballs. But Uncle Batty could be very industrious for the right reason."

"Was his name really Batty?"

"No. It was Beam. Lord Beam to you and me. The other mages called him Batty because he was slightly mad. And because he used to see bats when he smoked or drank too much. He hated other mages. Always quoted the old poem: *They are mired in corruption and full of bitter bile.* He stopped talking to Bright once he turned into a mage. Eff and I often wondered if that was why..."

Cats! hissed Katti. Two enormous glowing cat shapes came bounding out of the undergrowth to our right. Mooncats!

"Run!" I shouted, only to find that we were all already doing it.

"Bright!" I screamed as we ran. "Bright! Help!"

The cats were moaning out a low whining hunting yowl that chilled the soul. I didn't dare look back, lest I fall and be lost. But I was certain they catching up to us.

From further back came a huge roar.

Run, run! cried Katti's voice in my head.

As if I wasn't running flat out already. She kept close to my side and didn't leave me.

A turn in the path and there was Uncle Batty's house and, Lady's mercy, the glow of a fire in the chimney.

By now I had no breath left to shout, and the cats' yowling was so close I thought to feel their claws on my back. The roaring was coming closer.

My lungs screamed for air.

Up ahead came the fence. Shadow had reached it and was scrabbling with the latch through the slats of the gate. No, he was pushing it uselessly, because he hadn't realised there was a lower latch. I shoved him aside, pulled up the latch and shoved open the gate. The Mooncats came loping towards us with the intent stare of hunters.

We tumbled through the gate and Katti and I fell over each other. I rolled to shut the gate, but Shadow was already there, slamming it back and pushing on it with all his weight. The Mooncats let out a roar that made the trees echo. I scrabbled to the gate and shoved the lower latch down hard and shot the upper bolt. I couldn't see how the fence and gate would hold under their weight, but they had stopped coming. They were crouched outside, huffing and roaring.

Another cat roared away back among the trees. The Mooncats turned and with a flick of their tails were gone, pale glowing shapes padding quickly away into the shadowy forest as if to investigate the roaring. Or maybe the scent of a mage drove them off.

"Bright," I called, as I pushed open the door into the old miner's hut.

Someone was rocking in the rocking chair by the fire. His face was in shadow, but the shape was all wrong.

This wasn't Bright.

CHAPTER TWENTY

I STOPPED SO quickly that Shadow walked into the back of me.

"What...?"

"Come in, come in. Be welcome," said the stranger, waving at us but not getting up. I could not see his face in the shadows only his bare feet in the firelight. Bare feet that glittered with crystal dust. My heart froze in my chest.

He smells of cat. Katti crouched and glared at him.

"What are you doing here? Where is my cousin?" I demanded, ignoring the polite greeting. I was still panting from my run from the Mooncats. I put my hand on my knife.

"Ahh! You are one of the gentry. That explains it. Most

villagers would run back down the hill when faced with Mooncats," said the man in a completely unworried tone of voice.

He leaned over and put a taper in the fire and for the first time I saw his face. I didn't know it, had never seen him before. He was an older man. His forehead was smooth, without crystal or crystal scar—he had never been a mage—but by the light of the fire I could see specks of crystal glittering all over his skin. A rogue. My spine chilled.

As he reached out and lit the candles in a stand on the other side of him, I saw he was wearing a rough brown Blessing robe. He did not seem to be wearing anything underneath it. Graceson's brother, Dannel, had been dressed the same way the day I had met him in the forest.

Instead of hanging like normal hair, this man's grey hair hung in matted clumps, though it was tied neatly back from his face by a band very like that of the village shaman.

"Come, come, sit by the fire and warm yourselves. There is warm food here and drink. Be welcome."

Shadow's hand gripped my arm.

"Where's my cousin?" I asked again.

The man put his head to one side and peered up at me as if considering what to say.

"He's out looking for you," he said. I wasn't sure I believed him.

Behind us, we heard the gate click open.

"That may be him," said the man.

Another figure wearing long Blessing robes appeared in the doorway. Shadow and I sidled away from him, our backs to the wall. Katti sat, her ears back and her tail wrapped tightly round her haunches. One rogue alone would have been too much for the three of us. Two of them...

The new person was panting hard.

Then he spoke, and I knew him.

"These two are under my protection, First One," panted Dannel.

"Of course, my child," said the man by the fire. "This is Lord Beam's niece, is it not? We would never hurt one of his kin. Unless she hurt us first." He grinned. His teeth gleamed sharp in the firelight. "Your uncle was a great friend to me and my kin."

That'd be right. Uncle Batty was very easy-going if you left him alone.

"Please sit down, my dear. And introduce me to your pale and interesting companion. I've not seen a ghost in person before."

As Dannel stepped past us to go to his leader's side, he touched my arm and smiled at me. Probably the smile was meant to be reassuring, but... Shadow's hand gripped my arm even tighter and I heard a small hiss. He had a silver tube in his hand. He'd been gripping it when we'd been down the pit. I'd meant to ask him what it was, but I'd got distracted. Clearly it was some kind of lucky talisman.

"Where's my cousin?"

"I left him tidying up after you," said Dannel. "That

was a good shot. Marm Shine shot a mage right though the face," he said to the First One. "Blood everywhere."

The other man looked pleased. "Very good. But I assume she did not kill him."

"No."

"Even better." He gave me another of his strange smiles. "We prefer mages not be killed. It tends to bring the whole lot sniffing around. I do wish you'd sit down and have something to eat."

I wished I could too. The scent of the hot stew was making my stomach grumble about the delay.

"I'll wait for my cousin," I said.

"At least sit," said Dannel. "I promise you can trust us. Come on. You've known me all your life."

"You're rogues."

"We're shapeshifters," said the First One primly. "It's quite a different thing. There have always been Mooncats born in this valley. Even before the light bringers came. It's only the light bringers who call us 'rogues' and class us with criminals."

"I see. Well. Thank you. I'm fine here," I said, even though my feet were aching. The ghost, Katti and I stood there tensely, watching the two of them sitting by the fire and eating stew until the gate latch clicked again.

The door swung open and Bright came breezing in, with Stefan close on his heels. Stefan was carrying a big basket over his arm.

"Shine—praise the Lady! You're safe. I've been worried sick about you. And now I find you in complete comfort here, eating dinner with the Mooncats as if nothing's wrong. How typical."

I loved Bright, but sometimes he was so annoying.

But I forgave him quickly, because when he saw the bruises on my neck, he was furious.

"The dog. If I'd known he tried to strangle you, I'd have left him for the cats to eat."

Instead Bright had taken the still unconscious Illuminus back to Willow and left him on the front lawn for someone to find.

By then Dannel and the First One had gone and we were sitting by the fire eating stew. Stefan pottered about the cottage behind us as I filled in my side of the long sad tale of the Blessing festival and my attempts to hide the ghost from Illuminus. "It's been a bad Blessing feast," I said. "Blazeann tried to throw me over the balcony as well."

"And now she's dead. Poor old Blazeann," said Bright.

Bright knew all about that part of it. When Blazeann was found dead, Hilly had sent a runner up the mountain to tell Bright. He had flown down and lurked around outside the house to see if he was needed. Unfortunately Eff hadn't known he was there when she sent me off into the forest. By the time she found out and sent Bright after me, it was mid-afternoon and the whole business with Illuminus had played itself out.

Bright was shocked and angry at the way Great Aunt Glisten had spoken to his mother, but he didn't find it hard to believe that Illuminus was involved in crystal smuggling.

He shook his head and said, "Flara's get. They're capable of anything. They should make it their family motto."

"You shouldn't have stayed. They might have caught you."

"It's lucky I did, though, isn't it? I'm safe enough up here. No one's going to take me by surprise. Not with the Mooncats on watch."

"They chased us."

"They chase everyone they don't know. You were supposed to run back down the mountain, not up here."

I was beginning to get annoyed at the matter-of-fact way people kept telling me that our terror was all for nothing.

"I thought they were rogues. I went for the closest safe place. Who wouldn't?"

"Most of the peasants wouldn't. But they know all about Mooncats. Most of them are their friends and relatives."

"They're not rogues?"

"Not at all. Every now and then someone is born round here who changes into a cat at the full moon. It comes on like all magic, during puberty. If they cover themselves with crystal dust, like a rogue, they can change whenever they want. But they're not rogues— they protect the villagers, they don't prey on them. They keep bandits out of the forest, and in return, the villagers leave them offerings. Sometimes they even live among the villagers. But they're always dangerous at the full moon. That's when the cat side takes over."

"That's why Hilly told us never to go into the forest on the full moon? Does she know about Mooncats? Who else? How did *you* find out?"

"Stefan told me. Once I saw him with Dannel. All the mundanes hereabout know about the Mooncats. They never tell the gentry, because the mages would hunt them down and they... But Uncle Batty knew about them. Used to have little soirees with them up here, used to let them use his fire to cook on, that sort of thing. They live in the old mine workings. That's why Mother never worried about him up here by himself."

"Eff knows? Curse it, does *everyone* know except me?"

"None of the other gentry know," said Bright, shooting me a rueful grin.

"That's hardly a comfort. Surely I'm a bit more trustworthy than that lot."

Bright shrugged. "Don't be cross. The peasants trust you. It's just that no one ever needed to tell you."

"Does Klea know?"

"About the Mooncats? Of course not."

"About you still being here?"

"No. Thought it best to keep it among ourselves. She's a good woman but not... She's not a local. Did she find what she was looking for?"

"Oh, Bright," I said. "I'm so shocked about Klea. It's terrible. I don't know what to think."

The ghost looked up from his bowl. "Marm Shine, I'm sure she had her reasons."

"Maybe she's like the rest of the family. Maybe it *is* all about money."

"What happened?" asked Bright.

I looked at Stefan's back. We shared most things with him, but this was too awful. "I can't tell you here," I said.

"Why don't we go and look at Uncle Batty's grave?" said Bright, after a moment of difficult silence.

What with all the corpse lilies he'd planted up here, the little hillock where Uncle Batty had asked to be buried was easy to find even in the darkness of night. I lit a small stub of a candle and put it on the mound and said a couple of prayers for his soul.

Then I sat down and told Bright the whole story of Klea and the letter and the baby.

"Laaady. You *have* had an exciting Blessing festival, haven't you? Poor old Klea. What a mess."

I turned on him in shock. "Klea seems to have given, no, *sold* her own child for money and you say, 'Poor Klea.' Aren't you... I mean, I don't think I can speak to her again. It's too awful."

"Shine, listen to me." He took my hand and squeezed it. His mouth was scrunched up unhappily. "Klea had every reason to feel her child would not be safe growing up in the Family House."

"But money changed hands. That's... Isn't that shocking to you?"

"We don't know the real circumstances of that," he said. "It may have been a gift, or—"

"Why are you going so easy on her? She's done a terrible thing."

"Terrible things were done to her," he said.

"What things? I ask and ask and no one will tell me. Why is everyone keeping secrets from me?" I cried.

"I didn't know about it till I went up to live in the Family House. I was there when Klea ran off. Everyone was going round with long faces saying it was just what they expected. So I started poking around and... It's a horrible story."

"How?"

He took a deep breath.

"Well, you know how Flara and Radiant were always so big on mages mating with mages to breed pure?"

"Stupid snobbery that leads to sickly children."

"Well, Flara took it to extremes. She used to encourage Radiant to mate with his nieces. There's a good chance he sired both of Blazeann and Lumina's first children."

"Eww! But he was their uncle. That's disgusting."

"Radiant was very attractive. Like Scintillant is now. And the girls were very young. It seems Radiant likes them young. Blazeann and Lumina were both mages grown by then and so they had a choice in the matter. But apparently he was also mating with Klea."

"What? But she wasn't even a *woman* when they were deposed. Why would he mate with a child? That's horrible."

"It started when she was nine. They say she used to scream and cry to make him stop, but no one dared to interfere. Flara was so ruthless on the servants and she wouldn't believe anything bad about Radiant. She wasn't the first he'd done it to, either. But she was the only member of the family. You remember how we stopped going up to the Family House for Winter Solstice? That's because Hilly found out from the other servants what was happening. And because Radiant started showing an interest in you."

"In... me?" I remembered Uncle Radiant. *Lovely Uncle Radiant* was how I'd always thought of him. Sitting me on his knee and listening to me. He'd made me feel so special. And he'd spent several hours showing me the nicest books in the library, sitting with his arm round my shoulders, stroking my hair and back. The memory turned me cold.

I wasn't sure how long after that we left, but I do remember we left unexpectedly that year. Bright and I had been so disappointed when Hilly had bundled us onto the public mail coach before the big feast; and so upset that we never went back. Eff had told us that Flara had taken against us, which left Bright and me full of guilty anxiety over what we might have done wrong. Especially when we didn't go back the next year. That year, Uncle Batty joined us at Willow. He'd been Avunculus up till then. It had been his job to protect Klea.

"And Uncle Batty knew too? Or was he too smoked to care?"

I loved my Uncle Batty, but this was yet another unforgivable thing. And unfortunately I didn't find it hard to believe.

"Poor stupid old sod. I suppose he doesn't deserve my sympathy. Klea went to him for help, and I think he may have gone to Flara about it. Stupid man! Anyway, it blew up in his face. Flara accused him of skimming the household money. Batty was stood down as Avunculus. In those days, Granny had a different Premier, a mage, Great Uncle Gleam, who adored Flara. Wouldn't hear a word against her. It all got pretty ugly. Batty never got over it. You remember what he was like."

How could I forget? His room full of smoke. Those episodes where he drank too much Holy wine and kept hitting out at invisible bats. His building that funny little hidey hole in the wall.

He was a sad man.

"I thought he was always like that."

"He was never a strong person but... Anyway, I guess Klea never got over it either."

"Oh, Bright. Poor Klea. How horrible." Radiant became Avunculus once Batty was gone, and it had been another year before Flara and Radiant were deposed for mismanaging the family funds. They were sent into separate exile. Recently Flara had been allowed back, but Radiant was still out somewhere among the salt mines.

"So you see, there's a reason why she may have done what she did."

"Yes, I see." I said, shivering. "How can people be so terrible?"

Bright put his arm around me and gave me a squeeze.

"Shine," called a voice from behind us. The ghost was there, a pale figure in the lily light.

"What are you doing out here?"

"The hut is full of people with glittery skins," he said. "I got uneasy."

"There's only five of them," laughed Bright, clapping Shadow on the shoulder. "Don't be such a baby. They're not going to eat you. They just love Hilly's bread. Come on, Shine. I'll introduce you to the ones who tried to chase you off. Dannel seems to have taken up with a pretty woman called Bethel. I hope you won't be too broken-hearted."

I smacked his arm.

On the surface, everything was light and cheerful. Dannel and I talked deeply and satisfyingly of his life since he had left the village. He'd been many places and I was envious and impressed.

But when I lay down to sleep that night, I couldn't. Maybe I was overtired. I kept thinking about Klea and Batty and Uncle Radiant. Bright had said she used to scream and cry. Yet no one came. No one came. A dark, sick feeling grew in the pit of my stomach, and even the warm bulk of Katti curled against my back did not comfort me. It was a long time before I could fall asleep.

CHAPTER TWENTY-ONE

SOMETHING CRASHED AND I woke up. The door was an oblong of sunlight. The Mooncat woman was framed in it.

"Mage! Male! Coming up from the river," she cried.

"Illy!" cried Shadow.

That was a quick recovery, I thought as I grabbed my crossbow.

"Don't worry. I can take him." said Bright. "He'll still be weak."

"What if there're others?" I cried, making for the door.

"Good point! You better hide."

Shadow and I were outside before he'd finished speaking. We would have run for the old mine workings where they'd never have found us, but the mage was coming from that direction. We could already see his light through the trees.

Tree ferns carpeted the whole area around the hut.

This way, thought Katti, streaking down the hill into the ferns. Shadow and I threw ourselves in after her. Once underneath their canopy of branches, we could see a vague pathway through them. Katti had disappeared, but Shadow and I found a place to hunker down on our bellies watching the hut. I loaded a bolt into my crossbow. I heard him rummaging in his pocket and the strange little hiss that his talisman made again. Katti reappeared and hunkered down beside us. We all waited.

I heard the voice calling.

"Shine! Shine, Sweetie! Where are you?"

Scinty! It was Scintillant, not Illuminus. I felt myself relax and knew I shouldn't.

But I did lower my crossbow.

Bright must have heard the call too, because he came running out of the hut and stood in front of the open gate.

Scintillant was flying between the tree trunks, his long dark curls and his black and gold robes trailing out behind him. When he saw Bright standing at the gate, he stopped short, hovered for a moment and dropped down into the clearing, facing him.

The two men stared at each other. Even hiding in the ferns I could feel the hostility between them. This was something I hadn't known about...

"I wondered if you were up here," said Scintillant.

"What are *you* doing here?"

"Looking for Shine and her ghost friend."

"You've no need to worry about them. I've got it all under control."

"Have you, Bright? An unregistered ghost? I know you radicals like them, but have you considered that he might be out here to spy out the land for them?"

"Don't... don't try this, Scintillant," said Bright. "I'm never going to believe a word you say again. What are you really here for? Are you mixed up in the crystal smuggling with Illuminus?"

"He's simply worried about the ghost," said Scintillant. "He told me all about it last night. Asked me to come and sort it out."

"How touching! Hadn't thought you were so close. But I guess money will bring people together. Crystal smuggler!"

"All this talk about crystal smuggling is a scandalous libel."

"You'd know all about scandalous libel. All those things you said about Graceson."

Bright had told me someone in the family had accused Stefan of making advances on some of the family's young boys. He hadn't told me it had been Scintillant. After what Bright had told me about Radiant last night, the savage reaction of the family—throwing Stefan into jail without a trial—made much more sense.

"You didn't have to stand up for him, you fool," sneered Scintillant. "He's a mundane. Pretty mundanes are ten a penny. Or you could have broken him out of prison and sent him on his way. But no, you had to openly admit you were lovers. Some rubbish about his reputation! You're a fool like your mother."

"My mother is not a fool. And Stefan's my love. The love of my life. I couldn't leave him under the shadow of such a suspicion."

"So you threw away all your wealth and power for love. How very sweet."

"I wouldn't expect you to understand. You love no one."

"I'm tired of this conversation," said Scintillant. "Are you going to give me that ghost?"

"Of course not," said Bright. He threw a bolt of power at Scintillant, which Scintillant deflected with a wave of the hand. This was my cue. I was supposed to fire my crossbow at Scintillant while he was distracted. But I couldn't do it. Anyway, Bright looked confident.

Scintillant pulled something out his robe.

"A gun," cried Shadow. "No! Stop him!"

Scintillant was pointing a metal tube at Bright. The shape and colour of it reminded me of Hagen's firework tube. Even as I realized that, thunder boomed and a puff of smoke came out of metal tube. Blood spurted from Bright's shoulder and he fell, hands clutching his wound, face astonished.

"Bright!" I screamed. I stood up and shot at Scintillant but he was too fast for me and threw the arrow away wide.

I pushed forward to Bright's side. Getting through the trees ferns was horribly slow, like wading up a river.

Scintillant had his metal tube pointing my way, but I didn't care. I had to get to Bright.

"You slime rat!" I screamed. Scintillant was standing, watching me come, his metal tube pointing at me. He was grinning, the dog. I was so furious, I wanted to shoot him, but I had to get to Bright first.

"Hello, darling," said Scintillant. "Tell me about—"

Suddenly he jerked and something pushed out of his chest. Blood spurted and he staggered and yelled and fell back among the ferns.

Stefan Graceson charged out of the open door of the hut, crossbow in his hand, and fell on his knees beside Bright.

He was shouting Bright's name and tears were running down his face. When I reached them, Stefan had already pulled out a kerchief and was padding it over the wound. I loaded my crossbow quickly and went towards where Scintillant had fallen, just in time to see his bloodied, shaking hand rise up out of the ferns holding the metal tube. Thunder boomed three times and smoke filled the air.

The terrible thunder made me stagger back. By the time I'd got over to Scintillant, he'd dropped the tube and was unconscious, curled up on the ground, the crossbow bolt shuddering as it slowly worked its way out of his back.

The tube looked *exactly* like Hagen's. Remembering how hot the last one had been, I kicked it into the ferns with my foot and ran back to Bright.

"Is he alive?" I whispered to Stefan.

"Yes!" breathed Stefan back to me. He saw something over my shoulder. "Another mage coming! That must have been a signal. Quick, hide!"

"No! I won't leave you." I hoisted the crossbow to my shoulder.

I spun round to face the oncoming mage. In truth, it was too late to run anyway. From the speed she was coming, she must be a woman.

I could see her. Pale green draperies. Chatoyant! Of course, who else?

I stood over Bright and Stefan, crossbow pointed at her. Behind me, I heard Stefan loading his own crossbow.

Chatoyant didn't pay any attention to us until she had dropped to the ground beside Scintillant and checked that he was still alive.

That done, she came to us.

"You're really carving your way through my brothers, young mundane," she said wryly. It was the first time I could remember her speaking to me directly. I levelled my crossbow at her.

"Oh, please, spare me the heroics!" She flipped her finger and the crossbow was ripped from my hands so hard it stung and I yelped. She flipped her finger and I heard the same thing happening to Stefan behind me.

"Good. Now, no more silliness. I want that ghost."

"Why are you so obsessed with the ghost?" I said. "I haven't got one. He's gone."

"Nice try," sneered Chatoyant. "But we know about him. Illy saw him yesterday. You made a lovely mess of my poor little brother, but he was still able to write down what he saw. What are you thinking, hiding an illegal ghost?"

"And what are *you* thinking, crystal smuggling?" From the flicker in her eyes, my accusation had hit home; and yet she denied it.

"I don't know what you're talking about. All I know is that you and probably your aunt are endangering our empire by hiding an illegal ghost. And an exiled invert. Ladybless, girl. What sort of people *are* you, out here?"

"The ghost is all sorted. He's already on his way to Elayison. If you interfere, you will only create a scandal."

"I don't believe you."

"Well, I don't believe you. I *know* about the crystal smuggling."

"You are extraordinarily insolent for a mundane," said Chatoyant. She waved a hand and her crystal glowed. Her power plucked me off my feet and yanked me onto the ground, face-down before her.

She put her foot on my back. "Hasn't it occurred to you that I could hurt you? That I wouldn't mind a bit, hurting you?"

"I can't tell you where the ghost is, because he left here last night," I said through gritted teeth. I hated Toy. I was not going to tell her anything. Part of me knew I should be scared, but I was too furious.

"What if I offer you money?"

"Have you got any money?"

"Of course I've got money. I'm not like my brothers." She rolled me over with her power and her foot and bent over me. "Think of it. You could go to University. Everyone knows that's what you want to do."

This remark made me even madder.

"What are you going to do with the ghost when you get him?" I hissed. "Kill him?"

I was going to add *like you killed Blazeann* but some instinct for self-preservation stopped me.

Chatoyant's face lost its hopeful look. She let out a sigh.

"You children of Eff. You're both crazy. Such mad gallantry. Looks like we'll have to do this the hard way."

She pulled me upright, her power lifting me like a rag doll, till I stood before her with my back to her. I could see Bright from here, lying unconscious, eyes closed, limbs straight and arms crossed on his breast as if he was in his tomb. Stefan crouched beside him one hand on Bright's chest, looking up at us with wide, apprehensive eyes.

"Is the ghost your lover, that you protect him so?" Chatoyant whispered against my neck. "Did you inherit your mother's tastes?"

"No!" I retorted.

"They *use* us, the ghosts. They are dangerous. And greedy. Greedy for our crystal. Let's see how much this one cares about you." She picked up my hand in hers. I struggled, but it was no use.

"Ghost," she shouted. "I know you're out there hiding. If you value Shine's life, it's about time you showed yourself. I'm going to break her fingers, and if that doesn't bring you out of hiding, I will strangle her. Slowly. To death, if necessary."

"No! He's not here," I protested. "Aaargh!"

She'd chosen well. Having your little finger broken hurts like hell. You always hope you'll be bravely stoical at these moments, but I yelled. It helped with the pain.

"I'm here," said the ghost standing up in the ferns. He was holding his talisman up, pointed at us. Just like Scintillant had held the gun at Bright.

Suddenly Chatoyant screamed and let me fall on the ground, then seemed to collapse in a mass of green draperies and fur. A Mooncat was on top of her, growling and tearing. They struggled, its teeth sunk into her shoulder. As I gaped, another Mooncat leapt over me and onto them, blocking my view.

Something nipped me on the shoulder. Katti.

Come, come, stupid cub. She tugged at me. I staggered to my feet and ran up the hill after her. The ghost was already there; he took my hand. A long way in front of us, I could see Stefan running, and in front of him, a man carrying Bright in his arms. They were heading towards the mine. I started running too.

A cat screamed, a terrible sharp sound, and foliage crashed. A moment later I felt a pressure wave of power in my chest and saw the flash of crystal. I glanced behind me as another cat scream echoed though the clearing, and saw a glowing furry shape flying through the air.

Hide! They are defeated, wailed Katti. I threw myself face down into the tree ferns beside the path, and Shadow followed.

We hunkered down as still as we could be. I prayed that the ferns would stop swaying in time to not give away our position.

I could see the ghost's pale face shining in the dimness before me.

"You hurt?" he whispered.

I shook my head. My hand was stuffed in my shirt. It throbbed and felt twice its size, but there was no point fussing about it now. Katti crawled up next to me.

They are safe in the mine, her thoughts said to me. Lucky Bright and Stefan! I whispered the information to the ghost.

"Wish we were!" he murmured.

Down the hill foliage crashed like thunder. A cat squeaked and there was an explosion. Then the rush of foliage slowly dying away.

Chatoyant's voice rang out loud and clear. "Rogues. Hell bound rogues. Inverts, illegal ghosts and now rogues. Your family are the end, Shine!"

She gave a grunt: she was hurt. But not enough to close her down. Curse it! And now we had no weapons.

"Why do you have to make this so hard, Shine? Just stand up and give up that ghost. He's a spy, can't you see that? They're a danger to us all. You don't know their power. But I do. We need to kill him."

She sounded closer. She must be in the air. I peered up though the fern fronds.

Uncle Batty, or more probably the Mooncats, must have liked tree ferns, because the forest around the hut seemed to be full of them. Who wouldn't like them?

They were perfect cover. They grew to waist-and shoulder-height. We were hidden from the air as long as we didn't knock against their dark trunks and make them shake.

Unfortunately there were still things Chatoyant could do.

Suddenly the fern field just behind us exploded, showering us with hot bits of trunk and branch. I curled tight hands over my head, knees against my chest, trying to be as small as possible.

"I know you're in there somewhere," called Chatoyant from above us. My back ached with fear. My spine felt like a big soft vulnerable worm.

I put my face against Katti's fur. *Crawl away,* I willed her. She could get between the fern trunks without showing herself. We were too big and clumsy. The only answer I got from her was a soft hiss of disapproval.

Branches crunched away over to my right and, turning my head, I could see through the fern fronds to where Chatoyant had come to rest perched in a nearby tree. Her robe was torn at the shoulder and dripping blood, and she had claw marks down her cheek, but her smile was huge. She was safe in the tree. No Mooncat could jump her up there and she'd see any arrow before it hit her. She could destroy the fern field at her leisure. She was a woman. Her magical power would assuredly go the distance.

"Come on, Ghostie girl!" she called. "Come on out before I burn you out. I bear you no ill will, but I'll hurt you if I have to."

She threw out her hand and sent a blast of fire to a part of the fern meadow in front of us. Another rain of hot wood crushed the ferns close to Katti's side. I put my body over hers.

The ghost eased back towards me.

"How long can she keep this up?" he whispered in my ear.

"Long enough," I mouthed. "She's a woman. Their power, it's strongest."

Another blast of fire, another rain of burning wood. Shadow pulled his head back as a smoking fern tree fell towards him. The next blast could hit us.

"That's it, then!"

Shadow held up his small silver talisman. It hissed very faintly as if it breathed in. "I'm sorry, Shine. I know she's your cousin, but I'm going to have to shoot her out of that tree. Maybe kill her."

"With that little thing?" It looked nothing like Scintillant's firework tube.

"Sure," he hissed back. "It fires a bolt of light that burns. Just like she does."

No wonder he kept pulling it out when we were in danger. But that little thing? It was only a tenth the size of Scintillant's gun. Still, at this point I was willing to clutch at any straw.

"Go on," I hissed. The ghost held the tube up and took aim at Chatoyant, who was breathing in, marshalling her power in preparation for another blast.

"What in the Lady's name do you think you are doing, Chatoyant Lucheyart?" yelled a clear voice above our heads. A figure streaked into the tree and landed with a loud crackle of branches beside Toy.

It was Klea! Klea to the rescue! Lady be praised. I almost stood up and cheered. But Shadow gripped my arm and shot me a warning look.

"I might ask the same of you, my lady. Looking for something else to sell, are you?" sneered Chatoyant.

Klea hit her. Not with magic; she punched Chatoyant in the face, catching her completely by surprise. Chatoyant fell backwards out of the tree and crashed down into the fern fronds, but she must have saved herself before she hit the ground, because she was on her feet again very quickly. Klea hovered over her, hands on hips.

"How dare you?" she screamed. I thought her very glare would set Toy alight. "Shine and her friend are under my protection. Go away and stay out of my business, you horrible dog."

Chatoyant lifted her hand. Klea lifted hers to defend.

"What? You think you can take me? In the state you're in? Come on! Try it! Give me an excuse to hurt you."

Chatoyant's head drooped. She breathed out.

"That's right," snarled Klea. "Now get out here. And take your useless rooster of a brother with you."

"I'll get you for this," snarled Chatoyant.

"What? With poison, like you got Blazeann?"

"That was an accident! Nothing to do with me!"

"I know all about the poisoned smokeweed, Toy-Toy. Splendance's get are on to you, girl. Go running back to your mama and ask her what to do next."

The ferns bowed as Chatoyant flew away above us. A drop of her blood fell on my cheek as she went over. A moment later she flew back into view carrying Scintillant in front of her, and turned slowly away towards the river beyond the mountain. There was a town where you could catch a canal boat towards Elayison down there.

"Shine!" called Klea as she watched her go. "Shine! She's gone. It's safe to come out."

"Shine, Bright!" called another voice. "Please where are you? Someone please answer!"

Eff was calling! My darling aunt must have come up the hill with Klea.

"Eff! I'm here," I cried, standing up.

CHAPTER TWENTY-TWO

BRIGHT LAY ON Uncle Batty's old bunk. Stefan had washed and dressed the wound in his shoulder and Shadow had taken a look at him. The ghost marvelled again at how quickly my cousin's wound was healing. There was nothing much he could do to speed up the process. The *bullet*, which was the name the ghost used to describe the small pellet of lead that Scinty's *gun* had fired off, had already been expelled from the wound.

Eff and I hovered around, fretting, touching Bright's cheeks and forehead to make sure they weren't getting hot. Even a mage could get a fever.

We'd started talking to distract ourselves, but with both of us so on edge, maybe the argument that followed was inevitable. Eff started urging me to go up to Elayison and I said I needed to stay for the farm work as I always did. After I'd insisted the third time, Eff lost her temper and shouted at me.

"No!" she cried. "No, I want you to go up to Elayison with the ghost and stay there! Shadow could be ages finding your mother, and I won't have you staying here while he does. Surely that merchant woman will still take you on in some capacity."

"I don't want to leave you, Eff. What if you get sick again?"

"What? Is that why you stay? You ridiculous child."

I felt a moment of hurt at that, but she soothed it away by throwing her arms around me and planting a big kiss on my cheek.

"My darling child. It's not your job to look after me. I'm a grown woman and your foster mother. *I* look after *you*. And I won't have you staying here and sharing my exile. I couldn't bear the guilt. You deserve to have your own try at an exciting life, and I know you want it. You won't get that here in Willow."

I teared up. Me, tearing up. But I was very worried about Bright. And my finger hurt like hell even though Shadow had bound it up.

"I'm not sure I *want* to go," I said.

"Oh, Shine. Who are you trying to fool?"

I looked round the cottage. Bethel and the other Mooncats were standing around watching as Shadow washed and anointed the raw-looking burn on Dannel's side with some kind of magical ointment out of his bag. But I had a feeling they were all listening to Eff and me.

"Will you be able to cope without me?" I dropped my voice, but Eff didn't. She could be so indiscreet sometimes.

"Oh, pish! No, don't get offended again. Now you've set everything up, surely Thomas can boss everyone around. Or one of the peasants. They're not helpless, you know. Not helpless at all."

She was right about that. Jar the innkeeper could organise most of what I did, or even Old Man Jenkal. All Eff would have to do was chair the village meetings. And she loved doing that stuff.

"But..."

"Look, I promise you I won't get sick again."

"You can't promise that."

"True. But I'll order Thomas to send for you and Bright should I ever get like that again. Please. Go up to Elayison with this ghost and Klea. Deliver him to his embassy and find some kind of way to stay there. Auntie Four will help you. Go to that merchant. I can't bear to see you rotting away here. Even working in a counting house would be better than this."

"Stop that!" cried Shadow, but he wasn't talking to me. He was struggling with Bethel the Mooncat woman, who was trying to rub some ointment of her own onto Dannel's wound.

"It's rogue paste," said Eff, putting her glasses on her nose. "How interesting." She looked at the Mooncats as if she was seeing them for the first time. I had a feeling they were about to be studied.

"What's the matter?" I asked Shadow.

"She cannot put that on. She will dirty up the wound. Look, it's full of grit. Stop it!" cried Shadow.

"He must have it on," explained Bethel. "Otherwise he won't be able to change."

"Can you not wait for a couple of days till the wound is scabbed over?" begged Shadow. "That stuff will make it fester."

"There've been mages here. There's one still here," insisted Bethel.

"Oh, pish," said Eff crossly. "Be logical! If she was going to harm you, she'd have done it by now."

Typical of Eff. She always expected the world to run on logic, and it didn't. It ran on unreasonable things like love and fear.

"Couldn't you wait till someone attacks you, before he puts on the paste?" I suggested. "Surely you'd be safe enough hiding in the mine till then."

"I don't reckon you should worry about Lady Sparklea, Bethy," said Dannel.

"What about the other one? She's seen us now. When you are fit, we'll find another home."

Hard to know what Chatoyant would do. I could see her being malicious enough to hunt down the Mooncats, but I didn't really know her. Or Scintillant either. Was it possible to ever really know a mage?

I wasn't sure if I knew Klea any more either. I felt so sorry for what I'd learned about her and Radiant, and pity and understanding for what she'd done. Yet a part of me was still very shocked that she would give her baby to strangers. I mean, why not give it to me and

Eff? Perhaps it was because I was a foster child myself that I found it so hard to accept. The thought of money changing hands bothered me too. I knew what people were capable of doing for money. Lady only knew I'd seen enough of it in the last few days.

So I was in an uncomfortable place where someone I liked had done something I deeply disapproved of for reasons I understood. What stance should I take? How did I react? Was it even for me to judge?

You should go and thank Klea. Katti's thoughts intruded on my mind. *Isn't that what you monkeys do with your allies?*

I flicked her ear. She knew I didn't appreciate being called a monkey. But she was right about gratitude. And she must have known how uncomfortable I was about Klea, because when I went outside to talk to her, Katti came with me and sat with her head resting against my thigh for the whole conversation.

Klea was outside sitting on the branch of a tree. She'd gone out as soon as she'd seen how unhappy the Mooncats were with her. She was swinging her feet and enjoying the view of the valley around us, as if she didn't have a care in the world. *After all she'd been through*, said the mean part of me. *Shut up*, said the generous part of me. Why should she always be miserable because someone had done something terrible to her in the past?

She jumped up and threw her arms round me.

"Shine! So glad you're safe. And Katti." She scratched Katti's sweet spot and Katti allowed it. "Did Eff persuade you to come up to Elayison with us? Do come!

We'll have such fun. I know a good inn. We can see the sights."

The thought of the baby came unbidden to my mind.

"I'm not sure. I..."

She drew back and looked at me questioningly.

"What's the matter?"

"I found this. Hagen had it." I gave her the letter.

"Shine, my letter!" she cried, seizing it and pulling it open. "Oh, Ladybless you, Shine. You saved me." She threw her arms round me again and stepped back and held the letter up in the air. It burst into flame. In a moment it was ash.

"So that's that," she said, wiping her hands together.

"Klea?" I had to ask

"What's the matter?"

"She not dead, is she? You lied to the elders."

Her face hardened. She looked at me for a long moment. "So what? Since when did they deserve truth?"

"But why did you have to give her away?"

"I wanted to keep her safe from this family," she snapped. "They're poison, always plotting and watching. Look what happened to Bright. I didn't want her to grow up like I did. Everyone says it's fine now Flara's gone, but I know her. She's up at court whispering into people's ears, making friends. You don't know what she's like. She's scary. And she wants Radiant to come back, too."

"But Klea, you're a grown mage. What's that to you?"

She turned on me.

"Listen, I made my decision. It was the wrong decision,

but it's done now. And it's none of your business anyway. So if you want me to take you to Elayison, you can keep your disapproval to yourself, thank you very much."

"I'm not disapproving," I lied, unable to help myself. "I just don't understand."

She gave a bitter laugh.

"You don't know? I thought everyone in the family knew. When I was nine Radiant used to come into my room and get into bed with me at night..."

"I know, I know. You don't need to tell me about it. Bright told me. I'm so sorry."

She took me by the shoulders. "You're all the same, aren't you? Nobody wants to hear what it was like. How much it hurt, and how I wanted him to stop. But he was a mage and I wasn't, and the servants were all Flara's creatures. Blazeann and Lumi were at school, and they hated me anyway, and Mother was always away 'taking the waters' and when I went to Uncle Batty he told Flara. He didn't have the guts to face Radiant. Or maybe he didn't want to believe me. Nobody wants to believe me."

"I believe you," I protested. I had been willing to hear, to support her if she wanted it. But it had all gone wrong. I tried to tell her this, but she wasn't listening. She was shaking me, her face in my face.

"Flara beat me and told me to stop telling lies. Radiant... I thought he would strangle me. And he said he'd hurt Lucy if I told anyone else. And I knew I had to take it, because there was nobody to help me. So I took it. For almost two years I took it.

"Then they found out about all the money Flara was siphoning away for her own purposes. And then they found out that Radiant had been servicing Blazeann and Lumina." She let out an angry growl. "He'd sired children for both of them, Flara had encouraged him to do that, but it wasn't so bad because they were mages—they could have stopped him if they'd wanted to. Servants started talking, and Great Uncle Lucient came to see me and asked me if Radiant had done anything to me. And I was able to tell him. But he told me to keep it to myself for the sake of the family, because a mage mistreating a non-mage—and a child at that—breaking Shola's pact in an Imperial household... He said they'd send Radiant into exile and they did, but they should have taken his crystal for what he did to me. But there would have been questions, and a scandal, and there *mustn't be a scandal in an Imperial household...*"

Her voice had risen to a shout.

Her words felled me with pain. I was ashamed for even starting this topic.

"Klea, I'm so sorry, I... It's such an awful story. I didn't want to make you talk about it."

She dropped my shoulders and pulled away.

"Maybe it doesn't justify what I've done," she said. "I know I've made a terrible mistake. I didn't want to go back to the Family House. I wanted so much to be free of the family. And they offered me so much money and said they'd take good care of her. But I'd never have done it if I thought she'd have the same childhood I did. These people were friends of mine. I cared for the man.

334

It seems like a decent family. The children are happy and there's only the woman and her brother... The brother is the sire too, so she's got the safety of being a blood relation. I stayed with them in the country while I was pregnant and I promised myself that I wouldn't hand her over if there was anything amiss. And believe me, I looked."

Klea's voice broke. "I was a fool. I didn't realise how much I'd miss her. I went away, but I can't forget, and I long... It's like a physical ache. Mother never longed for us like this, I'm sure. I wrote and begged them and... It's like a madness. It's all I can do not to go and tear her from their arms."

"We can help you get her back. The family..." My voice dropped away as I realized where this was leading.

"Yes, I'd have had to live in the Family House, but I could have kept her close. If I'd known what it would be like, I'd never have agreed... But not now. Don't you see, I *can't* take her back by force. They have money and mages. I could make the family get her back, but then... Do you think they'd let me look after her after what I've done? Grandmother would never allow it. She'd be brought up in the Family House by nurses and governesses just as I was. She'd be completely at their mercy."

"Oh, Klea!" I said. I knew she was right and my heart ached for her. Even though I'd never had a child, I could imagine. People told me what it was like all the time, how much they loved their children from the very start.

"I've been such a fool," she said softly. She wiped the corners of her eyes with her fingers. "But I must try not to make it worse. She is safe and I have someone keeping a watch in case she ceases to be. That's all I can do now. I almost pray she will not be a mage so they will give her back to me."

I put my arms round her. All my disapproval had been washed away by her pain.

She leaned against me.

"Hagen read your letter. He'll tell Great Uncle Lucy."

"But they've got no proof. And they won't want the scandal. Thank you for the letter. I owe you one."

She squeezed me, but she didn't look at me. Perhaps she was afraid of what she'd see in my eyes if she did. I squeezed her back as warmly as I could, to try to counteract it. I felt guilty that my questions has chased away all her carefreeness.

"Thank you for coming after us," I said. "I owe you a lot more than you owe me. And please forgive me and take us up to Elayison. I promise..." I didn't know what to promise. I just wanted to make it better.

"I'll help you in any way I can." I added rashly, to be comforting.

THE MOONCATS CLEARLY wanted Klea gone, and Eff wanted to nurse Bright in the comfort of Willow, so that afternoon we left Uncle Batty's little hut. We loaded the semi-conscious Bright into his chariot, Eff and Stefan huddled into the back and Klea drove the chariot back down to the house. That left me and Shadow and Katti to walk back down the mountain alone. At least we didn't have to worry about mages following us now, and we'd arrive back at our destination before dark this time.

Despite the conversation I'd had with Klea, and all the troubling things that had happened in the last few days, my heart was light. My little finger might be broken and throbbing, my throat bruised and my body covered in grazes and cuts, but that old song, 'Goin' to the big town,' the one about how we'd all go somewhere exciting and drink and pleasure ourselves stupid, kept running through my head and making me hum. I was going to Elayison. Maybe Lucient would take me to the theatre. Or... I might just take myself. How much were tickets?

And if I left Willow for good? I felt like a world of possibilities was unfolding. My first plan was to go to that merchant friend of Eff's again and maybe go travelling across the world to the Spice Islands. Maybe even further. But even if that didn't work out, something else interesting was sure to happen. I would make it happen.

"You're happy," said the Ghost. "Excited about going to Elayison?"

"It'll probably all come to nothing," I said, to chase off bad luck.

"You don't believe that," grinned the ghost.

He looked like he was genuinely pleased for me. He gave my arm a squeeze.

In that moment it seemed like anything was possible.

"That silver thing of yours. Show me how you can shoot fire with it," I said.

He froze.

"I... do not want to," he said. "I'm not allowed to just fire it for fun. Only when my life is in danger."

"Says who?"

"It is one of our laws," he said.

"But those guns—the thing Scinty used on Bright and the thing Hagen used. That's ghost tech too, isn't it? Someone gave them to them."

"They were not supposed to," he said. "We have rules about these things, too."

I stopped and looked at him. "I don't really know anything about you, do I?"

His mouth was tense. "I am not trying to deceive you. It has just been... We have been busy."

"Yes, I know that... Can you at least teach me your language?"

He laughed. His laughter sounded relieved to me. "Sure, if you are brave enough to try."

"I already know one word. Bullet."

He pulled a face.

"Oh, and another. 'Wilk.'"

He laughed. "That's a swear word. Do you want to start with some swear words?"

"Definitely. Always useful. And yours sound really vicious."

He pronounced a couple: they were about shitting and turds, like our swear words. I did my best to pronounce them as he did. This was not going to be easy. I would have to start writing them down and practising them. But it could be worth it.

"Do you think, if I can learn your language, I can come to your country one day? Maybe I could find out for myself what happened to my mother."

He tensed up again. "I'm not sure," he said. "I do not really have the authority for that."

"Authority?" I asked.

"The way our government works is very complicated. Best to wait and see."

He doesn't want to take you, said Katti. She pressed her head into my hand. *Maybe it's dangerous*.

I watched the ghost's strange straw-coloured hair bobbing away down the path ahead of me.

I couldn't see how he could stop me if I really wanted to go. All governments have loopholes. But maybe it was too dangerous. After all, it had killed my mother. Still, wouldn't it be amazing to go somewhere no one else had gone?

"I could became an expert on all things ghost," I said to Katti. "Consulted by the government and everyone else important. Now that would be good. We could wind up eating the finest salmon, you and I."

I might never have to talk about mangle-wurzels again.

THE END

ACKNOWLEDGEMENTS

I'd like to thank my agent John Jarrold, my editor
Kate Coe, and all the other great people at Rebellion
Publishing who made this book possible.

ABOUT THE AUTHOR

Jane Routley has had a variety of careers, including fruit picker and occult librarian, and once lived in Germany and Denmark for a decade. Now she works at a railway station and is a keen climate activist. Jane has published six books and won two Aurealis awards for Best Australian Fantasy Novel. Her short stories have been widely anthologized and read on the ABC. Her current ambition is to visit an active volcano.

FIND US ONLINE!

www.rebellionpublishing.com

/rebellionpub /rebellionpublishing /rebellionpublishing

SIGN UP TO OUR NEWSLETTER!

rebellionpublishing.com/newsletter

YOUR REVIEWS MATTER!

Enjoy this book? Got something to say?

Leave a review on Amazon, GoodReads or with your
favourite bookseller and let the world know!